The Not Exactly Scarlet Pimpernel

A FIVE DIRECTIONS PRESS BOOK

The Not Exactly Scarlet Pimpernel

A NOVEL

C. P. LESLEY

ISBN-13: 978-0692375532
ISBN-10: 0692375538

Published in the United States of America.

A Five Directions Press book

Cover images: Baroque woman with fan © Nicoleta Ionescu/ Shutterstock; Winter at Harvard © rmbarricarte/Thinkstock.

Book and cover design by Five Directions Press
Five Directions Press logo designed by Colleen Kelley

FIVE DIRECTIONS PRESS

DEDICATION

In memory of Baroness Orczy (1865–1947), without whom this book, in the most literal sense, could not have been written. And with thanks to Carolyn Lougee, whose "The Would-Be Gentleman" first gave me the idea of a computer-based historical simulation.

Some dialogue in the first half of the novel is taken from Baroness Orczy, *The Scarlet Pimpernel* (1905), now in the public domain.

Spoiler alert: In the original novel, discovering the true identity of the Scarlet Pimpernel constitutes a large part of the plot, whereas here it is revealed early on.

MORE BY C. P. LESLEY
Legends of the Five Directions
The Golden Lynx (1: West)
The Winged Horse (2: East)
The Swan Princess (3: North)

Tarkei Chronicles
Desert Flower
Kingdom of the Shades

All my books are available in print and e-book formats. To stay up-to-date on my publishing plans for this and other novels, check my blog at blog.cplesley.com or my publisher's site (www.fivedirectionspress.com). I love to hear from readers, so if you have any questions about my books, please e-mail me. You can find current contact information on my blog. And if you are a Pinterest user, don't miss "Nina and Ian's Journey" at www.pinterest.com/cplesley.

CONTENTS

1. Cambridge

FIVE A, 5B, 5C, 5E, 5F: WHERE WAS 5D? I HAD CHECKED every seminar room on the fifth floor of Widener Library a zillion times. No 5D. I'd begun to think it lived in an alternate universe, restricted to the talented few like Avalon in the Arthurian legends and hidden from the uninitiated—meaning me.

I had no idea where I'd gone wrong. In eighteen months at Harvard, I'd never had this much trouble finding a seminar room. In fact, I rather prided myself on my ability to navigate the campus. Yet here I stood, on the brink of arriving late to my graduate seminar on the French Revolution. Which wouldn't matter, except that it threatened to sink me with David Houghton, the professor I wanted to supervise my doctoral dissertation. David had built a career on studying the psychology of committed revolutionaries—exactly the area where I planned to specialize. He'd also made no bones about having more students than he could handle. And since I had no less than four potential competitors for any remaining slots in his roster, I preferred not to grease the skids under myself by failing to show up on time.

To make matters worse, my feet hurt. I had bought my black fake-leather pumps two-for-one at Fantastic Footwear, since my usual thrift-shop forays didn't include shoes. Now I knew why the store put them on sale: they had an evil buttoned strap perfectly positioned to rub the bone above my big toe raw. A grad student income doesn't include funds for Manolo Blahniks, although I suspected that, if I could afford them, they might prove no more comfortable than my Hot Pincers.

My woes didn't stop there. The dust of century-old books made me sneeze, and my backpack had carved a permanent furrow into my left shoulder. I kept trying to shift it to the right, but it was one of the ergonomically correct one-strap sort that aligned to one shoulder or the other. Guaranteed to turn anyone into a hunchback. I imagined myself as Shakespeare's Richard III, doomed to limp around the fifth floor until I dried up and mingled with the dust on the shelves. In the distance I saw David's head clear the stairwell.

My heart accelerated, and with it my breath. A hollow cough alternated with the sneezes. I ordered myself to calm down. Obviously, I had located the general area where I was supposed to be. In a pinch, I could follow David there. So what if he held my tardiness against me? If he refused to accept me as his student, I could work with someone else. Not on the French Revolution, but on something. Turkish peasants, maybe. Sure, I wanted to know about the Jacobins, but I could adjust. No one would send me to the guillotine for arriving late to class.

Besides, I was exaggerating. David wouldn't turn me down for such petty reasons. Would he?

Clued in by the direction of David's footsteps, I spotted a tiny corridor that had escaped notice during my first sixty rounds and made a beeline for it. When I reached it, I discovered an index card, yellowed with age, bearing the notation 5D, with an arrow, in old-fashioned fountain pen. As I limped down the hallway, subdued voices guided me. I stumbled into the right room just as the campus clock chimed two. The usual library seminar room: one large oval-shaped table, a bunch of chairs, lights, and a white board topped with a tube that might hold maps. Not even a window opening onto Harvard Yard.

Four students looked up, startled by the clamor I created as I crashed through the door. Two thoughts darted through my head at the same time. One, they had found the place without trouble. Two, did I look as wild-eyed, shaggy-haired, and dirt-strewn as I felt? I headed toward the only other woman in the group: Suzanne Henderson, a cute brunette whom some people would describe as my opposite number. Whereas I spent my time trying to figure out what drove people to commit to a life based on violence, Suzanne focused on the victims. Specifically, she had an interest in the French noblewomen whose lives the revolution destroyed, who wound up penniless and often friendless in England, Austria, and elsewhere. After three semesters of shared classes, she was also the closest thing I had to a friend. She'd tell me if I resembled something the cat dragged in.

On either side of her sat Simon Gray and Tony Kent. Simon played football, although not well enough for him to attend some Midwestern school instead of quarterbacking our pathetic excuse for a team. Dark brown hair, gray eyes, solid, the kind of muscles you'd expect from a football player, big but not linebacker enormous. He and Suzanne had arrived at the same time, already a couple. I liked Simon, although I found it hard to imagine what he and Suzanne talked about. He had a gift for picking the kind of research topic that makes people think academics don't quite connect to the real world: crop failures that affected some itsy-bitsy village in the middle of nowhere from 1734 to 1736; age at marriage in Provence before and after the Fronde; the long-term impact of silk factories on shepherds—you get the picture. If Suzanne worried me to the extent that I doubted David would want to take us both on, Simon bothered me because if David succumbed to the lure of shepherds, I figured I didn't have a snowball's chance in the Inferno.

Tony—medium height and build, super-smart, African-American—tapped the conference table in front of him with long musician fingers. Marking rhythms for his next cello concert, I guessed. Or for the revolutionary songs that were *his* chosen area of specialization. "Ça Ira," "La Marseillaise"—Tony had a bottomless store of anecdotes about where they came from and how people used them to mobilize the poor. He was younger than the rest of us, but so knowledgeable and focused he seemed older than his true age. Under present circumstances, I had to consider him something of a triple threat.

That left Ian Campbell, my personal *bête noire*, although no one would think it to look at him. To reach Suzanne, I squeezed past him. Ian was very tall, with chestnut hair, hazel eyes, a mild expression, a charming smile that he didn't often show, and a hint of Scots accent even though he insisted he came from Chicago. Whereas Tony had squeaked past twenty-three last month, Ian had twenty-eight years under his belt, four more than I do.

That extra experience gave him a self-assurance I couldn't match. It had attracted me at first, before I tried and failed to get him to confide two words about his past. Since then, I'd gone out of my way to avoid him, only to discover that the structure of the Harvard history department made that impossible. He appeared in every class, excelled at every assignment, aced every exam. Naturally, I detested him. He even had the best-developed and most interesting dissertation topic: he wanted to learn more about the bystanders—conservatives, revolutionaries, ordinary citizens, whoever. If they played both sides, "spoke Jacobin" (to borrow a phrase) while retaining their previous loyalties, or just ducked under the radar, Ian yearned to find out what made them tick. An idea so appealing I wished I had thought of it first.

And unless David had developed a mad yen for crop failures, he would pick Ian for sure, leaving the rest of us, as usual, fighting not to end up in the cold. Another reason Ian and I did not get along.

"Hello, Ninel," he said as I pushed by. "Nice stockings."

Determined not to let him rattle me, I suppressed a groan. I hate my full name, imposed courtesy of my dyed-in-the-red-wool grandmother in memory of a certain famous Bolshevik (read it backwards). Other than Babushka herself, no one but Ian ignored my preference for Nina. And my leggings, until the library covered them in dust, had been a precious find at the campus rummage sale, held outside Memorial Church last month. Candy striped, like the ones you see on Christmas elves, hence in tune with my sweater (pine trees). A little off-season for February, but Boston, winter, dull snow-laden day—it worked. I had worn the leggings to give myself confidence. Now Ian Campbell made them seem garish.

"Thanks," I said, for lack of a brilliant comeback. Suzanne smiled in sympathy and patted the chair on her far side. "Do I look like a scarecrow?" I whispered as I slid onto the seat between her and Tony. She shook her head.

I'd skidded in just in time. The minute I stuffed my too-loud leggings under the table, David arrived. "Glad you could make it, Nina," he said by way of greeting. "Busy day?"

Drat. He'd seen me scurrying down the hallway—hobbled by the evil shoes. I hadn't gotten away with anything. But excuses wouldn't help me, so I bit my tongue and waited while he settled himself at the head of the table.

I should explain that David was in his early thirties. That's why we used his first name. A prodigy, he'd made his reputation even before he earned his doctorate. Brilliant, quirky, innovative. *The* bright young star in French revolutionary studies. Also outrageously handsome—dark, slender, blue-eyed, medium height—and blessed with one of those plummy English accents that make everyone sound like Lord Peter Wimsey. Harvard had lured him from across the Pond, offering tenure and freedom from the UK's routine assessments of faculty progress, and he'd been inundated with student requests since he arrived last fall. This was my first course with him. Of course, I knew not to get moony over a professor. But if I *were* to lose it, David Houghton would be worth the sacrifice. As he studied us, I had to work to keep my jaw in line.

He sat at the head of the table, pulled out a piece of paper, and called our names. "Pennington" didn't normally put me last, but this class was the exception. "Very well," David said. "Everyone's here. Before we start, I want you to understand something. All five of you have requested that I supervise your doctoral dissertations. I already have fifteen students, and with only so many hours in the day, I can't accept five more. So this course will, in a sense, determine your fate. The two students who come out on top—I'll explain what that means in a moment—will work with me. The rest need to find other advisers. The course centers on a computer simulation based on *The Scarlet Pimpernel*—"

A gasp went around the room. Only Ian made no sound. As if he already knew what David meant by a computer simulation. He would.

Childish, Nina. Stop grousing and listen. I listened.

"Yes," David said. "As a group, we are going to recreate *The Scarlet Pimpernel*, the Emmuska Orczy novel published in 1905. The original, let me add, not any of the film or television versions. The experience will be similar to a computer game, but live. At least, you will be performing live. The company running the simulation supplies sets, costumes, and players for the roles not covered by the six of us. The game lasts a fortnight—the final two weeks of the course—and will take place at a warehouse in Concord. Alert your families that they will not be able to reach you in that period, although they can contact the university in an emergency. If any of your other professors object, tell me, and I'll arrange a way for you to satisfy the requirements for their classes. If you drop out, though, you are also choosing not to work with me in the future."

Two weeks of running around in some warehouse in Concord in eighteenth-century dress—was the man nuts?

Nuts or not, David was still talking. "In week nine, based on the syllabus I'll hand out in a minute, you turn in a paper discussing how Orczy's novel shapes and distorts our historical perceptions of the French Revolution and contemporary England. To come out on top, you must write the best paper *and* win the game."

He'd lost his marbles, for sure. Syllabus, paper—those were old hat. But hanging my entire future on winning a game? And this was the guy I'd picked for my dissertation adviser!

At the same time, chills ran down my spine, and not just at the implicit challenge. Everyone has a book that defines a crucial stage in her life. Okay, not everyone—my sister Nessa probably has a ballet. But bookworms have books, and future historians tend to glom onto historical novels. Mine was *The Scarlet Pimpernel*, which I had loved ever since an aunt gave me a copy for my fourteenth birthday. The book marked my feeble attempt at teenage rebellion, in a sense. Since Babushka pretty much had a lock on the Radical Left, I moved right. Orczy made the perfect anti-Babushka—convinced that the French Revolution was a major international catastrophe, just as the collapse of the Soviet Union seemed to my grandmother. I devoured the book in secret (to avoid lectures about the downtrodden masses and the five social formations), relishing my wicked admiration for a long-gone and no doubt deservedly forgotten aristocratic past.

Of course, I had matured since then. These days, I understood that history looked different depending on where you stood. The downtrodden masses had as much right to life, liberty, and the pursuit of happiness as did the bluebloods and the merchants. Even so, I remembered *The Scarlet Pimpernel* with pleasure. I could ace this course in my sleep!

David moved on to asking each of us about ourselves. Again, as the "P" in the room, I came last. I half-listened to Ian summarizing where he stood with the bystanders. I paid even less attention to Suzanne, who shared her progress with me every other day. Tony, as always, had a few good anecdotes to share. Simon surprised me by abandoning the crop failures and the unwed teens, expressing an interest in the French royal family's intrigues with Austria. Then he threw in the silk industry and the shepherds, claiming he needed help deciding. The potential excitement of international espionage must have given him pause.

David gave a noncommittal nod and said, "Nina." Although I'd watched him on and off as the other students talked, his expression did not hint at how he felt. I had no clue whether one of us had impressed him more than another. Now that it was my turn to talk, how could I make my dissertation stand out, convince him I merited his attention?

"My grandmother was a revolutionary," I said, "in Russia. She still reveres Joseph Stalin today. Even though she lost classmates and an uncle in the Terror, she believes that the victory in World War II justifies their sacrifice. I want to find out how that kind of indoctrination happens, to study memoirs and letters—of people like Robespierre, yes, but also ordinary people who supported the revolutionary government even after the killing began. To understand how cognitive dissonance works. And how it doesn't: why some people draw back, as Marguerite does in *The Scarlet Pimpernel*."

Was that a gleam of approval in David's eyes? I subsided, happy with my succinct presentation. Big idea, method, mastery of concepts, last-minute reference to the novel chosen for this seminar (no one else had managed that)—and I'd left out the sticky stuff, like the fact that my grandmother was the family outlier. Only I showed any interest in understanding Babushka's point of view, mostly to figure out what kept her mired in the past.

David held up a plastic sandwich bag containing slips of paper. "So. Each of you has an area of interest that you can pursue through the simulation. We have revolutionaries, exiles, bystanders, and music as a motivating force. The factories won't get much play in Orczy's novels, but she does hint at high-level international politics. I suggest you focus on that, Simon, and worry about the shepherds later."

"Yes," Simon said, lacking any alternative. The only shepherd in a *Scarlet Pimpernel* novel would be Sir Percy in disguise.

"First step is to dole out the parts," David said. "Then you can keep your assigned characters in mind as you tackle the syllabus and the paper. *The Scarlet Pimpernel* has three major characters and numerous minor characters. There are six of us. This bag contains three male names and two female ones. The company running the simulation will fill the other roles." He handed the bag to Ian, sitting on his right. "Pick a slip of paper and pass it on. If the name turns out to be the wrong gender, pick again. If your selection strikes you as a horrible fit, feel free to switch with another player."

Ian picked Sir Percy, aka the Scarlet Pimpernel, right away. Simon landed Sir Andrew Ffoulkes, Sir Percy's chief sidekick—another good part, although Simon pulled a face that suggested he had hoped to play the hero. I suppressed a giggle. Who would have guessed Mr. Crop Failure concealed a longing to become Errol Flynn? (Not that Ian made a likely swashbuckler.) I wondered if Simon would try to talk Ian into switching, but I couldn't imagine why Ian would agree. Percy had the best part in the story, by far.

Suzanne showed her paper to the crowd: Lord Antony Dewhurst, third in command of Sir Percy's League of the Scarlet Pimpernel.

Tony reached across me and plucked it from her fingers. "I'll take that one. Seems like a natural." He grinned.

Suzanne yielded the slip with a laugh and reached into the bag again. Only two slips remained, and both were female. Would she get Lady Marguerite Blakeney, Percy's wife and the main woman's role, or Marguerite's best friend, Suzanne de Tournay? I doubted David would have chosen any women's parts except those two, since the others were little more than walk-on roles.

Suzanne's fingers closed around a second scrap of paper and drew it forth.

My stomach tightened. I was torn. On one hand, I had no desire to spend two weeks as Ian Campbell's estranged wife. On the other, Marguerite, a bourgeois radical who switched sides, fit my dissertation topic better than Mademoiselle de Tournay—just as Mademoiselle, a noblewoman sent into exile, was the better match for Suzanne. Could I persuade her to switch, if push came to shove?

Suzanne unrolled the paper. Her face lit up, and she held it out to Simon. "Suzanne de Tournay!"

Great. That left Marguerite for me!

"That's settled, then." David handed me the last slip and dropped the plastic bag into his briefcase. "Ian, Percy. Nina,

Marguerite. Simon, Sir Andrew. Suzanne, Suzanne de Tournay. Tony, Lord Antony. Let's talk about the syllabus."

"What about Chauvelin?" Ian asked. In *The Scarlet Pimpernel*, Chauvelin is the villain. Excuse me, Sir Percy's main antagonist. Chauvelin doesn't regard himself as evil. He genuinely believes that his opponents deserve to have their heads chopped off. Babushka's kind of guy.

David flashed his showstopper smile. "I'm taking Chauvelin. Your job is to thwart me. Change the plot, if you can. If I capture or kill you, you lose. If you capture or kill me, you win. Otherwise, the last two standing take the prize and—assuming you write decent papers—become my students. Got it?"

I was so excited at the thought of spending two weeks role-playing my favorite novel that I couldn't wait to talk the class over with Suzanne. It didn't surprise me to learn that as a budding specialist on the French Revolution, she too had read *The Scarlet Pimpernel* early and often. She loved it for the same reasons I did: the romance and the adventure. Sir Percy is the world's first dual-identity hero, the precursor to Zorro and Batman. Although a wealthy aristocrat, he risks his life to rescue Robespierre's victims from the guillotine by night, and by day he pretends to be nothing but a mindless fop. Each time he rescues someone—a duke or a count or even a revolutionary condemned by the regime for insufficient bloodthirstiness—he leaves a note signed with a five-petaled red flower: the scarlet pimpernel. So the Jacobins, having no notion of his true identity, call him the Scarlet Pimpernel, and the name sticks. The Jacobins are also gunning for him, not only because he's ruining their plans to rid their new republic of "undesirables" but because his rescues make them look bad. They dispatch Armand Chauvelin to hunt him down.

It's no easy job, though, to capture the Scarlet Pimpernel. A master of disguise, Sir Percy speaks flawless French, but what really fascinates me—and, I think, most people—is that his personality is so elusive. Just when you're sure you can predict what he'll do next, he flips on you.

By modern standards, the book isn't that well written: too much exposition and purple prose, not enough motivation. But literary flaws aside, Sir Percy has become a favorite of book, stage, and screen. I hear there's even a musical—there's a daunting thought.

So I had plenty to discuss with Suzanne—except that I soon realized I couldn't. We both wanted to work with David, and that made us rivals. For a few days, we tossed around a scenario in which Marguerite and Suzanne de Tournay banded together to defeat Chauvelin. In the twentieth century we'd have had no problem, but *The Scarlet Pimpernel* is set in the eighteenth. That threw the advantage to the guys. We could include Simon, as Sir Andrew—as I'd expected, Ian had nixed any offers from Simon to switch parts. But then we'd have three people and only two of us could win. When push came to shove, Suzanne would pick her fiancé over me. Or so I assumed.

The same caveat applied to Simon, with the additional hurdle that Suzanne would wonder if I was trying to steal her man. That left Tony, as Sir Percy's other henchman. I did sound him out, but he insisted he planned to play his role to the hilt and not worry about the outcome. Since I didn't believe him, I figured he must have some other alliance up his sleeve. When I overheard him exchanging details of horses and weaponry with Ian, I deduced which one.

I couldn't blame Tony. As a prospective ally, Sir Percy stood head and shoulders above Marguerite, whose espionage skills stopped with ferreting out the latest dress pattern. But Tony's decision left me in the lurch. I retreated into my shell, lonely and a bit hurt, and abandoned my halfhearted attempts to link up with one of the other players. With Suzanne and Simon inseparable, and Ian and Tony in cahoots, I saw no option but to go it alone.

Even then, I realized that the person I should approach was Ian. As Percy's wife, Marguerite had more to offer her husband, despite their marital problems, than she could reasonably promise Tony. But since I had no desire whatsoever to get closer to Ian, I rejected that option.

It didn't help that by nature I'm not a joiner: a childhood immersed in books had left me more comfortable with imaginary people than the real kind. And David had done an excellent job of setting his students at one another's throats. The game wouldn't begin for ten weeks, and we were already at daggers drawn.

I didn't think it was an accident, either, because David kept the pot simmering throughout the course. When we turned in our papers, two-thirds of the way through, he took them and graded them, then announced he'd return them when the game ended. No amount of pleading persuaded him to change his mind.

His recalcitrance annoyed me. I'd put a lot of work into my "Historical Errors, Emotional Truths," and I would have liked to get a sense of where I stood with my argument that Baroness Orczy had done a good job of creating compelling personalities, but not of explaining the revolution, *before* I committed myself to two weeks of nonstop costume drama.

But so be it. If I had to succeed on my own, I would. I pored over *The Scarlet Pimpernel,* dreamed *The Scarlet Pimpernel,* drew diagrams of *The Scarlet Pimpernel* on my laptop. I searched for intersecting story lines and traced the probable effects if, as Marguerite, I changed Plot Point A or interacted in a different fashion with Character B. In short, I became as obsessed with *The Scarlet Pimpernel* as any Jacobin I might study for my dissertation had ever been with the revolution. Throughout those ten fevered weeks, I had one thought in my head: how to come out ahead in the simulation and gain the prize of David's mentorship. Food, sleep, even my other course work seemed secondary—irritating distractions I had to fulfill as fast as possible in order to make time for my plans.

And boy, did I need time. My first re-reading revealed that Marguerite, as a part, imposed some serious constraints. The eighteenth-century woman thing was one, but Marguerite's personality caused me much bigger headaches. I had forgotten she acted like *such* a birdbrain. She's billed as the cleverest woman in Europe, but her behavior makes no sense. She supports the radicals because some aristocrat beats up her brother, then marries Sir Percy, a wealthy English nobleman who hates the revolution. But she doesn't marry him for his money, or even because she loves him, rather because *he* adores her, and she likes the feeling. How lame can you get?

But Marguerite is just hitting her stride. Once she's got Percy safely married (no divorce in those days), she celebrates the wedding by telling him she turned in the aristocrat who beat up her brother and sent the man's whole family to the guillotine—a major confession that we later discover is not even true. So why does she say it? The novel slides over these crucial details, but it does make clear that Marguerite is surprised when Percy disapproves. She runs off, leaving him to stew for weeks. When she trots back home, Percy receives her with icy courtesy, and she responds by taking potshots at him whenever she can. An apology is out of the question. It's all his fault. He should have trusted her!

She travels with Percy to England, where she moons over the Scarlet Pimpernel, not realizing she's married the dude.

But despite her infatuation, she ends up betraying the Scarlet Pimpernel to his enemy, Chauvelin. To protect her brother. Which, when she figures out at last who the Scarlet Pimpernel *is*, sends her dashing around France until Percy can rescue her. At this point, Baroness Orczy's Victorian readers swooned in maidenly delight, whereas the whole sorry performance inspired in me a desire to smack Marguerite hard, then smack her again for good measure.

By the time I finished that first read-through, I wished from the bottom of my heart that David had not forced us to respect gender differences. As Percy, Andrew, or Tony, I might have had a chance. As Marguerite? Forget it.

An attack of gloom followed. But a few days before the class was due to leave for Concord, my diagrams and plot tracing turned up one chance of success. That became my plan. Whatever happened, I would refuse to help Chauvelin find out that Sir Percy was the Scarlet Pimpernel.

Because, despite the fancy talk about simulations, in the end the assignment boiled down to a play—sets, plot, costumes. People could hand me a script, but I didn't have to follow it. Change the lines, and I'd win the game. It was as simple as that.

What could go wrong?

2. Concord

THE NIGHT BEFORE LEAVING, I TOOK THE PLUNGE AND phoned my mother. Experience convinced me to wait till the last minute. Like many immigrant parents, my mom was a "helicopter mother" before anyone invented the term. It didn't help that my father, whom Nessa and I called Henry VIII because of his unending stream of wives, had left her in sole control years ago when he departed in search of his first bimbo. So I could guarantee that the news that I was acquiring a fake husband would freak her out. As a result, I downplayed that bit, emphasizing David and the seminar and how my dissertation depended on my doing well.

Let slip that my professor wanted to guillotine me, even as a bad joke, and I'd turn around to find her on my doorstep with Babushka in tow.

My restraint did me no good. Mom seldom let facts get in the way of her fears. "Two weeks?" she asked. "How can you take off for two weeks?"

"It's a class, Mom. The professor cleared it with the university."

I had predicted her reaction with pinpoint accuracy. "It sounds dangerous," she said. "I don't like it. Can't you tell him your mother doesn't approve?"

"Mom, I'm twenty-four. No way I'm saying that. Besides, no worries. The university wouldn't let us do anything dangerous." Stretched out on my tattered rose-pink sleep sofa, I touched my copy of *The Scarlet Pimpernel* for inspiration. I wore slacks today, brown wool moth-eaten on one cuff but otherwise fine, and a fisherman turtleneck in a shade of green not seen in nature. Marguerite, fashionista *extraordinaire*, would have had a heart attack at the sight of the bobbles on my socks. I loved them.

On the far wall, the early evening sunshine cast a serene glow over an impressionist chalk drawing of the Kremlin Annunciation Cathedral. I was lounging in the living room of my cherished one-bedroom apartment. It occupied the first floor of a gorgeous Brookline brownstone, built a century ago—the kind that look identical on the outside but are architecturally distinct on the inside, with built-in bookcases and china cabinets and fireplaces and all the other accoutrements of nineteenth-century life. The apartment consumed most of my graduate stipend, but it repaid every penny in comfort and quiet.

"I still don't like it," Mom said. "A married woman? What are they thinking? Who is your husband?"

The telephone signal bounces from San Francisco to a satellite in the sky and then returns to earth in Boston. I could hear her teeth grinding at a distance of 46,000 miles. I have, without question, the only mother on the planet who believes her twenty-something daughters are virgins.

I didn't correct her delusion. She was giving me enough trouble as it was. "Honest, Mom, not a problem. The guy playing Percy hates me. Ian Campbell. Whenever we meet, we spat. He calls me Ninel."

"Ninel is your name," Mom said. "Why shouldn't he use it? But this marriage thing bothers me. He'll get ideas."

"He wouldn't dare," I told her. "Besides, Marguerite and Percy can't open their mouths without saying something rude. She thinks he's an idiot and obsessed with clothes. He believes he can't trust her to tell him the weather. It's a competition. I want to beat the jerk, not sleep with him."

"Oh, Nina, you're so judgmental." If it wasn't like Mom to switch in midstream. "You can't spend your life as a bluestocking. How will you get married if you scare off all the nice boys? I'm putting Nessa on the phone. I can't stand this."

Bluestocking. Nice boy. Ian, the same guy who'd had ideas thirty seconds ago? Not to mention that life as Henry VIII's daughter would scare anyone off marriage. U-curves like these explained why conversations with Mom left me with mental whiplash.

I braced myself. Most of the time, Nessa chattered for about five minutes before handing me off to Babushka, in this case primed to deliver a long lecture in Russian about the degeneracy of the aristocratic lifestyle. I was plotting means of deflection when my sister came on the line. "How'd you get Mom going like that?" she asked.

I told her, sure the game wouldn't appeal to her. She hadn't cracked a book for pleasure since she left first grade.

But I was wrong. "Oh, fabulous," she said. "What's the story?"

Encouraging. My excitement returned as I summarized the plot. "Sir Percy, an English aristocrat who lives during the French Revolution, falls in love with Marguerite. She's a French actress with leftist sympathies. He marries her—"

"He marries an *actress*? During the French Revolution? I thought they were like dancers, one step above whores."

Another implausibility that hadn't troubled the baroness. "Yes, of course," I said, because Nessa was right. "But Marguerite has her brother to chaperone her, so she's a virtuous actress, and Percy has no family living, meaning no one's around to object."

"Oh." Nessa sounded as if a virtuous actress wasn't much fun. "I see."

"I bet he regrets his choice, though," I said, to cheer her up. "The day after the wedding he discovers she got some guy killed. His wife and kids, too. So the next year, when his conscience demands that he set up a secret identity and save people from the guillotine, he doesn't tell her. She writes him off as a fashionable nincompoop. She's supposed to be next best thing to a genius, but she's a bigger dolt than Henry's favorite bimbo."

"Oh come on, Sparrow." Nessa laughed. "Be fair. Who'd guess she's married Batman? Go on. So he's hiding from her. What next?"

Sparrow. I detest that name. Not least because Nessa uses it to put me in my place. To remind me I'm not as beautiful as she is. Well, that was the one thing I did expect playing Marguerite to give me: I'd find out how life as Nessa felt, if only for two weeks.

I picked up the paperback, studying the cannons and guillotine on the cover while I went on with my summary. "Marguerite runs into this sinister character she knew in Paris, Armand Chauvelin. The professor's playing him. He's Robespierre's chief agent, come to England to find the Scarlet Pimpernel. Sir Percy. Chauvelin discovers Marguerite's brother is one of the Pimpernel's men, and he threatens to have the brother executed unless Marguerite helps him learn the Pimpernel's identity. She ends up betraying her husband without knowing it."

A yell sounded in the background from the SF end of the line. "Gotta go," Nessa said hurriedly, "Rehearsal. Good luck."

"Bye. Kiss Babushka for me. And tell Henry if you see him." Whew. No lecture. I dropped the handset onto its base. My lucky day.

I went to pack. In the morning I had to meet the rest of the class to catch the bus to Concord for the simulation. Excluding Ian, who owned his own car and planned to meet us there. Which was great, because it postponed the moment when I'd have to deal with him.

Come to think of it, maybe the prospect of having me as his wife appalled him, too.

But I didn't care how he felt. By tomorrow, I'd be swanning around London poking fun at Sir Percy as I got ready to win the game. What could top that?

My plans went haywire the moment I woke up and realized my alarm clock had failed me. I hauled on the first clothes I saw: gray pants, burgundy V-neck, faded-flower socks in multiple colors. Burgundy was in there somewhere, or rose—close enough.

Damn, where were my other shoes? Not the demon straps! My toes ached at the thought.

I'd packed the other shoes. I had to unzip the suitcase and rummage until I found them at the bottom of the bag. By then, everything else had tangled into an inseparable heap, and I had no time for breakfast. I stuffed my feet into the shoes (the other half of the two-for-one sale, but wearable), forced the suitcase back into zippable shape, and ran. Halfway down the street, I remembered I hadn't locked the door to my apartment. Grumbling, I retraced my steps.

The day I searched for the seminar room, I'd skidded into it just in time. Not so this morning. As soon as I staggered across Massachusetts Avenue, I saw the bus, more properly a van, parked behind Witherspoon Hall. I raced toward it, bumping my suitcase along the sidewalk and dodging the Harvard Square traffic. Boston drivers are exciting at the best of times, but the square has the added attraction of hundreds of highly intelligent youth waiting to hurl themselves like lemmings into the stream of oncoming cars.

Including, at that moment, me. A blue-haired grandmother gave me the finger when, in a fit of desperation, I picked up the suitcase and dashed in front of her SUV. I waved an apology, but she was already threatening someone else's life.

As I dragged my bag over the last curb, I stumbled into David—pacing in front of the van, checking his watch. He grabbed the suitcase from my hand and hurled it into the trunk while I mumbled excuses. Seconds later, I lurched into the back seat. David slammed the bus into gear and honked his way through the Cambridge snarl. Simon, bless him, passed me a styrofoam cup of coffee. I was weighing schemes to woo him away from Suzanne when Tony produced a muffin and I decided to set my sights on him instead.

A jack-knifed tractor-trailer on Route 3 delayed us further. By the time we pulled up to a set of buildings that, according to David, had once formed part of the Concord Iron Works, he was growling in frustration.

Cuckoo, really, to fuss about a schedule he'd set himself. I hadn't delayed them by more than fifteen minutes. But I felt guilty about being late, so I stared out the window for most of the trip and tried to avoid drawing attention to myself. As soon as he threw the van into park, I pushed open the door and clambered down. Last in, first out. I collected my bag and surveyed the place where I would spend the next two weeks.

Ian waited by a door under a big banner that proclaimed *Dreamlife Productions* in curlicue white script against a royal blue background. For the first time, I noticed his muscles—long and lean, like a gymnast or a dancer—and the way his hair fell into his eyes. I found myself wondering what sport he played. I'd assumed Simon was our only athlete, but looking at Ian, so tall and poised, that seemed unlikely. How had I failed to recognize that his self-assurance extended to comfort with his own body?

Of course, my attempts to find out more about his past had gone nowhere. He had no use for me, and I had no interest in him. By eighteenth-century standards, we made the perfect married couple.

Besides the van, the parking lot contained only a small red Ford, probably Ian's. A California-surfer type approached, dressed in a sweatshirt of the same royal blue as the banner. He took my case, asked my name, attached a label to the bag, and placed it with the others. I thanked him and followed Suzanne to the door where Ian waited. A wiry man in his forties, whose baseball cap topped out somewhere in the region of Ian's biceps, introduced himself as Jeb Singer, Dreamlife's owner. He ushered us inside.

Jeb's office was a study in vintage geek: neutral shades, books piled on the floor, blueprints and papers warring for surface space with empty pizza boxes and crumb-strewn plates, massive banks of computers blocking any wall that could have housed bookcases. A set of seven chairs, the foldable metal kind that people put out for extra guests at dinner parties, teetered among the piles.

We took our seats in a rough circle. I ended up next to Ian—appropriate, I guess, given our soon-to-be not-intimate relationship. Figuring I'd honor the occasion with a stab at friendliness, I said, "Hi," which provoked an answering "Hi" but no conversation.

So much for effort. Turning away from him, I picked up a flyer that lay on the pile next to me. Against a background of blues and greens, large white letters proclaimed: "Role-Play *The*

Scarlet Pimpernel. Two Weeks in the Past." A picture of Anthony Andrews as Sir Percy—gold satin coat, lace cravat, quizzing glass in one hand—adorned the front, flanked by smaller stills from the same film. Jane Seymour in a ball gown and pouffy hair looked out of place next to Andrews disguised as an old hag or in action-hero mode with leather breeches and waistcoat, blood dripping from his forearm. Chauvelin raised Seymour's hand to his lips while she beamed at him as though he were her dearest friend.

I imagined myself looking like Seymour. Did the world contain that much makeup? Deciding there was no way, I flipped the flyer over. On the back Ian's name appeared in small white print. Until then, I hadn't realized he had any connection with the company.

I held out the flyer, tapping his name with one fingernail. The surfer type had followed Jeb Singer into the office and was distributing coffee, so we had a few minutes before the presentation started. "What's this?" I asked.

"I worked for Jeb," Ian said. "The summer before I started grad school. Historical consulting, some programming. Nothing major. I told David about the simulation."

Well, that answered a question I hadn't thought to ask: where David Houghton got the idea of turning his seminar into a live role-playing game. We were guinea pigs, in effect. I didn't point that out to Ian—or the fact that his connection with the company might give him an unfair advantage. I was too busy pondering another question. *Programming?*

When David talked about the simulation, he'd used the phrase "computer game," but what he described sounded more like a play. I distinctly remembered him mentioning costumes and sets. If I had to spend two weeks manipulating a joystick, I'd let David guillotine me just to keep from being bored out of my skull.

I leaned forward to prod Ian further, only to draw back when Surfer Dude handed me a cup of coffee. "So how does this work?" I asked.

Ian shrugged and pointed to Jeb Singer, who'd taken his seat behind the overloaded desk. "Jeb will explain."

I cradled the coffee in my hands, savoring the delicate steam-borne aroma and brooding. If only I had taken any other seminar. At this point in the semester, I didn't have too many options. If I spent money I couldn't afford on a taxi and ran off home, I'd flunk the course and have to choose another adviser (which didn't seem like such a bad idea right then). And I'd have to admit to my mother that she'd been right— well, except for the part about Ian getting ideas. I could handle Mom by lying low for two weeks and not confessing a thing, but that didn't solve my academic problems.

Blast. Even if I arranged to get guillotined right away, I'd have to find another adviser. Who wouldn't want a student with a crummy grade in her second-year seminar. No, I'd have to see it through and hope for the best.

Jeb launched into his introductory talk, thanking us for helping his group test their program. He went on at length about the software, its history and his goals—and praised Ian, who blushed. That was rather cute, actually. I'd never seen him embarrassed before. Maybe I'd try complimenting him sometime and see what happened.

Simon spoke up first. "Tell us what makes the game work."

David leaned against the wall, arms folded across his chest, and looked smug. I wondered what he knew that the rest of us didn't. Well, except Ian, presumably. I scowled first at one, then the other, but they had both focused on Jeb.

Could I claim that Ian's prior involvement with the company constituted foul play? But Ian didn't work for Jeb now. A software program would change a lot in two years. And complaining wouldn't, most likely, get me where I wanted to go. I decided to keep my mouth shut and see what happened.

Jeb answered Simon's question about how the simulation worked. "We've programmed a virtual-reality environment. It replicates the novel—characters, dialogue, scenery—in a way that appears completely lifelike."

"I can't wait." Suzanne leaned forward, her dark eyes alight. "When do we don our costumes?"

"You don't need costumes." Jeb held up a small disk, showing it in turn to each member of the group. "We attach these to your temples, wrists, and ankles. The computer feeds data to them through a wireless connection, and they transmit the information to your brain. You wear your regular clothes, but you see them as historical dress. It's like being swept up in a 3-D movie. You'll wonder whether you've time-traveled."

Suzanne gave a cry of surprise, unless that was me. I hadn't anticipated anything so high tech. No joysticks, though—that was good. "So it's not a computer game per se?" I asked.

"It is," Jeb said, "but not the kind you sit at a desk to play. You live your characters—become them, in a sense. You have complete freedom of movement within the computerized scenario. Everything looks and feels real. Once you become familiar with the environment, you can manipulate your surroundings with your mind. Think of yourself dressed as a stable hand, and a stable hand's clothes will soon appear."

"How do we eat?" Tony asked. "Sleep? Do we stay in the eighteenth century for two weeks straight?"

"The staff brings you food and clothes," Jeb said. "You'll think they're servants, or innkeepers, or whatever fits the game. The book starts in September 1792, so you'll see the props as late eighteenth-century. The computer will direct you. You can walk around the big room over there and into the various cubicles."

He waved at the wall opposite me. I guessed it hid the big room from view. "But the surroundings will look like scenes from *The Scarlet Pimpernel.* You may drive or dance or ride: whatever the story requires. The one thing that does stay the same is the number of people, so if you find yourself alone, or with one other person, you are. Otherwise, you'd have no privacy. We monitor the simulation to prevent accidents and gather information, but the computer filters out anything personal."

Simon jumped in again. "You don't expect us to quote from the book, I hope. I expected a script, so I didn't memorize more than a handful of lines."

Jeb shook his head. "The computer supplies the words."

Wait. If a machine controlled my brain, what hope did I have of influencing the results, winning, or even stopping Marguerite from acting like a birdbrain? I asked, "How is it a game if the computer tells us what to say?"

"Sorry," Jeb said. "I put that badly. As with the props, the computer sets the parameters, but you can maneuver within them. It feels like a conversation between you and your character. You can't tell her what's going to happen. You can't change her personality. But you can influence her behavior and decide what comes out of her mouth—if you learn to negotiate with her. That's part of the challenge."

Negotiate with the birdbrain? How's that supposed to work?

But I wanted to finish in the top two, so I had to find a way.

"Ready?" Ian stood and held out a hand to me. For a moment, I could have sworn he gazed straight into my eyes. An unaccustomed huskiness edged his voice.

Was he more interested in me than he'd let on? Startled by the thought, I took his outstretched hand. He released me as soon as I stood steady on my feet. I shook my head, convinced I had imagined that heartfelt gaze.

The other students crowded around the door, David in the lead and Ian at my heels. As I joined them, Ian spoke over my shoulder. "Show time," he said.

3. Dover

THE SHIFT TOOK PLACE IN THE BLINK OF AN EYE. ONE minute, I sat on a chair inside a warehouse, hearing voices from behind a screen but seeing no one other than the computer tech strapping wireless disks on my head, arms, and legs. The next, an unseen hand pushed me into eighteenth-century Dover.

Shocked, I gasped like the heroine in one of Baroness Orczy's novels. My ears felt blocked, and I shook my head to clear them. My breath came and went in short, rapid pants, like a diver surfacing after her oxygen tank gave out. *What was happening?*

At my back, torrential rain fell, and I ducked onto the porch to my right. Long velvet skirts dragged at my feet, although the lantern on the porch didn't give off enough light to see colors. An ostrich plume brushed the side of my face.

A portly man, short enough to seem almost square, blocked my path to the fireplace in the room beyond. He attempted a bow, but his out-thrust left arm unbalanced him, rocking him back on his heels. He kept sputtering, "My lady, my lady," as though he couldn't think of what else to say.

My lady? Me?

Then it hit me that he meant my character, Lady Marguerite Blakeney. I needed to pull myself together, fast.

A keening, practiced wail sounded amid the downpour, a blind man begging for charity. As I registered a flash of compassion, my mouth opened and I heard myself say, "Let the poor man be, and give him some supper at my expense." My voice, low and musical, had a distinct French accent, strong enough to be attractive without making words difficult to understand.

That was weird. How could I talk without planning what to say? I'd read the book, but like Simon I'd expected someone to hand me a script. I hadn't memorized every word. The electrodes connecting me to the computer couldn't have turned me into a different person, but it sure felt as if they had.

Having disposed of the beggar, the stranger in my head, Lady Marguerite Blakeney, turned her attention to the portly man. In her thoughts I heard his name: Mr. Jellyband, innkeeper of the Fisherman's Rest—the building sheltering me from the rain.

Not enough. Cold water dripped from ostrich feather to neck, and I shivered. The fire in the taproom glowed against the dark clouds outside. Impatience tightened Marguerite's chest, and without having decided to move, I found myself tapping the beribboned cane I held in my right hand inches from Jellyband's toes.

"Why are you standing there?" I demanded. "Stop hopping about like a turkey with a sore foot and let me pass!"

Again the words emerged without conscious thought. Jellyband ducked sideways, and Marguerite swept past him without a second glance.

No, not Marguerite. Me. My body, my voice. But not my personality. Not my instincts. How was that possible?

The strangeness of the experience sent me spinning into something close to panic. I fought the impulse to tear the sensors from my head, to flee back to Concord, to quit.

Jellyband coughed. Behind me, rain streamed from the eaves of a centuries-old building. Heavy oak beams supported the planked ceiling above my head; paneled walls closed me in on either side. Down the corridor, I could see the glow indicating the taproom beyond, where voices traded jokes and flirtatious comments in a broad, lower-class English accent familiar from *Masterpiece Theater*. Tankards clanked at the raising of toasts. I smelled cinnamon and nutmeg, the tang of hard cider, the malty scent of ale, and the rich, complex aroma of mulled wine.

Quit? Give up the opportunity of a lifetime—not just to see the past but to touch it, smell it? To relive my favorite novel, remake it in a way that suited me? Even if I lost, I'd keep those memories forever.

But I wouldn't lose. I knew the book as well as the other students did. I had a plan. The only way to lose was not to play. Negotiate, Jeb had told us. I could negotiate.

"Onward," as the Russians say. "To victory!" As Marguerite propelled my feet along the hallway, I imagined my babushka cheering me on.

"Brrr." Marguerite walked through the taproom door, shaking off the rain. "I'm as wet as a herring. *Dieu*, has anyone ever seen such a contemptible climate!" She headed for the fire, shedding moisture.

The room contained a dozen people or more, most of them locals dressed in loose clothes, worsted trousers, and leather gaiters. The five who stood between Marguerite and the fire belonged to a different social class altogether: three young men, two tall and fair and one dark-haired with an exotic air; a pretty young lady whom Marguerite recognized as her dear friend of convent days; and a formidable older lady who resembled nothing so much as a dragon, especially in the glare she bestowed on me. All five wore traveling costumes, the women with silken hooped skirts peeking out from under their fine wool cloaks and the men sporting the pantaloons, short-waisted jackets, and knee-high boots made famous a few years later by Beau Brummell. The women had elaborate coiffures, and the men tied their hair back—their own hair, though, not powdered wigs.

Three of them had to be my classmates: Simon, Suzanne, and Tony. But only Suzanne looked anything like herself: a slender brown-eyed brunette.

Meaning they looked at me and saw Marguerite, who at that moment seemed wholly alien to me. How strange to realize that the self-image in my head didn't match what everyone else perceived. Like *Invasion of the Body Snatchers*, with a twist.

Marguerite stopped mid-track and held out both her arms to the young woman. "Well, if it isn't my dear Suzanne," she said with a girlish enthusiasm I couldn't imagine exuding on my worst teenage day. "*Pardieu*, Citizeness, how came you to be in England? And Madame, too!"

Suzanne extended her hands in turn, until the dragon pulled her up short. "I forbid you to speak to that woman," she said in a voice that could have stopped clocks. Marguerite's shock flowed over me. My heart pumped as she fought for control. Suzanne looked stricken.

Marguerite soon rallied. "Hoity-toity, Citizeness! What fly stings you, pray?"

The dragon snapped, "We are in England now, Madame, and I am at liberty to forbid my daughter to touch your hand in friendship."

I blinked at the hostility in her voice. The two young Englishmen squirmed, and I heard a hiss from Mr. Jellyband, who had followed me into the room after doing his insufficient best to prevent disaster. Marguerite's chin trembled, but she kept her head up as the dragon swept us an imperial curtsey and headed for the door.

As the shock of immersion ebbed, my discomfort eased and my confidence creeped into the light once more. The lines, the actions—I recognized them from the original novel. Not things I would say or do myself, but words I would have read from a script if I were playing Marguerite in the conventional sense. Jeb's flat statement that "the computer supplies the words" hadn't prepared me for being taken over, body and soul, by a doppelgänger with instincts different from mine, but it was accurate. I could predict what would happen if I put my mind to it.

I might not *like* what I predicted, but I was not flying blind. I could take my time getting used to this bizarre sensation while I figured out how to supplant Marguerite and regain control of my body.

The story rolled along. The dragon demanded her daughter's presence. Suzanne trailed after her mother, but when she reached the door, she ran back and kissed Marguerite on both cheeks. Then, with a quick look over her shoulder, she dashed from the room. Marguerite smiled, and the tension among the young men eased.

She turned toward the blonds, Sir Andrew and Lord Tony. While pondering who played which of these interchangeable young men, I spared a moment to wonder how Tony felt about his change of race. Funny that it hadn't occurred to me to ask him. Had David considered that element when he came up with his scheme? Percy, Andrew, Tony: Baroness Orczy obviously had a thing for blonds, but that didn't excuse the rest of us acting oblivious.

Although, knowing Tony, he might well view the whole thing as a hoot.

Marguerite hauled me back into the game. "So that's it, is it?" she announced with forced gaiety. "La, Sir Andrew, did you ever see such an unpleasant person? I hope when I'm old, I shan't look like that!"

By "unpleasant person," she meant the comtesse. I went along for the ride as she stalked to the fireplace and said over her shoulder, "Suzanne, I forbid you to speak to that woman!"

The two Englishmen clapped. I had to admire her skill as an actress. She'd caught the comtesse's intonation precisely, as Sir Andrew and Lord Tony didn't hesitate to point out. But the effect wasn't quite what she intended. The third man— Suzanne's brother, the Vicomte de Tournay de Basserive— took an impetuous step forward, his hand on his sword. Marguerite's attempt to save face had stirred him up, not calmed him down.

Inside her head, I weighed the pros and cons of intervention. The comtesse had earned every nasty word, but her son? It seemed a shame to let Marguerite take out her snippiness on him.

Only I had no idea how to stop her. I had yet to make a single remark of my own. And I had a clear goal for this game, one that didn't include protecting the vicomte—who was probably a computer projection anyway. I should hold off until I could turn the plot in a direction of *my* choosing. Most of the time, Marguerite concentrated her attacks on her husband, and he gave as good as he got. Birdbrain or not, she'd do no real harm.

An inane laugh signaled Percy's arrival. Marguerite glanced to our right. For an instant, her mouth dropped open as I stared, stunned by my first sight of Percy.

Six foot odd of gorgeousness—so Baroness Orczy had described this tulip of fashion—lounged in the doorway. Blond and broad-shouldered, Sir Percy looked like the cover model on a men's fashion magazine, circa 1795. In him I saw the hero described in the novel, the man sketched in the line drawings of old editions, Percy as an actor might play him in a movie—anything but Ian Campbell in eighteenth-century dress.

When he caught me staring, he gave an elaborate court bow. Amusement lit the bland, beautiful face. A Russian adage describes the eyes as the windows to the soul, and for an instant I experienced the flash of recognition people mention when they talk about love at first sight.

Nonsense. I'd caught a glimpse of Ian, no more. Keep your eye on the ball, Nina. It's a game, not a fantasy.

From the doorway, Percy surveyed me from my coiffed head to my two-inch heels. A knowing smile curved his perfectly molded lips. My stomach tingled. The romantic novels I devoured in college teemed with men who undressed the heroine with their eyes. I'd written it off as hyperbole, but Percy stripped Marguerite's half-dozen layers off with a glance. I gazed at him, mesmerized. Flickers of desire shot through my body.

A game, not a fantasy. I took deep breaths, trying to slow my heartbeat. Ian was doing his best to undermine my confidence, drat him, and if I didn't take care, he'd succeed.

Percy dropped his wet greatcoat over the back of a handy chair and pulled his quizzing glass from a pocket, observing the scene through heavy-lidded blue eyes. Sir Andrew and Lord Tony went to shake his hand. He greeted them by name and with a disparaging comment on the weather. Any minute now, he would pick up the tension Marguerite's mimicry had revived and start asking questions.

Not that it mattered. This scene existed to introduce the characters and the setting, to show the sympathetic victims rescued by the Scarlet Pimpernel and contrast them with the nasty, murdering Jacobins. I could give Marguerite her head or take a stab at altering a word here or there, just to test the waters. Either way, I wouldn't change the outcome.

Nasty, murdering Jacobins. The thought distracted me from the surrounding scene by sparking a memory of my grandmother, her broad face ringed by thinning hair under the ever-present scarf, her body thickened by hard work and heavy food. The image faded as I recalled her prized possession, a silver-framed picture of herself at twenty: a slender redhead with curly hair, huge brown eyes, and slanting Slavic cheekbones she'd bequeathed to Nessa, lucky duck. In the photo, Babushka wore a red Komsomol scarf around her neck and a white shirtwaist that must have taken hours to starch and iron. A dark skirt but no stockings, because they didn't have nylons in Russia in 1948, so the girls drew lines down the backs of their legs to mimic seams. Some nameless official pinned an award on her chest. Heroine of Socialist Labor, maybe. She was a revolutionary, like Marguerite. And a voluntary exile, also like Marguerite. They would have lots to say to each other, including how it felt to have your best days behind you.

As the thought formed in my brain, the oddest thing happened. I felt the air shift between me and my character, the way one might if someone opened a distant window, long closed. Startled, I drew back. The window swung shut, but I sensed a slim thread of connection I hadn't noticed before.

Was *that* what Jeb meant by negotiation? And if so, what could I do with the information? I couldn't manufacture emotional intimacy!

Percy interrupted my thoughts, raising his quizzing glass and examining the company. The glass magnified his eye to monstrous dimensions. "Lud," he announced, "how sheepish you all look ... What's up?"

Marguerite's cue. She produced an affected giggle and said, "Oh, nothing, Sir Percy. Nothing to disturb your equanimity— just an insult to your wife."

Oh, dear. Percy didn't like that. He, the Scarlet Pimpernel, too cowardly to defend his wife's honor? I saw his hand clench where he held the quizzing glass, but he forced it to relax long enough to deliver his lines. With complete indifference, he drawled, "La, my dear, you don't say so! What brave man dared tackle you, eh?"

He stabbed better than she did. Marguerite winced. Before she could respond, the Vicomte de Tournay, outraged masculinity in motion, pushed past Lord Tony's restraining arm and cast the fat firmly into the fire. His mother, he admitted, had "offensed" Marguerite, and he would gladly offer up his life in support of the woman who bore him. As a man of honor (midget of honor, more like—his head topped out at Percy's breastbone), he offered the husband of the woman scorned the only gentlemanly resolution to the conflict.

He couldn't have underlined Marguerite's implied insult better if he'd tried. The vicomte would defend his mother's honor to the death. And he was spoiling for a fight, most likely with swords, given the way he'd thrust the hilt of his dress rapier forward.

Marguerite burst into laughter and pointed at the vicomte. "Lud, Sir Andrew, look on that pretty picture—the English turkey and the French bantam."

What was *with* this fixation on turkeys? A birdbrain obsessed with birds!

Percy didn't acknowledge his wife's ill-judged attempt at humor. Instead, he brought the quizzing glass into play again and scanned the vicomte from head to foot before asking incredulously where the man had learned English. "I vow I can't speak the French lingo like that. What?"

The vicomte stiffened. He lengthened his spine, gaining a whole half-inch, and thrust out his chin. The poor guy must think he'd landed in a lunatic asylum. Didn't Percy realize he'd been challenged to a duel?

But that was the point of Percy's faked incomprehension: to distract this boy, stop him from doing something stupid by refusing to take the bait. Admirable goal, fulfilled with aplomb. My respect for Sir Percy grew.

"I'll vouch for that," Marguerite chipped in. "Sir Percy has a British accent you could cut with a knife."

Another cheap shot, but Percy ignored this one, too.

"Monsieur," the vicomte said in his stilted English, "I fear you have not understand. I offer you the only possible *réparation* among gentlemen."

Again, Percy left the verbal gauntlet on the floor. I watched him drop the quizzing glass into his breast pocket and pull out a snuffbox, from which he extracted a pinch of snuff with exaggerated care. He looked nothing whatsoever like Ian.

The vicomte had reddened like a proverbial beet by the time Percy drawled, "What the devil is that?"

"My sword, Monsieur." The vicomte, losing patience, thrust the hilt of his rapier down until the sheathed blade ran almost parallel to the floor. His chest puffed out in anger, increasing his resemblance to a bantam rooster.

Marguerite opened her mouth once more. For the first time, I heard the words of her retort form in her head. As a test, I suggested an alternative. She clamped her lips shut, considering.

Success! I'd delayed her—not long, but enough for Percy to step in. One tiny victory.

Percy gave no sign of noticing the missing dialogue. From his great height, he gazed at the angry vicomte through sleepy eyes and asked, "Lud love you, Sir. What's the good of your sword to me?" He slid the snuffbox into his pocket and turned his back. You'd have sworn the whole fuss made him want to take a nap.

"A duel," the vicomte said to that expanse of gray wool.

Percy settled next to the fire. "Oh, is that what you meant? I never fight duels." He glanced at Lord Tony. "Demmed uncomfortable things, duels ... ain't they, Tony?"

Like his cat-and-mouse game with the French was not one extended duel.

Marguerite didn't react to that. I spared a moment to wonder what she heard and didn't hear. My earlier suggestion had stopped her, as if she listened to an inner voice, but I had aimed that right at her. And the memory of my grandmother had touched her emotionally, even though she didn't respond in words. The "cat-and-mouse game" comment provoked neither action nor feelings, though, so it must have passed her by. Jeb had said the computer wouldn't let us give away the plot, right? Another set of boundaries to test as the game progressed.

Meanwhile, the vicomte sputtered like a kettle about to boil. In those days, no gentleman worth his salt refused a challenge. Dueling may have been illegal in England, but most people paid the law less attention than we pay to parking signs. Refusing a duel was itself an insult: it implied you considered the would-be opponent beneath your notice. Which in this case he was—Percy looked as if he could pick up the vicomte in one hand and squeeze him into submission.

While the vicomte simmered, Marguerite returned to the fray. "I pray you, Lord Tony," she said with a mocking laugh. "Play the peacemaker. The child is bursting with rage and might do Sir Percy an injury. The British turkey has had the day. Sir Percy would provoke all the saints in the calendar and keep his temper the while."

In my mental isolation cell, I groaned. Did she have to be *such* a bitch? I felt irritation rising. Not only was this *my* body, but if I had to listen to two weeks of birdbrain "humor" coming out of my mouth, I'd go round the bend.

Annoyance flashed in Percy's eyes in response to her latest assault, though he didn't express it. On the contrary, he joined the laughter at his own expense and praised her to the vicomte. Which was good, since it meant we were still following the script, my one small deviation notwithstanding.

Still, I had to do better than this. Marguerite's idea of witty conversation made my jaw hurt, and so far I hadn't a hope of fulfilling my plan.

Lord Tony steered the vicomte away from Percy with more soothing words. In a minute, the two Englishmen would have averted the crisis.

Unless Marguerite stirred the pot once more. Hearing another round of thinly veiled insults form in her mind, I reacted on instinct. «Don't say a word!»

To my astonishment, it worked. She shut her mouth, the words the baroness had written for her unspoken.

Eureka! I might pull this off after all.

Without Marguerite tightening the screws, the reconciliation among the men proceeded apace. Percy demanded a bowl of punch and invited the vicomte to share it. Jellyband, waddling in to take the order, mentioned that he had spotted Marguerite's brother, Armand (to whom Baroness Orczy, oddly, had given the same first name as the villain), coming down the road with Percy's skipper. I recognized an approaching scene shift.

Percy's casual invitation to join the punch party extended to Armand, but Marguerite refused. Several times. Aglow with my recent victory, I left her to it. She didn't land *too* many barbs.

"In fact," she finished, "you are such merry company that I trust you will forgive me if I bid my brother goodbye in another room."

Good idea. Get her out of the way for a while and give me a chance to practice.

The men bowed, acquiescing. Good manners required that they push her no further. With a flourish, she lifted the velvet skirts (blue, I noticed) in her right hand, took the beribboned cane in her left, and swept from the room. The ostrich plume caressed her cheek as a breeze blew from the open doorway. The rain had disappeared into radiant sunshine.

At the last minute, a whisper from me made her look back. Otherwise, she would never have seen the yearning passion with which Percy watched her depart.

4. Seashore

MARGUERITE RELAXED AS SOON AS THE DOOR CLOSED behind her. Her shoulders released, and tears slipped from beneath her closed lids. The whalebone corset jabbed into her ribs, and she pulled her spine upright with a sobbing breath. Until then, I hadn't realized how much strain her marriage placed on her. I found myself sympathizing with her.

She wasted no time pondering the expression she'd surprised on Percy's face. Her thoughts drifted past me like the occasional wispy breeze, whereas emotions billowed like clouds. Unhappiness, disappointment, resentment swirled around me. Anger. Fear that life would never get better. Wistful memories of her lost home in Paris, heightened by the unexpected meeting with Suzanne and by Armand's impending departure, intermingled with confusion at her husband's coldness and the impenetrable customs of this alien island. Bittersweet recollections of happier times when Percy had gazed at her as though she meant something to him.

Like my grandmother. She, too, pined for her lost youth, the home left behind. Why had I failed to realize that nostalgia drove her to maximize the good from her past and deny the bad?

Nostalgia and defensiveness. I guessed that Babushka, like Marguerite, felt constantly under attack, a representative of a country and a time no less excoriated in the twenty-first-century West than revolutionary France had been in secure, monarchist England. A point I hadn't understood before my hour in Marguerite's corset.

Another unaccustomed question flitted through my mind. Why *did* I dislike Marguerite so much? Sure, she zigged and zagged and sniped and made stupid decisions, but wasn't the real problem that she reminded me of my sister? Nessa and I pretended to get along, but bad blood lay between us. She had pushed me off a set of monkey bars when I was six, and things went downhill from there. My family expended time and scarce funds to support her desire to dance, whereas my love of books provoked at best an uncomprehending shrug. In truth, I was jealous, of Nessa and of Marguerite. A humbling thought.

This was weird. I'd entered the game with one goal in my head: surpass everyone else and earn David Houghton's agreement to act as my dissertation adviser. Yet here, one hour in, I'd already discovered things about my family that had eluded me for years.

Again I felt the wispy thread of connection strengthen, the window between myself and Marguerite swing open. This time it remained ajar.

From the inn porch I admired the scene before me. White chalk cliffs rose sheer out of the blue-gray sea. The ground glistened from the recent rain, and the late afternoon sun shaded the chalk to the pearl-pink of an abalone shell, reflected in the frothy waves that pounded the beach. The town—more like a village by my standards—had the charm of a picture postcard: peaked slate roofs and cobblestones. Only the occasional clop of a horse's hooves and shouts from those arriving at the inn broke the stillness. No cars, no motorboats, no machines.

Out on the water, a yacht drifted at anchor, graceful as a sea eagle, waiting to carry Marguerite's brother to France. Here and there, lanterns and candles cast golden circles behind the shutters. The inn kitchen gave off the appetizing scent of cooked beef and fresh bread. Fifty yards or so along the path, two men walked toward us. The older—middle-aged, with a ruddy face, short gray beard, and pipe and clothing reminiscent of Popeye the Sailor—rolled along with a typical seaman's gait. The younger, as short as Marguerite's "bantam" but less choleric, with crisp dark curls and lively eyes, had to be Armand. Marguerite, shedding depression as she'd earlier shaken off the rain, glided toward them, skirts swishing against the cobbled street.

The scene surrounded me, yielding not a hint of the other, real world where until now I had spent all my time. Jeb and his staff had done an astonishing job. I could have sworn the technology to produce this level of illusion didn't exist.

Armand ran to embrace Marguerite, as though they hadn't seen each other little more than a day ago. They took their leave of the boat captain and walked, arm in arm, along the cliffs. Dover was a transit point, Britain's gateway to the English Channel. Except for Jellyband, everyone I had met so far had another destination: London, Richmond, some ancestral estate. But no one had as far to go as Armand, due to depart in half an hour for the revolutionary inferno that had engulfed Paris, City of Light.

At first, the emotions that reached me glowed rose pink. Armand, eight years Marguerite's senior at thirty-two, had raised his sister after their parents died while he was in his teens. None of the tensions that marked my family relationships carried through into Marguerite's love for her brother. For the first few minutes, I let the tide of feeling sweep me along, awash in a warmth I had never experienced.

The joyous pink developed dark edges of fear. Without Armand, where would Marguerite turn for love? Not to her indifferent husband. Not to society, either. The comtesse's snub, delivered with such conviction, underlined that point.

Desperate, she pleaded with him to stay. "I am not going far, sweet one," he said. "A narrow channel to cross—a few miles of road—I can soon come back."

But she knew he was lying—and he knew it, too. The distance in miles meant nothing. From here, France lay closer than Richmond and the beautiful, soulless house Marguerite shared with a man she could not understand. The difference between Dover and Calais lay elsewhere. Between a world still ordered and one filled with chaos, a place where today's hero could fall from grace tomorrow, his head split from his neck while the mob howled for his blood. Unbearable if the head were Armand's.

"Our own beautiful country, Margot," her brother said. "When France is in peril, it is not for her sons to turn their backs on her."

Like most of the dialogue I'd heard to this point, the line came from Orczy's novel, and the artificiality of it struck me. Marguerite spoke that way too, in high-flown phrases I found it difficult to believe anyone had used, even in the eighteenth century. But with Marguerite I could sense the emotions that drove her and, as time passed, the thoughts that lay behind the unnatural speech.

"Oh, Armand!" She sounded wistful, as though she knew he no longer heard her. "I sometimes wish you had not so many lofty virtues. I assure you, little sins are far less dangerous and uncomfortable. But you will take care?"

Her sorrow rolled through me, drawing me into her life and thus into the story. I felt like a person awakening from a coma, without hands or feet, unable to communicate, locked in a head that wasn't my own—yet, in some unfathomable way, reborn into this new, different body.

"As far as possible," he said. "I promise you."

Marguerite shuddered. "Remember, I have only you." The words choked in her throat, but after a while she whispered, "to care for me."

A startled expression crossed Armand's face. "Sir Percy cares for you."

Marguerite hesitated. "He did once." She gripped her hands. I sensed her already regretting her slip of the tongue. "Don't let me distress you, dearest. Percy is very good."

"Good! A strange way to characterize the man who loves you above all others!"

She shuddered again.

"Does he know of the part you played in the arrest of the Marquis de St. Cyr?" Armand asked.

I perked up, eager less to hear her words, which I had read many times, than to discover what lay in her uncensored thoughts. For truth be told, I'd never grasped what Marguerite thought she was doing when she denounced the marquis. If she had denounced him—even that wasn't clear. The baroness, not content with a single explanation, had supplied at least three, blissfully unconcerned that they contradicted one another.

Yet I wanted an answer. The question went to the heart of my dissertation: how does a decent, ordinary person support, even defend, an ideology permeated with violence? Marguerite was not cruel. Yet somehow she had justified the murder of an entire family, children included.

No, I was wrong. I heard guilt in her bitter laugh, in her refusal to mince words. "That I denounced the Marquis de St. Cyr to the tribunal that ultimately sent him and his family to the guillotine, you mean? Yes, Percy knows. I told him myself after our wedding."

Be careful what you wish for, people say. And there, on the hillside, I saw why. My half-baked plans smashed like coracles against the reef of her despair. I reeled under the memory of her confession: the effort of mustering her courage, only to discover that Percy had already tried and condemned her; her horror on learning that a simple error—trusting the wrong person with information—had killed her fairy-tale love story almost before it drew breath.

Armand's face softened as he said, "And you told him the circumstances, so he understood you were not to blame?"

She stared at the roiling waves of the English Channel. Under her feet, I felt springy grass and the crumbly chalk cliff. "It was too late to talk of circumstances. He had already learned the tale from others and believed every word." She raised her chin. "I could not demean myself by trying to explain."

Another birdbrain moment, I'd thought when I read the book. More fool me. In Marguerite's eyes, her behavior made perfect sense. Why babble excuses Percy had proven he had no interest in hearing? Better to seek refuge with Armand, who loved her.

Not that it did her much good. In the end, she had to go home. An eighteenth-century wife had no residence, no legal existence, apart from her husband. But by the time she returned, she might as well talk to an icicle hanging from the roof. From that moment on, Percy shut her out of his life. Their marriage was a show, mounted every day for the *ton*.

I shivered. A year. It must have felt like a century.

"But Sir Percy loved you, Margot," Armand said.

I wondered if Armand had that right. Would a man in love condemn his beloved unheard?

"Well, I thought so," Marguerite said. "Otherwise I would not have married him."

Indigo waves of bitterness swept me into her head. A gallery of pictures formed before my eyes. Percy, handsome and elegant, tweaking the flower of the Paris intelligentsia at Marguerite's salon. Percy in a garden, his eyes darkened with passion, pulling her into his arms. I felt her excitement at having found something hidden, previously unsuspected, not only in him but in anyone. The thrill of pledging herself to this intense, fascinating man.

The contest, Ian and David, my goals, my future—all disappeared. Marguerite's distress tossed me into the past, trapped me in coils of loss.

Nessa letting go of my hands, so many years ago. She'd looked stricken. How had I forgotten that? I heard a man's voice, raised in fury.

No, not that. Anything but that. I wrapped both arms around my head and let the fog swirl around me, shutting the images out.

"And now I have the satisfaction, Armand," Marguerite was saying when I came back to the present, "of knowing that the biggest fool in England has the most perfect contempt for his wife."

«It's not true,» I told her, remembering the quizzing glass. «Look at his hands. People mask their faces, not their hands. Watch for the fleeting expressions he can't control. You'll see. Every time you prick him, you draw blood.»

I sensed a little click, like a light switch flipping on, followed by a vivid memory of the yearning in Percy's face as she left. The indigo waves faded.

Marguerite was thinking, at last.

❀

Marguerite talked with Armand until the skipper called him away. Then we stood for almost an hour, watching the yacht glide into infinity, crimson-gold sunset casting sparks on the water and echoing off glowing brass and satiny paint. Nostalgia and grief at Armand's departure mingled with simple reluctance to return to the world of pretense represented by the Fisherman's Rest.

Throughout the hour, I explored her thoughts, searching for paths that would release me from the confines of my own mind. With the subsidence of emotional storms, my goals for the seminar returned.

I realized my plan needed serious work. When I'd thought of the game as a kind of eighteenth-century *Risk*—me and my fellows in costume negotiating in real time—I'd had no doubts I could keep from betraying the Scarlet Pimpernel to Chauvelin. But with my character so real and so powerful, my ability to communicate with my own body so variable, it would be a miracle if I could achieve that level of control.

If I could not change the plot, Marguerite would ally with Chauvelin. Which would do me no good, since to win I had to thwart Chauvelin's plans. With my back against the figurative wall, I realized that, much as I hated the idea, my best bet was to forge a partnership with Ian. If necessary, I could double-cross him later, but so long as the two of us worked together against Chauvelin, we would both win. Suzanne had Andrew on her side, and even if I could drive a wedge between them, I wouldn't do it. Marguerite, though, could derail Tony's collusion with Ian without much effort. And since I'd offered Tony an alliance and he'd turned me down, he was fair game.

Yet the idea stuck in my craw. Not because Ian would, as my mother said, "get ideas." More likely, he'd refuse to cooperate, leaving me back at square one. And if he agreed, there I'd be, cooperating with *him,* instead of staying nicely estranged as the baroness had planned. Besides, I liked Tony. Liked him better than Ian. I felt guilty about elbowing Tony out of the way.

I should give it a shot, though. I was a scholar, not a soap-opera queen ruled by gummy emotions. Like my fellow-students, I wanted to win. The others would defeat me if they saw the opportunity. I couldn't afford to go easy on them. If Ian agreed to a partnership, fine. If not, I could keep striving to achieve enough control over Marguerite to revert to Plan A.

That decided, I concentrated on moving so much as a finger or toe. Changing the script seemed like a pipe dream when I had yet to lift a hand or take a step.

As the sky darkened, Marguerite turned back toward the inn, walking slowly at first, then picking up speed as she looked around and realized how empty the streets had become. Long skirts shushed in rapid rhythm against the stones as Marguerite kicked them before her. Lights glowed in many windows, and the smells of dinner seeped from the houses as we passed.

About half a block from the Fisherman's Rest, a cough sounded behind us. Marguerite turned, skirts swinging, to face a stoop-shouldered man twisting a tall hat in restless hands.

From the book, I knew we had encountered the villain. Monsieur Armand Chauvelin—former marquis, dedicated revolutionary, chief agent of the Committee of Public Safety, special envoy of the republican government of France, and Robespierre's right-hand man. That cough indicated we were entering an important scene.

Chauvelin looked like nothing so much as one of the Puritans you see parading themselves before tourists on

Plymouth Rock. The cuckolded parson from *The Scarlet Letter*, perhaps—they both gave me the creeps. I found it difficult to imagine handsome, arrogant David in that scrawny figure. He'd have a fit the first time he looked in a mirror. The thought heartened me enough that I could focus on the present.

Dressed in black except for a plain white shirt, Chauvelin appeared relentlessly unfashionable, worlds apart from the elegant Sir Percy. As Marguerite curtseyed, Chauvelin produced a perfunctory bow, as if manners were an aristocratic vice he could no longer justify.

He fixed Marguerite with his pale eyes. The baroness, who favored animal metaphors, likened Chauvelin to a weasel. He looked every inch the villain, impermeable as steel.

"*Citoyenne* St. Just," he said, using the French for "citizeness" and my character's maiden name. To remind her of her revolutionary past. Or to deny the reality of her husband. Had Chauvelin learned of the quarrel between Percy and Marguerite?

Marguerite, true to the baroness's characterization, laughed and extended both arms, cooing over her dear Chauvelin. He lifted one of her hands to his mouth and brushed his lips across her fingertips. She giggled in the girlish way that made me yearn to slap her.

"But tell me," she asked, "what in the world are you doing here in England?"

"I might return the subtle compliment, fair lady," Chauvelin said, although Marguerite hadn't complimented him as far as I could see. "What of yourself?"

He walked at her side as she turned back toward the inn. Anger grew inside me as I listened to her laughing and flirting. Ugh! The woman was a birdbrain after all.

"*Je m'ennuie, mon ami,* that's all," she said. I'm bored, my friend. Only when she switched back to English did I notice that she'd been speaking French since the moment she left the yacht captain an hour and a half ago. Much more fluent French than I could have managed on my own. Another gold star for Jeb's staff.

Chauvelin feigned surprise at her declaration of boredom. "And this within a year of a romantic love match!"

"Yes." Marguerite sighed. "A romantic love match. That's just the difficulty."

Watching Chauvelin—oily, cynical, manipulative—I felt dislike burgeon inside me. Marguerite seemed oblivious. Not thinking of how it would help my plans but out of pure fellow-feeling, a desire to wake her up to Chauvelin's malice, I reached out to her. «Look at him!» I urged. A sardonic smile pulled at his lips. «You're playing into his hands!»

No dice. I danced with impatience as Marguerite compared her marriage to the measles, easily contracted and as easily forgotten.

Hmm. What to do now?

I had opened a window before through empathy and shared experience—mine and my grandmother's. It was worth a try. «You're lonely,» I said. «You want to go home, where no comtesse dared snub you; you were the toast of Paris before you met Percy. But Chauvelin is not your friend. He can't help.»

A crack appeared in her mental walls. Meanwhile, Chauvelin oozed sympathy, teasing and prodding her, highlighting her frustration, dangling her past happiness before her the way one holds out keys to distract a baby. The chatter from the taproom, the shouts for Sally the barmaid, and Sir Percy's inane laugh punctuated the French agent's words with uncanny perfection.

«You need friendship,» I said. «I understand. But you won't get it from Chauvelin. Trust me. I can help you.» The crack in the walls widened. I inserted an imaginary foot, then a leg. I could almost step through.

Chauvelin pressed on. "I have a most perfect prescription against the worst form of *ennui*, but..."

He paused, and Marguerite rose to the bait like a hungry trout. "But what?"

Chauvelin took snuff. "There *is* Sir Percy."

Uh oh. Given the amount of discord between Marguerite and her husband, an offer like that might prove too good to resist.

But I'd underestimated her. Wary, she drew back. And when, a few minutes later, Chauvelin casually dropped into the conversation his mission—both official (to act as France's ambassador to the Court of St. James) and unofficial (to capture the Scarlet Pimpernel)—I felt her hesitate.

"Find him," Chauvelin urged, meaning the Scarlet Pimpernel. His eyes glowed with fanaticism. "Find him for France." His narrow hands rubbed, one against the other. At any moment I expected an evil cackle to emerge.

Marguerite drew herself up, almost his equal in height. "La, man, you are astonishing!" She gave another infectious chuckle. "Where in the world am I to look for him?"

Chauvelin's narrow face creased, weasel smile well in evidence. He'd withdrawn when she spoke, but now he leaned in again, as if sharing confidences. "Lady Blakeney is the pivot of social London, so I'm told. You see everything, *hear* everything."

What an absurd remark. Surely a diplomat had attended enough society parties to know that the people you meet there don't say anything that counts. They certainly don't sneak up behind you whispering drunkenly into your ear, "Guess what, sweetie? I'm that dashing anonymous hero, the Scarlet Pimpernel." And if they did, any normal woman would dart behind the nearest potted plant, secure in the belief that wrestling a cactus beat having to evade an admirer even more potted than the plant.

As for that unctuous hint that Marguerite would agree to become his spy—well, for two pins I'd whack that cane of hers against his head.

«Oh, let's!» Marguerite said, her voice clear in my mind. Her hand twitched on the beribboned cane, and Chauvelin took a hurried step back.

Yes! Could we be talking? Stuck in the background, I did a celebratory two-step.

She waved the stick. Chauvelin looked alarmed, but alas, Marguerite didn't hit him.

"What you propose is horrible, Chauvelin," she said with dignity. "Whoever the man may be, he is brave and noble, and never—do you hear me?—*never* would I participate in such villainy." She pulled in her skirts, turned her back, and stalked into the inn.

«Oh, good for you,» I told her. Indeed, she'd hit exactly the right note. Better than using the cane, I supposed, although the thought of smacking Chauvelin still made me wistful. That weasel smile infuriated me.

My professor lurked behind that smile. I should show some restraint.

Marguerite had pushed open the door when Chauvelin managed one final shot. "Do you prefer to be insulted by every French aristocrat who escapes to England?"

Marguerite's head snapped round. I felt as startled as she. How had he known about the snub she'd received from the Comtesse de Tournay? He hadn't been in the taproom when we entered. One of us would have noticed him.

Wait. What was I thinking? David had read the book even more often than I had.

But that would mean David had succeeded in contacting his character more quickly than I. In which case they made a dangerous combination.

I'd underestimated David as well as Marguerite. If he had control of Chauvelin, then I needed to take over my body right away. And if success meant allying with Ian, then allying with Ian was what I would do.

"That's not your last word, *Citoyenne*," Chauvelin said. "We meet in London." It sounded like a threat.

Marguerite spoke over her shoulder. "We meet in London, but it is my last word." And with that, she stepped over the threshold and swept into the dark passageway beyond.

5. The London Road

WHEN WE RETURNED TO THE TAPROOM, WE FOUND SIR Andrew and Lord Tony standing around the table, which bore a large and almost empty punch bowl. As I watched, the innkeeper's daughter arrived from the kitchen, a tray balanced on her left shoulder. She swung it down to unload lemons, a bowl of sugar, and various bottles onto the table—already set with places for five, a loaf of bread, and a large joint of beef. A few slices, their centers pink and steaming, invited diners to partake. The vicomte had given into temptation and stood to one side, munching a sandwich.

Sir Andrew and Lord Tony ducked their heads toward Marguerite before pouncing on the bottles and pouring them into the bowl, not wasting time on measurements. She nodded at them. The vicomte abandoned his sandwich long enough to produce an elaborate bow.

"Ah," Percy drawled from his seat near the fireplace. "So you're back, m'dear? Armand get off all right?" He rose languidly to his feet and subjected me to his heavy-lidded stare.

Again his scrutiny tightened my stomach and curled my toes. I had to stop this. Yes, Percy had been the hero of my teen years, but I should not let him have this effect on me.

Otherwise Ian *would* get ideas, and with good reason. And that was the last thing I wanted.

No, untrue. When I first met Ian, I thought he was hot. But his combination of indifference, barbs, and silence soon convinced me he had no interest in me. If I were honest with myself, wasn't *that* when I decided I had no interest in him?

And when I thought of Ian that way, I realized something else. Percy treated Marguerite in exactly the same way. Maybe she and I had more in common than I'd believed.

Some part of my response captured Marguerite's attention. At last she'd noticed I had reactions of my own. «What *are* you?» she asked. «An angel or a demon?»

A reasonable question: she must wonder about her sanity. But hard as I tried, I couldn't supply information about myself. It felt peculiar, as though the computer had raised a chain-link fence around my thoughts.

«A friend,» I essayed after a while. «I'll help you if I can.»

I sensed some skepticism, although she didn't question the statement as much as I would have. Perhaps Jeb's software accounted for her ready acceptance; Marguerite seemed so real, her control of my body so perfect, I kept forgetting that she had no existence outside a computer program.

Percy bowed, Ian's teasing glint lighting his eyes. Marguerite curtseyed as I struggled to remember his opening remark. Something about Armand. I sighed.

"Armand left with the tide," I said through Marguerite's mouth. Hey, things were looking up. I'd managed to produce actual words.

Percy's calm gaze discomfited me. The world, and even his wife, might think him stupid, but in my view those lazy eyes saw far too much. Looking around in an attempt to break the spell, I recalled a detail from the book. One—two?—of Chauvelin's agents lay concealed somewhere in the room, ready to spring out and attack Andrew and Tony as soon as the rest of us left.

Of course, the agents had told Chauvelin what the comtesse said. David need not have established contact with his character at all.

Or had they? In my pre-game obsessing over the plot, I hadn't wasted a moment on that particular detail. But since the men had not left the taproom, I didn't see how an agent in hiding could have sneaked out from under his table for a quick confab with Chauvelin.

Another puzzle. So while Marguerite walked toward the fire and extended her hands to the blaze, I checked the room for potential hiding places. The tablecloth beneath the punch bowl came down to the floor, and one of the benches did seem large enough to conceal a grown man. Should I coax Marguerite to tell Percy? But odds were about even as to whether I could manage anything so complicated, and much poorer that she could explain her knowledge if I did. It wasn't as though Chauvelin planned to do his captives any harm. Something had to push the story forward, so in the end, I said nothing.

Andrew and Tony dropped the last lemon in with a flourish and offered Percy a glass. He turned his disconcerting stare on them, giving me a moment to breathe.

The vicomte had finished his sandwich. At a wave of Percy's hand, he joined them. They stood around quaffing, jocular and aristocratic and male, while Marguerite sank gracefully into a chair and waited for them to return to earth.

With a certain degree of concentration, I raised her hand to touch the pink ostrich plume that brushed the side of her face. «Take it off,» I thought to her, meaning the hat. «The thing's as big as a hippo and twice as awkward. I swear that hatpin's sticking into your skull.»

«It wouldn't be proper,» she said. «A lady doesn't go out without hat and gloves.»

«At this rate, we're not going anywhere.» Darn, I sounded grouchy. «Those guys»—I corrected myself—«those *men* will be standing there drinking when the Last Trumpet sounds.»

I heard a small giggle, quickly suppressed. Well, at least *we* were talking.

Two rounds later, the men recalled our existence. Percy put his glass on the table and extended his arm, drawling, "Come, m'dear. We'd best be on our way."

Marguerite rose, graceful as ever, straightened her hat, and placed her fingertips just below his elbow. After curtseying to all concerned, we sashayed out of the room.

I watched as Percy and Marguerite stood under a clear, cool sky. He'd sent for his carriage, but it had yet to arrive from the stable yard. More stars than I'd ever seen blanketed the heavens above us. For the first time since the game began, I was alone with Ian. I shivered. I should be pursuing my new plan for an alliance, but I couldn't. Familiar as I was with the plot, I hadn't absorbed this reality: that I would spend hours, even days, with a man I didn't much like.

"Lud, Madam, are you cold?" Percy's sleepy voice sounded from somewhere over my head.

"It's nothing," Marguerite said. "A passing breeze."

Percy didn't respond. Again wrapped in silence, I returned my attention to the unfolding scenario. Crystalline evening embraced me. Wildflowers perfumed the air, until obliterated by the unmistakable smell of horse. The carriage had arrived.

Just like that, the game spun out of control. I'd read the book. I'd walked around Dover for almost two hours.

Marguerite had shown me, in the bluntest terms possible, what it meant to inhabit a body that appeared to belong to someone else. Nonetheless, I hadn't prepared myself for the carriage.

On the whole, I deal pretty well with life. All right, plants don't live long when I tend them. My family sees me as an incorrigible bookworm. I get touchy when compared to a sparrow. And some people think I have no taste in clothes. But despite the usual set of idiosyncrasies and flaws, I have only one real phobia, and it was staring me in the face.

Why, by all that was holy, had the baroness decided to make her hero's particular quirk that he liked to drive himself home? And why, despite the open conflicts that dotted his marriage, did he insist on having his wife next to him while he did so?

The issue wasn't the horses. I have no special affection for horses, but no antipathy for them either. Well, except that their backs seem unnecessarily far from the ground and themselves overfond of toppling people onto it.

No, my problem was heights. Since Nessa pushed me off the monkey bars, I've been terrified of heights. Even heights that don't meet most people's criteria for high, like the box of this carriage, the platform of which started somewhere around my chest. The seat was level with Percy's head. But a small, narrow shelf destined to be dragged at speed over rough and unpaved roads was enough to send me into a funk. I panicked if asked to stand on the fire escape outside a second-floor apartment, and now I was supposed to leap onto this ... this *ledge*?

Don't get me wrong. Percy could drive from Dover to Ulan Bator with my perfect good will, so long as he did it while I sat inside the coach. Dover to Richmond with me on that box was a different proposition. I glanced up at the fairy-godmother equipage that had pulled up in front of us and wondered how the blazes he expected me to get up there, and what I would do when I did.

Marguerite, drat her, didn't seem to care a whit. On the contrary, she was looking forward to the journey, and I could see why. It represented one of the few pleasures in her tortured relationship with Percy. Oh, I could feel her reacting at some level to my hysteria, but even then, so early in our relationship, I understood that she didn't share it.

The young man who'd driven the coach in from the yard hopped off the box and headed for the taproom, Percy's largesse stowed securely in a pocket. A pair of men in livery ran from the inn and jumped onto a step at the back of the coach. Two hands closed around Marguerite's waist from behind, and her husband, who had so far shown the energy of a somnolent turtle, tossed us six feet in the air and onto the seat the young man had just vacated.

That answered the "how." I ignored Percy's leap onto the box next to me and focused on settling the miles of hoop skirt into something approaching decorum. I was here. Percy was here. The coach would start moving any moment. If Marguerite had one area of her life where she enjoyed spending time with Percy, I shouldn't mess it up for her, right? I already knew she would survive the drive. Baroness Orczy guaranteed it.

The ridiculous hat tipped sideways. As Marguerite moved to catch it, the corset shifted and jammed whalebone into her ribs. She sucked in her breath. Percy snapped the reins across the horses' backs. In that instant of pure fear, Marguerite tumbled into me and we became one. I sobbed and covered my face with both hands.

When I'd read in the book about a coach and four, I'd anticipated something like Queen Elizabeth progressing at a sedate pace toward Westminster Abbey and waving to the crowd.

These horses were not walking. They were not trotting. They dove for the inn gate like a quartet of Triple Crown winners, scattering grooms in all directions. The coach rolled from side to side. The sensation of being catapulted into space was worse than anything I had ever imagined. I thought of roller-coasters, or one of those switch railroads so popular at Disney World. When I was ten, my father lured me onto that train with the idea that it would cure my fear of heights. Let's just say it didn't work. Nessa was furious. He never invited us on holiday again.

"Bit fresh, aren't they?" Percy drawled.

The box was only about three feet wide, pushing us together until our collar bones touched. Hoop skirts filled most of the available space. I adjusted the hippo hat to catch a glimpse of his profile. It should have reassured me to see him concentrating on the infernal horses. I'd lost all sense of Marguerite.

Maybe I could ditch the hat. But as my hands closed on the ribbons, I felt her again, like a tiny doll inside my mind. «Don't,» the doll said.

We'd switched places. My terror had pushed me forward and left her in the background, and she wasn't any happier about it than I had been. I let go of the hat.

"Road's clear," Percy said. "I think I'll give 'em their heads for a bit. It'll calm 'em down."

The horses leaped forward. The coach rocked more violently. My velvet skirts slid toward the edge. Instinctively, I grabbed Percy's arm. He shook me off. To control the horses, I hoped, but in my pitiful condition it didn't matter. It felt like rejection.

The corset constricted my ribs. Skirts tangled round my feet, trapping me in this awful place. I thought I'd never breathe again. Fog closed in. Rejected or not, I buried my face against the capes of Percy's greatcoat, closed my eyes, and prayed.

❀

It seemed like an eternity before the horses slowed. As the air returned to my lungs, I again became aware of Marguerite, whispering consoling thoughts at the back of my mind.

Her mood switched as soon as she realized I was paying attention. «What is this nonsense?» I heard her grumble. «We're barely six feet from the ground. What do you think you're doing, clutching Percy that way? Don't you have any pride?»

But Marguerite could no more keep me from grabbing her husband than I could stop her from flirting with creepy Chauvelin. If not for the raw terror, I could have rejoiced at finally gaining control of my own body.

With my face pressed against Percy's coat, I felt rather than saw him rein in the team. I heard boots hit the road as the grooms jumped from the back of the coach and ran to the horses' heads. "Something wrong, Sir?" a rough voice said.

"Not with the horses, Matthews. Pull them to one side, there's a good chap, and let them graze for a minute." Percy's drawl had vanished, the tone that replaced it as cool and crisp as the evening air. "I must tend to my wife."

A muttered, "Yes, Sir," greeted this statement. The coach moved sideways and then, mercifully, stopped.

Percy caught my wrists and pulled them away from his coat. I was trembling and couldn't make myself stop. At first, I could hardly bear to look at him. What could I say? Marguerite didn't behave like this. On the contrary, she sat seething in a corner of my head, arms crossed and back ostentatiously turned.

I took deep breaths, trying to concentrate. Percy was speaking now, his voice neither the habitual lazy drawl nor the businesslike tone he had used to the groom. Puzzled, husky— that slight Scots burr sounded like Ian. An Ian I would have sworn didn't exist. The shield of my dislike clanged in response to this latest buffet. Perhaps I had misjudged him.

The words were impersonal enough. "Are you ill, Madam?" My head tipped back. I gazed straight into Percy's eyes. And realized with a frisson of shock that, for the first time since my arrival in Dover, the lazy stare had given way to alert, focused intelligence.

The Scarlet Pimpernel. Or Ian. I couldn't tell which.

He watched me—silent, unmoving. When I shook my head to indicate that I wasn't ill, long fingers undid the ribbon under my chin and slid the surgical-steel hatpin from tangled curls. Marguerite, in her corner, emitted a yelp of protest.

"Here, let's get rid of this. I can't see your face." His hand brushed my cheeks, where tears lay drying in the evening air. "Ah, don't cry," he said, still in that husky voice. "You know I can't stand to see a pretty woman cry."

Words twisted into knots in my throat. "Thank you," I managed after what seemed like an endless pause. I wondered where Marguerite kept her handkerchief. A velvet bag hung from her arm, but rummaging in it would require me to pull my hands away from Percy. I couldn't do it.

He released me long enough to toss the hippo hat at a groom. It sailed through the air like a mammoth cloth Frisbee. "Put it inside," he said. Marguerite was still complaining when he retrieved my wrist.

One glimpse of my face, and he again dropped my arm to dig out his handkerchief. Soft linen touched my cheek, soaking up the tears. "Tell me what's wrong, my dear. This isn't like you."

The warm strength of his fingers centered me. Without the motion, with him filling my vision and my senses, I no longer noticed our distance from the ground. And amid the jumble of thoughts, I realized he'd given me an opening.

Marguerite sulked in her corner, and for the moment I controlled my body. Find the right words, and I'd be able to hint at the alliance I wanted. Sound him out, so to speak. But what should I say? What *could* I say, with the computer monitoring my words?

"The horses," I choked out at last. "When they dove forward like that, they frightened me. I'm sorry I reacted so badly."

"Would you prefer to ride inside, then? I can let you down now." The husky tone slid away, replaced by his usual drawl.

I should have said yes. Anyone with sense would have. But I could hear the hint of pain that lay behind the surface chill, and even without Marguerite stomping around in the back of my mind, I couldn't bring myself to break this last bond between them.

"No," I said. "I'll be fine." The tears returned, thickening my voice. "I've just had a hideous day. First the comtesse…"

He released my wrists and handed me the handkerchief. While I mopped up the renewed onslaught, he shifted sideways, rested one elbow on the coach roof, and regarded me quizzically. "The incident you insisted meant nothing?"

"I lied." I didn't think it was news. "Suzanne held out her hands, and I was delighted to see her, and then her mother snubbed me something dreadful and told Suzanne not to talk to me. You'd think I were some kind of leper. And she's known me half my life!"

He could have brought up St. Cyr, but he didn't. Instead, he pressed his thumbnail against his teeth and waited.

"Then I had to say goodbye to Armand, and that made me feel terrible. I'm afraid he won't come back."

"Don't worry about your brother, my dear. He can take care of himself." Percy twisted the reins in his free hand. From the road, I heard stamping hooves and grooms jollying the horses.

The door of opportunity was closing. Marguerite, who despised Percy by that point in their marriage, had not told him about meeting Chauvelin in Dover. If I wanted to change the way the game played out, maybe I should break that pattern. "Then, as though that wasn't bad enough, I ran into Armand Chauvelin, right outside the Fisherman's Rest."

That earned me a raised eyebrow. The drawl returned in full force. "That funny little man I met at your salon? The one who dressed like a crow? Well, 'tis true that his jackets would torment a saint, and his cravats are an even greater assault on a discerning man's senses. But worse than saying farewell to your brother, m'dear?"

His voice *dripped* sarcasm. Raw fury kindled in me, fueled by disappointment. I let myself be vulnerable, only to have him—Percy, Ian, whatever he called himself—respond with more barbs. How dare he?

My reaction spun Marguerite around in her corner. In my mind, I saw her staring at me. As if she couldn't understand what made me so mad.

But as I opened my mouth to tell Percy what I thought of him, I recalled the advice I'd given her and glanced at the hand he had twisted in the reins. The knuckles stood out, white with tension, every nerve visible.

I bit my tongue and gazed at that telling fist. He'd provoked me on purpose, then braced himself for my anger. But why? Did he hate his wife *that* much?

No, Percy loved Marguerite, even though he pretended otherwise. The baroness had made that clear. Ian was the one who disliked me, as I did him. It would take more than one sentence to convince him to trust me.

And with Marguerite under control, maybe I didn't need him. I could wait and see. Try again tomorrow. Or not.

From the road, the rough voice I'd heard before said, "The horses are getting cold, Sir."

Percy glanced at me. "With your permission, my dear."

I closed my eyes, fighting nausea. We couldn't spend the rest of our lives sitting by the side of the road. If I couldn't survive another stint on the box, I should get down and let him drive.

Marguerite intervened. «I'll help,» she offered. «Lean on me.»

Her husband, her life. And with Percy choosing to be difficult, I'd need her cooperation more than ever. Best not to upset her. "Go ahead," I said through clenched teeth.

"Stand away, Matthews," he told the groom. "Let's hope they've got some of the fidgets out of them by now."

The grooms stood away, Percy flicked the reins, and we were in motion once more. I heard the men leap onto their perch behind the coach as we passed. As the horses picked up speed, the carriage began to rock.

Oh, no. I scrunched my eyes shut and prayed that I wouldn't throw up all over the box.

With the possible exception of Marguerite, no one was more amazed than I when Percy transferred the reins to his right hand and pulled me against his shoulder. As soon as his strong arm closed about my waist, I took as full a breath as the corset would permit and pressed my cheek into the soft wool of his coat. He had relented. Had I misjudged him again?

«Relax,» Marguerite said. «Worry about it later.»

The wool under my cheek felt as comforting as a pillow, and with Percy's arm around me, I no longer had the sense that the rocking of the coach would send me flying into the hedges.

Marguerite, I could tell, was as tired as I was. We'd both had a pretty rough day.

«We can decide what to do next in the morning,» I said to her.

«There's nothing *to* do. Percy isn't going to change. And we don't have many social engagements—just the opera and Lord Grenville's ball. It should be a nice, quiet day.»

I pressed my cheek against Percy's shoulder and tried not to laugh out loud. *Quiet? Hah!* Marguerite was in for a shock.

6. Blakeney Manor

SOMEONE WAS SHAKING ME. BLINKING, I STRAIGHTENED and found myself gazing at Percy. My head felt fuzzy, and my neck ached when I moved. But the strangest thing was my new relationship with Marguerite. First she had controlled everything, and I'd merely observed. Then my fear pushed me forward and sent her to the back. But now, in some odd way, we had become equals. I could hear her thinking and—I tested—yes, I could engage her in conversation, but when I lifted her head, it felt like my own. Hooray!

I untangled my hands from Percy's coat. His mouth quirked as he glanced my way. "I apologize for waking you, m'lady, but as you see, we are home."

Ahead of us, a long pathway stretched between trees and opened into a wide circle. The most beautiful house I'd ever seen stood on the far side. Blakeney Manor, I assumed. A brick house built, like many Elizabethan homes, in the shape of an E, with slate roofs and wood and stucco patterns on the facing, it blazed with light, however late the hour. As the coach pulled up in front of the massive oak door, young men came running from the far side of the building to grab the horses' heads. Percy tossed one of them the reins and jumped down.

He held out his arms. I paused. It looked like a long way to the ground. While I hesitated, Percy reached up and grasped my waist. "Odd's fish, m'dear," he said, "you don't think I'd drop you, do you?"

Actually, yes. But I was already in mid-air, so I put both hands on his shoulders and let him lift me down. Fear of heights aside, I saw few chances of getting off that box on my own while clad in a corset and two dozen petticoats.

I'd have to put my feminist sensibilities on hold for the rest of the simulation. I couldn't help but giggle.

Percy's lips twitched. But when I glanced at him, his blue gaze was distant, his mouth set in a straight line. I sighed.

As soon as my feet touched the pavement, Percy let go of my waist and stepped back. We hadn't yet returned to the plot laid out by Baroness Orczy, who skipped from the Fisherman's Rest directly to the Royal Opera House at Covent Garden with only a paragraph mentioning the recently completed carriage ride. As a result, I wasn't sure what to do next.

Subconsciously I'd assumed the game would skip, too, but it looked as though we would live through a whole day before I could again predict what would happen.

"Thank you," I said. Percy responded with a small bow.

«Go inside,» Marguerite told me. Only then did I realize that he was waiting for me to precede him.

The great oak doors stood open, flanked by a slight old man whose name escaped me. The butler, presumably. Chivers? Brinker? Those came from the films. I don't think he ever had a name in the books.

I responded to the butler's "good evening" and let him take Marguerite's shawl. A footman brought in the massive hat and dumped it on a sideboard. The butler looked startled, but even Marguerite didn't think we needed it to walk up the stairs.

The soul-baring had taken its toll, and I wanted nothing so much as to get out of the uncomfortable clothes, undo the elaborate hairstyle, and find some food. Marguerite had eaten nothing at the Fisherman's Rest. After hours of angst, we were emotionally worn out and starving.

«Where are your rooms?» I asked her. «Or is there something we have to do first?» I doubted that Percy and Marguerite shared quarters, in part because of the fight over St. Cyr but more because aristocratic eighteenth-century couples preferred connecting rooms, or even non-connecting rooms. Love matches like the Blakeneys' didn't become the norm until later, but I didn't know if the desire to avoid an unwanted spouse or simple affluence was the driving motive for giving each person his or her own space.

«One moment,» she said.

Percy handed his hat and gloves to the butler whose name I still hadn't caught and held out his arm. «Now,» Marguerite prompted. I placed my fingertips on his elegant sleeve and allowed him to escort me up the stairs. It seemed needlessly formal, but who was I to object?

He stopped in front of a door, raised my hand to his lips, and said, "Good night, m'dear."

The whole touching scene in the carriage might never have taken place. "Good night, Percy," I replied. "Thank you for helping me earlier."

For an instant, he leaned toward me, as though unable to stop himself, then quickly drew back and walked toward the far wing of the house.

Not sure what to make of his reaction, I watched him go, then marched through the door. My head had started to ache.

❀

To make matters worse, I found myself fighting with Marguerite as soon as the door closed. «What did you think?» she shouted. I could see her in my mind, hands on her hips, her face contorted in anger. «That you're better than me? You could say a few words and he'd fall right into your hand? I've been struggling with this for a year!»

«You're right,» I said to her. «That *is* what I thought. And it was stupid. I'm sorry.»

She put both hands over her face. «I want him to love me. Forgive me. He's so polite and so kind—»

«And he treats you like dirt,» I finished for her. «It's horrible.»

Marguerite looked up. «It is?»

«Sure. Courtesy is fine, but an honest fight clears the air. All that politeness tells you nothing about what's upset him.»

She gave a deep sigh, like someone encountering words she'd expected never to hear. «Yes, that's it exactly. I feel ungrateful, but his restraint makes me crazy. I hate myself for picking at him, but at least then he responds.» Her lips drooped. «If only to take jabs at me. I wish he'd talk seriously, but he won't.»

«Talk to you?» I said lightly, trying to lift her spirits. «Not kiss you? Make love to you? Anyone as competent and controlled as that has to be good in bed.»

Her cheeks flushed, which felt quite bizarre, as they were my cheeks, too. My outspokenness had embarrassed her. She must be the only married woman on the planet who had less sexual experience than I did. She and Percy hadn't completed twenty-four hours of married life before their big blowup.

Perhaps that was why she chose to respond to the other point I'd raised.

«Competent,» she said. I could hear her astonishment. «*Percy?*»

I laughed. «Think about it. You saw him handle those half-wild horses, and the half-wild vicomte as well. Haven't you figured out yet that his idiocy is for show?»

Leaving her to ponder that one, I surveyed the room.

A pretty girl in a mob cap and frilly apron beamed at me from the fireplace. Mary?

«Louise,» Marguerite said. She sounded distracted.

Louise bobbed a curtsey. "Evening, m'lady. Won't you come over here and let me loosen your stays? You look quite worn out, Ma'am."

A lovely child, with a good sense of priorities. My examination of the room could wait. I glided over to her, pulling pins from my hair as I went.

"I'll brush it out for you, shall I, m'lady?" she asked.

Louise, I decided, was worth a dozen Sir Percys.

«Two dozen.» Marguerite's sarcasm was back. «No, three.»

«You're feeling grumpy,» I said. «We need comfortable clothes and some food.»

"Please do," I told Louise, answering her question about brushing my hair.

I took a deep, exultant breath as the wicked corset abandoned its death grip on my ribs.

The maid removed layers of velvet and petticoats, leaving only a chemise as sheer as a spider's web. From a wardrobe next to a fireplace she produced a clinging silk negligee and wrapped it around me. The headache retreated.

"Is anyone still in the kitchen, Louise?" I asked.

The girl nodded. "Are you hungry, Ma'am? Shall I tell Mr. Alphonse to prepare something?"

"Anything," I said. "It needn't be fancy. An omelet would be wonderful, or bread and cheese. I didn't eat in Dover."

The girl's face lit up. "Mr. Alphonse will be that happy, m'lady. He's always complaining that you eat like a bird."

Marguerite giggled, her spirits returning as the headache receded.

«Goodness,» I said. «Anyone who spends half her life encased in whalebone *would* eat like a bird. I can't imagine how you breathe in that contraption.»

Louise toddled off, promising to return in a jiffy and brush out my hair. I took advantage of her absence to search the room for chamber pots. With Marguerite's help, I found one hidden behind a pretty Chinese screen, and the negligee proved no impediment, which made me feel better.

Since she was still pondering the bombshell I'd thrown about her husband being smarter than he let on, I took the opportunity to examine my surroundings. Its appointments spoke of wealth, discreetly applied, and excellent taste. If anything, it seemed too perfect, like one of those houses in magazines where no one drops a book on the coffee table or leaves children's toys in the hall. The place needed a fuzzy Persian on the bed or a messy pile of research notes spread across the spotless surface of the escritoire. Nothing would convince me that Marguerite or anyone else escrited there. The colors were exquisite, though: gold, white, and blue.

Above the vanity hung a mirror. Curiosity overwhelmed me. Whom would I see? Brown-haired, brown-eyed, snub-nosed Nina, pretty but no showstopper? Merle Oberon, the classic brunette from the 1934 film? Jane Seymour, another lovely brunette? Baroness Orczy's redheaded beauty? I headed for the bureau and, although I'd prepared myself for the sight, recoiled in astonishment.

Yikes! Marguerite was stunning. If you can conceive of Oberon with blue eyes and red-gold curls tumbling past her waist, you can approximate the reflection I saw in the mirror. I couldn't begin to describe the effect it had on me. I'd never looked that beautiful in my life. Nessa paled by comparison.

Who could fail to be pleased? And yet ... I felt uncomfortable. My mother, my father, Nessa and her "Sparrow"—years of disparaging remarks about my appearance flitted through my mind. I couldn't connect with the beauty in the glass.

That reflection was *not* me.

Louise returned with a fragrant tray, which she plunked on a small table next to the unused escritoire. "I'll brush out your hair then, m'lady, and let you be. Charles will pick up the tray in the morning, if that's all right with you."

"That would be wonderful." I dropped onto the ottoman in front of the vanity and closed my eyes as she eased the brush through Marguerite's long curls. The headache faded to nonexistence.

Louise braided my hair for bed and slipped from the room, taking the chamber pot with her. I washed my hands again in the sink behind the screen and turned my attention to Mr. Alphonse's offering, warm under its metal cover. As the aroma of buttery cheese omelet wafted past my nose, I realized how hungry I'd been. I finished it, plus the roll that sat on the plate next to it. Someone had thoughtfully provided a glass of white wine. I finished that, too. If the cook thought Lady Blakeney didn't eat, he should be overjoyed.

I picked up the tray, intending to deposit it outside the door for Charles to collect in his own good time. Marguerite let out a shriek of protest, and I dropped the tray back on the table. A silver knife rolled onto the floor.

«Can't I put it in the hall?» I asked her. «The smell of food will keep me awake.»

But Marguerite wouldn't hear of it. With a sigh, I returned the knife to the tray and left it on the table.

The bed called to me. I slid between satin sheets and tried to adjust to a too-soft mattress made largely of feathers. For the first time since my arrival in Dover, nothing demanded my attention.

I inhaled slow, deep breaths as in a yoga class. Above me, painted cherubs frolicked among fields and woods to tunes piped from the god Pan's double flute. Was there any detail Jeb's programmers had missed?

So much had happened since I tumbled out of bed that morning. The trip to Concord. Winding up in the body of a woman I despised, only to discover that she wasn't the birdbrain I'd thought her. Realizing that winning might require an alliance with a man I disliked. Trying and failing to make that alliance—only to succeed in breaking through in the end.

Or not. The results seemed ambiguous. Percy (Ian?) had rejected my overture but then comforted me on the box of the carriage. And someone had acted as if he wanted to kiss me (Marguerite?) in the hallway just now.

It was too confusing, the multiple names and personalities. I could separate myself from Marguerite, but I decided to think of the others as their characters for as long as the simulation lasted. I'd drive myself crazy trying to figure out how much of Percy's behavior came from Ian or Chauvelin's from David, and it didn't matter anyway. Chauvelin would kill me if he could. Percy could defeat me with both hands tied behind his back, but he'd shown signs of softening. I'd focus on making use of that and leave the rest for later.

Maybe I didn't need the alliance, with negotiations between me and Marguerite proceeding apace. Much better to win the game on my own, without owing any part of my success to Percy.

No. Even if that choice worked for me, it wouldn't benefit my character. Marguerite needed Percy. After my quarrel with her earlier, I grasped that she loved her husband, even if she denied it. His coldness hurt her. When I despised her too, I hadn't cared. Now I did. Allying with Percy would help her.

An alliance might help me as well. At worst, it couldn't harm me. I could still pursue my original plan of not betraying the Scarlet Pimpernel to Chauvelin.

Which raised the question of how to proceed. Percy distrusted Marguerite because she had denounced St. Cyr, but he hadn't said what bothered him about the denunciation. However disillusioned he felt, he must know she wasn't a fanatic revolutionary like Chauvelin. Did he feel shamed because he heard the story first from his friends? Trapped, because she hadn't told him before the wedding? Abandoned, because she ran off?

I had no idea. But the trouble between them began there. So my attempt at reconciliation had to start there, with the explanation and the apology that Marguerite had withheld. And I must give them as soon as possible, before the baroness's script resumed. Tomorrow morning, in fact. I bit the tip of my finger, plotting how to create the opportunity I needed.

After a while, I remembered I hadn't brushed my teeth. Hadn't snuffed the candles, either. Not a good idea to leave them burning while I slept. I hauled myself out of the satin sheets and explored the area behind the screen, which yielded a ratty toothbrush and something that Marguerite assured me qualified as tooth powder. A trip to an eighteenth-century dentist was a horror I refused to contemplate.

My nap on the ride home kept me from feeling drowsy. My exhaustion had been emotional; an hour alone, combined with food and physical comfort, sent it into retreat. I blew out every candle but one, which I used to light my way to the window, then snuffed before I opened the velvet drapes. Lit only by moon and stars, the grounds of Blakeney Manor, serene and lovely, spread for what appeared to be miles. On the far stroke of the E, the lights shone in Percy's rooms, and I watched them until they doused, one by one, and I could no longer see him. Even then, I sat for hours, thoughts drifting and mingling with Marguerite's, before walking across the moonlit room to return to the satin sheets.

I woke at an ungodly hour to the first hint of dawn visible through the open curtains. A small figure, mostly mob cap and shoes, squatted beside the fireplace. She made no noise, but I couldn't rule out the possibility that some clank or crunch had wakened me.

«Young Betsy,» Marguerite said with a sigh. «She can't stay quiet, however much she tries. It will upset her if you move.»

That seemed reasonable. Nor did I want to get up. From the gray light, I put the time at about six in the morning. After Betsy left, I fell asleep again and dreamed of Percy. My subconscious, proving it has no sense whatsoever, gave him Ian's face.

The next time I woke, I heard the clock in the hall strike nine. With Marguerite's help, I located the bell pull and summoned Louise, who soon appeared, a steaming cup of chocolate in one hand and a plate of rolls in the other. In response to my gestures, she placed the food on the night table next to my pillow, handed last night's tray to the footman waiting at the door, and began fussing around with clothes while I ate.

"What will you wear today, m'lady?" she asked. "'Tis a fine day. See, the sun is shining!"

A rare and glorious event, I gathered. Since eighteenth-century fashion was not my forte, I turned the question over to Marguerite. "The apple-green sacque," she said.

"Yes, m'lady." Louise drew the sacque from the wardrobe. "I'll do your hair simply, and we can leave your stays loose. You'll be comfortable despite the heat."

"Heat" didn't mean the same thing here as it did in Boston, I deduced. But minimal corset sounded good, and the gown was lovely. I rubbed the silk between my fingers, enjoying its texture. The apple green set off Marguerite's red-gold hair and creamy skin and turned her eyes almost turquoise. The mirror still seemed like a liar, and I was weeks from accepting I could ever be that beautiful, but at least whomever it was reflecting looked good.

The sunny morning seemed fraught with promise. Lifting green silk in both hands, I left Louise to clean up the room and descended the stairs as quickly as my full skirts allowed.

7. Rose Garden

THE ORIENTAL RUNNER THAT CARPETED THE STAIRS SPREAD
out at their base to cover most of the hallway, although I could
see patterned wood in bands under the windows that shed light
along one side. A sound from the far end drew my attention,
and I began to walk the length of the hall, apple-green silk
frou-frouing around my feet.

As I passed a door about halfway down on my right, it
opened. Percy stood there in buff breeches and jacket, brown
leather boots, and crisp white shirt and cravat. When he saw
me, he bowed in the exaggerated fashion I had noticed the day
before. Then I had written off his artificial politeness as part
of the mask that hid his true personality, but now I wondered.
Did the exquisite manners express sarcasm in a different way?

"Sleep well, m'dear?" he inquired.

I curtseyed, matching his formality. "Very well, and you?"

He nodded. Amusement gleamed in his eyes. Not mockery,
something warmer and more genuine, unexpected from either
Percy or Ian. Disconcerted by the sight, I said "good day" and
continued my walk down the hallway. As I reached the end, I
heard him moving toward the stairs.

From the window, I saw gardeners and manicured grounds
that looked even prettier in the sunlight than they had under

the moon. Since I know just enough about plants to be dangerous, I can't identify most of the wonders I saw, but they included rose gardens and herbal borders, fountains, and, in the distance, an ivy-covered folly in the style of a Greek temple that I ached to examine in detail.

In the driveway a boy held the reins of a magnificent chestnut Arabian. As Percy reached the bottom of the front steps, the boy handed him the reins, pulled his forelock, and stood back. In a single fluid motion, Percy mounted and set the animal moving toward the iron gates where we had entered the night before, now barely visible through the trees. For a moment, I stopped to admire him. Irritating he might be, but no one could deny that Sir Percy knew how to ride.

For half an hour or so, I roamed around the second floor, then the rooms below, getting in everyone's way. Not that I meant to. I didn't interrupt anyone or stop them from performing their tasks. Quite the contrary. Every time I showed my face in a room, maids jumped to their feet and footmen bowed, wanting to know what they could do, m'lady. After a while, I felt like a colossal nuisance, even if the servants' deference evinced the same feudal principle that had kept me from having to make my own bed or empty my own chamber pot.

Marguerite wasn't much help. I didn't detect many domestic urges there: no trips to consult with the cook over the day's menus or the housekeeper on the state of the linen, like the wives you read about in historical novels. If it had been my house, I might have done something about it, but since it wasn't, I gave in to Marguerite's urgings and headed for the sunshine.

Louise leaped after me with a parasol. I accepted it without protest. It seemed unlikely that Marguerite, a literary character, could die of skin cancer, but she probably freckled, which

eighteenth-century society considered almost as bad. Parasol overhead and silk skirts swishing, we strolled into the grounds, staying well clear of the gardeners.

Dolphins and cherubs and gryphons and such spewed crystal drops into warm air redolent with the mingled aromas of hundreds of flowers. The folly proved deliciously cool but otherwise disappointing, more fascinating from afar than inside.

Sometime in the early afternoon, I found myself in a rose garden. A small fish pond lay in the middle, and I could see the golden flash of carp as they swam by.

Although a plant murderess, I have always loved roses. These old-fashioned scented flowers drew me with their aroma and their beauty. I found a stone bench and sank onto it, silk skirts spread around me. Eyes closed, I inhaled roses.

From half-sleepy contemplation, I opened my eyes to find Percy, still clad in riding dress. I straightened, surprised as much by his having approached me as by his having already returned from his ride.

«What's this about?» I asked Marguerite, but she had no answer.

He produced that affected half-bow. "Would you care to stroll in the gardens for a while, m'lady?"

Promising. I took his arm, hoping for an opportunity to apologize as planned. "So long as we don't walk far or fast," I said. "I've been wandering around the house and grounds since I ran into you this morning."

He didn't, as I'd half-anticipated, refer to the carriage ride last night or, indeed, say much of anything. We wandered among the flowers, my hand tucked snugly in his arm.

As we walked, I wondered where to start. I couldn't ask him why he'd sought Marguerite out, as it implied that under other circumstances he wouldn't or shouldn't have, and that might not be true. But I didn't want to let this moment pass—even though Marguerite, when I shared my plan with her, thought it was cuckoo.

«You need to explain why you denounced St. Cyr,» I said, watching her slam around inside my head throwing fits. «Otherwise, he's *never* going to trust you.»

«He won't respond.» She sounded like a sulky teenager.

Shocked, I realized that when Marguerite denounced St. Cyr, she was twenty-three and the toast of Paris, fêted and courted and told she could do no wrong. Was it any wonder she'd taken Percy's adoration for granted?

Great. Here was I, ex-high-school geek, trying to advise the Homecoming Queen on how to handle her love life. I couldn't decide whether to laugh or cry.

«I know you tried,» I said, remembering what I'd seen during her conversation with Armand. «But let's try again. You hurt Percy when you ran off. Did you expect him to go down on his knees and beg you to come home? When he was already disillusioned?»

«Yes!» She almost threw the word at me. «He said he loved me, but he didn't wait to find out what happened before he condemned me. Because his *friends* accused me! What sort of love is that?»

«You're right.» I'd wondered the same thing myself. «But if we're ever to fix your marriage, we have to help him understand what went wrong.»

«It won't work. He hates me.» Marguerite sounded more sad than sulky now. Despite her resistance, I could sense fantasies of better times forming in her mind.

«Then you have nothing to lose.»

«Oh, very well,» she grumbled. «Do what you think best.»

❁

Percy and I had circled our small part of the garden and returned to the roses. He withdrew his arm—preparatory to leaving, I thought.

"Wait." I caught his sleeve. "Please. There's something you need to hear. I should have told you ages ago."

He raised an eyebrow but didn't object, just sat on the edge of the pond and gestured to me to join him. I trailed my fingers among the weeds, watching the goldfish bubble to the surface. The sun glinted off their backs.

"The Marquis de St. Cyr—" Marguerite's reluctance weighed down my words.

He interrupted me, a discourtesy. I must have touched a nerve, although his tone was level and remote. "Forgive my slow wits, Madam, but the time for explanations of that incident would seem to be past."

«What did I tell you?» Marguerite stamped her foot.

Although tempted to do some stamping of my own, I refrained. "In a way, yes," I said, "but one mistake does not excuse another. I've owed you an explanation since our wedding. Will you not listen to me now?"

Percy stared, not at me but at the stone bench on the far side of the garden, his shoulders hunched forward as though he anticipated assault.

Discouraging, but I decided to take his silence as a yes. Hands clasped in my lap, I began, drawing on my memories of what Marguerite had experienced. "Armand and I lost our parents when we were quite young. In effect, we brought each other up."

"As I well recall." Percy continued to study the bench. His voice lacked all inflection. It was like talking to a robot.

A sigh escaped me, but he didn't turn his head. "We moved to Paris before my eighteenth birthday." Briefly I closed my eyes, the better to access Marguerite's memories. "Armand, as you know, has always been hotheaded. About five years ago, he fell madly in love with St. Cyr's daughter."

Percy stuck his hands in his pockets and listened. I could sense Marguerite watching, her fear mixed with hope. "One day he wrote her a poem, a silly ode to her eyelashes or something. Nothing disrespectful, you understand. He wanted only to adore her from afar. But the marquis objected."

"A plebeian approaching a descendant of his illustrious house? What did you expect?" Percy's monotone shifted into the sardonic drawl I disliked. I sent my sympathy to Marguerite.

Hands clasped in my lap, I pressed on. "He sent a band of thugs to teach Armand a lesson. They beat him within an inch of his life. I swore vengeance, but I never expected to carry it through."

Percy raised a brow. My heart sank. "The revolution began. The public liked me. I was becoming established as an actress. Armand and I had an apartment in the Rue de Richelieu. You visited me there."

"My memory may be faulty," he said, "but I do recollect that."

You'd think we were discussing the weather, not the incident that had turned his life upside down and driven him apart from his wife.

«See?» Marguerite said. Arms crossed over her chest, she emitted a belligerent glitter.

"I'm trying to explain," I announced with dignity.

"Very well." He returned to his research project, the bench. "Explain."

One step forward, two steps back, as my Bolshevik namesake liked to say. Or was it the other way round? "A few years after the incident with Armand, I heard someone say that the Marquis de St. Cyr was plotting with Austria. To save the royal family."

"Naturally." Percy straightened, settling one foot on the stones that ringed the pond and resting his elbow on the raised knee. "A man like that, so proud of his ancestry. He *would* support the royalist cause."

I hesitated. What I had to say next formed the heart of Marguerite's story. If Percy didn't accept it, I had no idea what to do next.

"I mentioned it to some friends." My voice shook despite my efforts to control it. Marguerite stopped glowering and moved closer, reaching for me. "Including Chauvelin. The government was less radical in those days than it is now. I didn't expect people to react as they did."

Percy watched me, silent, unbending. Did it make sense to go on? If I stopped talking, the script would force Marguerite to make the explanation herself within hours.

But by then she'd have done more damage and would have more secrets to conceal. And if Percy refused to believe her now, what difference would a few hours make? So I pushed myself to continue, Marguerite's remorse roughening my voice. "I don't know who reported the marquis. Chauvelin had connections, even then, so I suspect he was the one, but any of them could have done it. Troops raided the St. Cyr house and arrested everyone inside. The tribunal ruled his family guilty by association."

"Even the children?" Percy pulled his right hand from his pocket long enough to raise his quizzing glass at me.

"Yes." I gritted my teeth at the sight of his magnified eye. His skepticism rubbed my nerves raw. "Even the children.

Then Chauvelin spread the rumor that I had denounced them. I was horrified, by the tribunal's ruling more than the accusation. I had supported a democratic revolution. I couldn't support a new and more violent tyranny."

When I glanced at Percy to see the effect of my confession, I found that he had switched his unswerving gaze to the water. Ignoring the large lump in my throat, I gripped my hands together. He'd told me last night that he hated to see women cry, and I would *not* indulge in cheap tricks to overcome his resistance.

Marguerite lay crumpled in a ball on the floor of my thoughts. Her tears flowed freely.

I raised my chin and took a deep breath. "I tried to save them. Right up to the moment when they went to the guillotine. The marquis, too, although I knew there was little chance that the tribunal would spare him. By their lights, he had committed treason."

Percy watched the fish, his face set in tense lines. My fingers brushed his sleeve.

«I told you,» Marguerite said. «He won't forgive me. The man is an icicle. Or too stupid to understand.»

«But he's not,» I told her. «Look at his face. At his hands. He understands perfectly. Why won't he relent?»

I turned back to Percy. "I thought perhaps they would release St. Cyr's family. I called in every favor I could, but to no avail. Robespierre was coming to power then, and he wanted to make an example of them."

"A sorry tale indeed." In her corner, Marguerite shook like one of the ivy leaves that dangled from the folly. Percy's hands weren't much steadier. When he saw me looking at them, he thrust them into his pockets again.

"Most of the people who attended the salon believed in the republican cause," I said. "They exaggerated my role. That was the story you heard."

Having run out of words, I stopped. Whoever bore the ultimate moral responsibility for the marquis's death, I couldn't deny Marguerite had contributed to the tragedy.

"Again, no doubt 'tis my wits that are all to let, but I fail to see the value of revisiting the past." Percy's voice carried the warmth of a Moscow winter. I wondered if he realized how much his words stung.

I had just about given up on Percy when Marguerite decided to help. In response to her prodding, I leaned forward and said, "How indifferent you are! Is it possible that love can die? Once you swore I had your heart, and now, see how coldly you treat me."

It worked, after a fashion. Percy's chilly courtesy acquired a bitter edge. "You did not regard my heart so highly when you had it, Madam. On the contrary. You demanded from me a humiliating allegiance, and when I refused to sacrifice my honor, you spurned my affections and returned to your brother's house."

Marguerite let out a wail, but overt anger I could deal with. I stared him down and said, "I hurt you. I'm sorry. You acted as if you cared nothing for me, and I was ashamed."

Marguerite sat up, astonishment overwhelming her grief. «How did you know?»

Percy glared at me, his usual composure quite lost. "Ashamed? You said nothing of it. Instead you laid the blame at my feet."

"Ashamed," I said firmly. "Upset, too, at your readiness to believe the worst of me. After our parents died, no one but Armand loved me. None of the men who paid court to me ever touched my heart. I thought you were different, but you weren't."

He made a small sound of protest. "I want you to understand," I said. "Whatever it looked like, I felt terrible. I assumed you would hate me because I hated myself."

"No," Percy said, every trace of the fop gone from his voice. His head drooped, and he went back to staring at the bench. I could see only his perfect profile. "I hoped for an explanation. I would have accepted anything you said. But not silence. Nor the weeks when you left me and went back to Armand."

He didn't add, "And I was devastated." He didn't have to, and of course, I didn't expect him to. Men don't talk like that. None of the men I know, anyway.

"I'm sorry." I touched his elbow, felt the fine grain of his riding jacket under my fingers, and withdrew when he didn't respond. "I wish I could undo it, Percy, but I can't."

Unable to think of any other way to reach him, I took it out on Marguerite. «You behaved like an idiot,» I told her, «and me too, thinking I could explain it away. Why wouldn't Percy be devastated? The poor man falls like a ton of bricks for the prettiest, most scintillating girl in town and wins her hand, only to hear on his wedding day that she's such an avid republican that she's proud of having sent an entire family to the guillotine. Then, when he confronts you, you throw the denunciation in his face, refuse to give any explanation for it, and trot off home to your brother, leaving him alone for weeks to ponder what a fool he's been. You asked him to give you unconditional support without explaining what you'd done to deserve it. What *were* you thinking?»

«You're right,» she said. «I behaved abominably. I was unhappy, and I didn't know what else to do.»

Blast. What gave me the right to chastise her?

«Why? What have you done?» she asked. I could almost see her spirits rise.

«Messed up one romance after another. My mother insists I'm too quick to judge. Like Percy.» As the words formed in my head, I recognized their truth. Percy blamed his wife for not meeting his expectations—for being human, in effect.

Another line flitted by. I caught his sleeve again. "Ah, the madness of my pride!" I said. "I realized I'd made a mistake as soon as I reached Armand's, but I couldn't bear to admit it. And when I returned, you were so changed, so cold. I should have apologized then, but pride held me back."

Percy pulled one hand out of his pocket and pressed it against his temple. Remembering last night, I wondered if his head ached. I released his sleeve and rubbed his neck, beneath the black bow. Hair, fine and soft, caressed my hand, but Percy, while not rejecting my touch, remained pulled in on himself, silent and self-contained.

I had decided I was getting somewhere when he straightened his neck and looked at me. His sardonic smile made me flinch.

"Lud, Madam." He had the nerve to yawn. "How distressing."

The shock caused by his rapid shift of mood undermined my fragile self-control. Disappointment ignited a flash of fury, and I leaped to my feet and pushed at his chest. I meant only to shout at him, the irritating man. No one was more startled than I when he toppled backward into the pond.

Oh, lord! I reached for him, but before we could connect, Marguerite thrust me into the background. She picked up her skirts in both hands and raced out of the rose garden.

«Wait!» I said. «Aren't you going to make sure he doesn't drown?»

She whirled, not so much stopping as hovering, like a hummingbird in flight. «He's not drowning.»

Indeed not. Percy sat in the middle of the fish pond, weed dripping from his elegant suit, the look on his face somewhere between amazement and anger. I hadn't seen that much expression from him since I'd entered the simulation.

In her rage, Marguerite didn't acknowledge the change. While I sputtered suggestions for helping him, she completed her turn and ran straight for the house.

Great. Wonderful. Fantastic. Just when I'd had a smidgen of hope. Locked inside Marguerite's brain, I dropped to my knees, wrapped both arms around my head, and ran through every swear word I could remember.

Unless I came up with something fast, I was going to find myself heading into the pivotal scene with Marguerite in control and Percy not speaking to me. There went Plan A. And given Percy's complete lack of response, our potential alliance was dead in the water. So much for Plan B.

As we reached the front steps, Marguerite slowed to a walk. Dropping the silk skirts, she sauntered into the front hall. She was breathing hard, but the butler deigned not to notice.

"Sir Percy fell into the fish pond," she said as though this were an everyday occurrence. "I believe he may require assistance."

The butler didn't even blink. "Indeed, m'lady."

She swept up the stairs, silk skirts lifted in one graceful hand. On the fourth step, she turned. "And ring for Louise, Simmons. I will eat luncheon in my rooms."

After a short while, Louise appeared, tray in hand. Sorrel soup and homemade bread. Steam rose from the soup, and pale gold butter lay near the bread. My stomach rumbled.

Nevertheless, I thought I should show some concern for my absent and no doubt water-logged fake spouse. «You're going to eat?» I asked. «Aren't you worried that something might have happened to Percy?»

«No,» she said callously. «Didn't I tell you there's no talking to him? It's not as simple as you think. The man's an iceberg. All that apology, and he didn't so much as thank you for telling him!»

She walked to the window. Watching him trudge into the house, leaving a trail of weed and water behind him, she giggled.

«He did have it coming,» I said, «brushing me off that way. I didn't intend to push him into the pond. He was off-balance.»

The Marguerite in my mind looked skeptical. «So you regret it?»

When I lie, I try not to lie to myself—or to people living inside my brain who know what I've done. «Not really,» I admitted. «Do you?»

«Not for one minute! I wish I'd shoved him myself.» She looked out the window again and let out another batch of giggles, then laughed harder. Soon she was holding her sides. «Oh, dear, did you see him?»

Until then, I hadn't let myself recognize how funny he'd looked, sitting hip-deep in water with that astonished expression on his face, as though a rabbit had turned around and chomped on his toe.

Louise had left by then. I laughed as hard as Marguerite.

The hall clock had chimed four before I disposed of the delicious lunch. At my suggestion, Marguerite again rang for Louise and requested a bath. «We need to plan,» I explained.

She shook her head. «More plans? None of the ones you've tried so far have worked. In fact, I think you've made things worse. *I* never pushed Percy into a fish pond!»

«That's rich,» I said. «I could have sworn that was you laughing yourself silly a few minutes ago.»

«Well, it was funny,» she admitted. «But I don't see why I should stand by and let you make more plans that involve my body and my words.»

I couldn't argue with that. The idea that the body and the words belonged to me wouldn't convince her. And so far, my advice had gotten us exactly nowhere. Ian had not responded to my offers to team up, which meant I had to hit a home run with Plan A. And although I had a clear goal, the details were doing their usual infernal dance.

Within a few hours, Marguerite and Percy would leave for the Royal Opera House and the plot sketched out by Baroness Orczy would resume. Following the script, Chauvelin would threaten Marguerite; Marguerite would hem and haw before deciding that her brother's life meant more to her than the mysterious stranger who hid his identity behind the mask of the Scarlet Pimpernel; and when she reached Lord Grenville's ball, she would give Chauvelin the information he sought, not realizing that in doing so she was endangering Percy. And— not coincidentally, from my point of view—deep-sixing my plan to win the game and finish my dissertation under David Houghton's supervision.

I hoped to intervene before she reached that point. But I couldn't do much without her cooperation. If the computer wouldn't allow me to warn her, and she didn't trust me enough to give me a free hand, how was I going to steer her in the right direction?

She's like Nessa, I thought as I sat in the back of Marguerite's mind and watched her drum her fingers against the windowsill, waiting for Louise and her pails of water. Although I'd learned to get along with Nessa over the years, no one could describe us as friends. Yet here I was, stuck with finding a way to make peace with a woman like my sister. Not just a demilitarized zone but a real working relationship. Where did I start?

The enormous wardrobe caught my eye. Nessa liked clothes. Marguerite did, too. Maybe I could do something with that. Because I too wanted Marguerite to look her best. The most beautiful woman in Europe was about to cross swords with the Great Manipulator, and I shouldn't send her into battle with only half her arsenal at her command.

If she also knocked Percy's socks off, so much the better.

8. Opera House

WHILE I PLOTTED HOW TO ESTABLISH A PARTNERSHIP WITH Marguerite strong enough to attack the Weasel, Louise came in, trailed by half a dozen footmen carrying steaming buckets. They disappeared behind the Chinese screen, where I could hear them pouring water into a copper tub, then bowed themselves out of the room sputtering "m'ladys" left and right. I waved them away, my attention focused on the pile of gold and cream fabric cradled in Louise's arms.

She spread the gown on the bed, stroking out the slightest wrinkle. Enchanted, I brushed the skirt with one finger. Cinderella couldn't have asked for better. One detail that never made it from book to screen was the change in women's fashion around the time when *The Scarlet Pimpernel* took place. Admittedly, Baroness Orczy had muffed the date of the change by a year or two, as she tended to do. Nevertheless, she'd been quite emphatic about what Marguerite wore to Lord Grenville's ball.

The dress that Louise was caressing did not resemble yesterday's bell-shaped skirts or even the Watteau sacque I'd worn to tip Percy in the fishpond. A cloud of gold lace topped a cream tunic with a high waist and low neckline. Puff sleeves closed with satin ribbons, and the lace overdress opened down the front, revealing tiny gold leaves embroidered with painstaking care around the hem below. It was the style familiar from every Austen movie ever made, the neo-Classic style known as *Directoire* or *Empire*. And it was stunning.

"That's the loveliest dress I've ever seen," I whispered.

Baroness Orczy had described Marguerite as unusually tall, with a slender figure and queenly bearing. As near as I could tell, we both stood five foot six, which did qualify as unusually tall in 1792. But there the resemblance between us ended. Marguerite—so said the mirror—had the body of a cover girl. Long legs, slender waist, full breasts—the *Directoire* style might have been designed for her.

Like Nessa—another point I'd failed to realize before I entered the simulation—Marguerite's love of attention hid a fundamental insecurity, not helped by her husband's frigid withdrawal. She soaked up my open admiration like a sponge.

«Can we make a pact?» I asked her. «I won't bully you, and you won't exclude me? There are things I don't know, and others I can't tell you, but if we don't find a way to work together, something horrible will happen. Agreed?»

Bilious green waves of suspicion clouded her thoughts. «Who *are* you?»

But the computer clamped onto my brain, and I couldn't tell her.

«You don't have to trust me,» I essayed after a while. «It will be your choice. If something bad happens, you can ask me for help. And if it doesn't, you'll do fine without me.»

That seemed to reassure her. I felt her tension ease, her mind open. We again became equals. Humming, I stepped behind the Chinese screen to take my bath.

❁

Percy was waiting for us when we made it to the front hall an hour later. I had the satisfaction of watching his eyes widen, and this time when he bowed, I could see that he meant it. Even the starchy butler gave Marguerite a second glance, only to turn around and snap at the footman, who was goggling.

She deserved it. Louise had sent her out the door in a storm of cooing and fluttering, and I felt a good deal like cooing myself. Thrift-shop clothes didn't hold a candle to this. But then, who could have anticipated the effect of satin and lace, diamonds around my neck, a ruby scarlet pimpernel pinned to the black velvet bow that held back my hair, and a hand-painted ivory fan dangling from my wrist?

Marguerite, head high, glided toward Percy, placed her fingertips on his arm, and let him lead her out to the carriage. To my relief, he didn't attempt to drive this time.

«He only drives home,» Marguerite said. «It's not acceptable to show up at a social function windblown and dust-covered.»

«Wonderful. Something else to look forward to at the end of this hideous evening.» Darn, I hadn't meant to sound so bad-tempered.

«Why hideous?» she asked. «I like music. Dancing, too.»

I didn't answer, having no way to alert her more than I had already.

Percy did look fine, I had to admit. One of the pleasures of watching the BBC version of *The Scarlet Pimpernel* had been wondering what Anthony Andrews would wear next. Beau Brummell had made his mark in the early nineteenth century by decreeing that the true dandy wore nothing but black evening dress and white shirts, but he sure took the fun out of men's clothes. No more getups like Percy's: cream satin, beaded embroidery, and pearl buttons. No flowing lace cuffs or long hair tied at the nape of the neck. No full-skirted coats, clocked stockings, or powdered wigs.

I couldn't imagine living in this fantasy world forever. For two weeks, though, it made for a spectacular vacation.

Despite Percy's avoidance of anything that might encourage intimacy with his wife, I half-expected him to bring up the incident at the fish pond, but here, too, Marguerite had read him better than I. He treated us with the same cool courtesy he'd demonstrated since Dover.

«Can't we apologize?» I asked her.

«Hah!» She brushed me off. «What good would that do? He'd say something polite and meaningless.»

«You don't think it might have an effect on him later? *Not* apologizing didn't work so well.»

She produced another cynical laugh. Then again, she was probably right. If Percy had a chink in his emotional armor, I hadn't discovered a way to pierce it. If our relationship kept heading south at this rate, I could count myself lucky if he didn't feed me to Chauvelin.

«You promised not to make me do things,» Marguerite reminded me.

«True.» Let her think she had the upper hand. I had bigger battles to fight.

We drove first to the Covent Garden Opera House, where Marguerite would try to listen to Glück and be forced to confront the Weasel. As in the book, Sir Percy wandered off after about ten minutes, and I sat amid a crowd of Marguerite's young acquaintances, whose limited powers of perception didn't seem to prevent them from having a great deal to say. After a while, she chased them off. I'd have welcomed the move if I hadn't known what came next.

Sure enough, Chauvelin slunk in right on cue. In fairness, I suppose he had the baroness to blame for his clothes, but maybe he should have asked for a rewrite. In his little black number he looked every inch the crow of Percy's description, foreshadowing Brummell's stipulations with none of his style. To mark the occasion, he'd dolled up the black waistcoat with some black embroidery, but that was it.

The image of David in that getup did provoke an indecent urge to grin, although Chauvelin's grim stare soon drove out thoughts of my professor.

True to my promise, I let Marguerite handle him and didn't interfere. There wasn't much I could do, and perhaps it would reassure her that I had no plans to take over our body again (not true—I'd do it in a flash if I saw an opportunity). Chauvelin sat behind us so he could mutter threats in Marguerite's ear without being seen and went immediately into his act. For the first few beats she spun him a series of lines, most of which boiled down to "leave me alone so I can enjoy the music." Chauvelin paid no attention to these.

Throughout the aria, his smooth voice formed a sinister bass line, the effect only highlighted by my inability to see him, his voice droning in the space behind Marguerite's right ear. "Your brother, St. Just, is in peril," he began.

He had Marguerite's full attention from that moment. I felt her hands tense on the sticks of her fan and wondered that the fragile ivory didn't snap under her fingers. Her skin crawled.

She strove for a casual response, although her voice trembled. "Another of your imaginary plots, Chauvelin? I thought we were friends. Why involve Armand?"

Instead of answering, he produced what would have seemed like a non sequitur, had I not read the book a zillion times in the last ten weeks. "'Tis not two days since we met in Dover. France asked you for help, and you refused."

Marguerite yawned, tapping her delicate fingers against her upper lip in pretended indifference. "Indeed. Are you suggesting this has some connection with my brother?"

"My men made an interesting discovery after you and Sir Percy left last night," Chauvelin said. "Sir Andrew Ffoulkes and Lord Antony Dewhurst did not, it would appear, happen on the Fisherman's Rest by chance."

Marguerite's left hand abandoned the fan and tangled in the gold lace at her side. Inside her head, I frowned. As circuitous as Chauvelin was trying to be—almost to the point of incomprehensibility—he wasn't repeating himself as much as he had in the book. So most likely, I was listening to David, not the character as written by the baroness.

Creepy. Did I want to write my dissertation under the eye of this manipulative fanatic?

"Lud, man," Marguerite said. "Were we not talking of my brother? Do get to the point!"

"Patience, dear lady. We progress, I assure you." Chauvelin's voice made me think of machine oil. "Sir Andrew and Lord Tony are your husband's friends. Does it not disturb you to find out they may not be what they seem?"

Marguerite made a small, annoyed noise. Her tormentor's voice became slicker. "My men intercepted them after you left, bound and gagged them, and relieved them of their papers. We found those papers quite interesting."

I glanced over Marguerite's shoulder and saw the side of Chauvelin's mouth twisted. A shiver ran through me. Could any man look so irredeemably evil?

"La, robbery *and* violence! In England?" Marguerite kept her voice flippant, although her hand clenched the gold lace so tightly I thought it would rip. Chauvelin had mentioned papers for a reason. Images of Armand raced through her mind. *What had he done?*

I tried to comfort her. «Trust me, we'll find a way to save Armand.» But she couldn't relax enough to hear me. Can't say I blamed her.

Chauvelin waved a letter in front of her face. "Irrefutable proof, *Citoyenne*. Your brother, St. Just, has aided the League of the Scarlet Pimpernel. He is compromised beyond hope of pardon."

We both knew what that meant. Arrest, imprisonment, the guillotine. Nightmare memories of bloodthirsty mobs crowded Marguerite's thoughts. They scared *me*, and Armand wasn't my brother.

«Careful,» I said, doing my best to allay her fears. «Don't let Chauvelin manipulate you. He wants you to believe he has Armand at his mercy and only you can rescue him.»

She dropped the abused fan in her lap, turned in her seat, fixed him with her big blue eyes, and extended a pleading hand.

Chauvelin ignored it. "Irrefutable proof, *Citoyenne*." His smooth voice had hardened, and his face had the chilly, implacable lines you see in statues of the nastier Roman emperors. "And I will use it."

He paused for effect. "Unless you care to undertake that little service for France that we discussed yesterday afternoon."

"Find the Scarlet Pimpernel." Marguerite had none of Chauvelin's deviousness, for which I blessed her. Even though I'd read the book and could predict what he'd say next, the effort to follow his twisty mind left me dizzy.

"And if I do?" she added. "You will give me Armand's letter?"

Chauvelin's frigid calm slid away, leaving an unpleasant smile. He leaned back in his chair and rubbed his hands together. "If you do, I will give you the letter. Tomorrow."

Marguerite raised both eyebrows. "You do not trust me?"

He inclined his head. "The stakes are high."

She tried common sense. "Suppose the Scarlet Pimpernel doesn't go to the ball?"

Chauvelin pulled another scrap of paper from his pocket and held it out. "He'll be there. My men took this from Sir Andrew's pocket."

In the near-dark of the opera house, Marguerite and I squinted at the distorted handwriting. "Remember, we should meet no more often than is necessary," the note said. "We" meant Sir Andrew and the writer, I assumed. "You have all your instructions for the 2nd. If you wish to speak to me again, I will be at G's ball." A small, five-pointed flower was stamped in red ink in the lower right corner. The symbol of the Scarlet Pimpernel.

"Lord Tony and Sir Andrew do want to speak to their leader, I expect." Chauvelin plucked the note from my fingers, folded it, and returned it to his pocket. His weasel smirk sent chills down my spine. "My men took them, bound and gagged, to a deserted house on the Dover road. We freed them this morning. No doubt they will head straight for the ball."

«Pig,» I murmured to her. «Wouldn't you *love* to smash a cream pie into that grin?»

Her left hand relaxed its grip on the gold lace.

«You're doing a great job,» I went on. «No one would know how scared you are. Still, Chauvelin looks disgustingly smug. Would you mind if I tried something?»

«What?»

«Nothing you would dislike. We can discuss how to handle his whole blackmail scheme later. I want to shake his confidence a bit. You could do it yourself, but I bet I can do it better. Being ladylike isn't as highly regarded where I come from as it is here. Also, Armand is your brother, so naturally you care more.»

Keeping a firm hold on my patience, I waited for her to work through this line of reasoning, knowing I couldn't push her too far or we'd be fighting again. We were going to have enough trouble figuring out what to do next without complicating the decision by arguing.

Percy had left the box a long time ago, so I expected him to return soon. Should I talk to him? But coaxing Marguerite to reveal Chauvelin's scheme to her husband would mean another tussle with her. An exhausting thought, especially since I no longer felt certain that telling Percy would solve anything. I'd made huge efforts already and gained almost nothing in return. The time had come for him to make the next move.

Still, I didn't see why Chauvelin should have everything his way.

Fear pounded me, each retreat followed by another assault. I'd almost given up hope of persuading Marguerite by the time I sensed tentative agreement.

Chauvelin had laid out his plan by now. Not much of a plan, as it seemed to consist of Marguerite showing up at Lord Grenville's ball and waiting for something to transpire, knowing that if nothing transpired, her brother's head would roll in a basket at the Weasel's convenience. The government of republican France didn't put much faith in the idea of *positive* reinforcement.

The Weasel shifted his legs in a manner that suggested he might be about to rise. "I'll have the Pimpernel's head or your brother's," he announced, like the villain in a melodrama.

«Here goes,» I said to Marguerite. I leaned forward and pinned him to the seat with the scowl I'd developed during four summers as a camp counselor. It had once scattered a dozen illicit beer drinkers, so it should get my point across, even with the Weasel. "Don't you mean, the Scarlet Pimpernel's head *and* my brother's?" I asked. "Or do you think I trust you to keep your promises? I think *you* were the one who turned in St. Cyr. Then blamed it on me! How dare you ask me for help?"

One wild guess after another, but I seemed to have struck a chord. My accusation stopped Chauvelin in his tracks. He sat straighter and for the first time looked at me with respect.

«*Dieu*,» Marguerite said. «I think you shocked him.»

I thought so, too, although he'd already raised his guard again. To be expected, alas. The scowl is good, but not *that* good. An unscrupulous villain can survive it.

Smarmy as ever, he tipped back his chair. "You refuse, then?"

"Not in the least," I said. Prompted, Marguerite stood. Some hidden residue of manners caused Chauvelin to drop the chair forward and spring to his feet. From the other side of the box door, I heard footsteps approaching—Percy's, I hoped.

Twenty minutes' association with the Weasel had proved, in my view, nineteen minutes too long. Next to that, an hour with a chilly, withdrawn husband in whom I couldn't confide looked like a walk in the park.

The Weasel awaited his answer. "I will naturally do the best I can." I summoned my most saccharine smile and curtseyed. "For France, Monsieur Chauvelin."

«*Brava*,» Marguerite said. Percy's arrival shut off any retort Chauvelin might have made.

"Won't you introduce me, m'lady?" Percy's lazy, heavy-lidded gaze rested appreciatively on the neckline of the *Directoire* gown.

Chauvelin made an odd sound, as though grinding his teeth. Percy's aristocratic drawl—representing as it did everything republican France had spent the last three years destroying—

probably had the same effect on a Jacobin as dropping him in a bed of poison ivy. I doubt the cream satin and pearls helped much.

«Shall we give Percy a hand?» I asked Marguerite. «He seems to have a gift for making Chauvelin squirm.»

«Yes, let's,» she replied. Her fear had receded for the moment, although I sensed it massing in the background.

Marguerite gestured with her fan, indicating the Weasel. "Why, Percy," I said. "This is Armand Chauvelin, the French special envoy. You remember, I told you I ran into him in Dover. He used to visit us in the Rue de Richelieu. Didn't you meet him there?"

Percy raised his quizzing glass and surveyed Chauvelin from head to foot. "Ah, yes, now I recall." Percy wagged the glass in the general direction of the Weasel's neck. "The jacket. The breeches. And the cravat!"

Chauvelin, perhaps unconsciously, touched his neckwear. "Do you object to it?"

"Object to it?" Percy seemed stunned at the mere question. "Sink me! The thing's an abomination. As limp as a boiled noodle. Starch, my dear man. You must speak to your laundress. Really!" He put up the quizzing glass once more and shuddered.

To be honest, I couldn't tell the difference between Chauvelin's cravat and any other in the concert hall—not counting Percy's magnificent creation—but the Weasel looked so put out I had to fight my giggles. Marguerite's laughter, I noticed, edged into hysteria.

Having disposed of Chauvelin's pretensions to fashion, Percy announced in his lazy drawl that he had come to collect his wife, whose sedan chair waited outside.

"I suppose you will want to go to that demmed ball," he said as if nothing could be farther from his own mind.

Marguerite flinched at the return of Percy's inane laugh. As in the book, she quickly considered and even more quickly discarded the idea of seeking his aid.

I saw no point in arguing with her. She would only tell me why it couldn't work, and I had to admit that after my experiences of the last day and a half, I had no inclination to ask Percy for assistance either.

Although one anomaly had not escaped me. That speech about breeches and cravats didn't come from the novel. Ian had emerged from his character's shadow.

Could dunking Percy in the pond have released Ian, in the same way that my heights phobia had let me develop a new relationship with Marguerite?

I didn't know. But I decided to offer him one last chance to establish a truce. For Marguerite's sake. And to ensure I'd have alternatives if Plan A fell through.

Of course, he might turn me down again. In that case, I'd have to do whatever it took to finish the game on my own.

"I'm ready to go," Marguerite told Percy. After promising to meet Chauvelin later at Lord Grenville's ball, she put her hand on her husband's outstretched arm, and we walked down a deserted corridor toward the door.

Halfway to the lobby, where the two side staircases met in a wide platform, stood a large dracaena. Percy swept me behind this plant. His words came out low but forceful. "Are you all right? When I arrived, you looked as though you'd seen a ghost."

Marguerite blinked at him, so startled by his intensity that she couldn't think of anything to say.

«It's your chance,» I urged. «Tell him!»

«You do it.» I felt her trembling. On top of the terror Chauvelin had inspired, her husband's personality shift overwhelmed her, but she didn't block my path.

My chance, then—and a better one than I'd expected. The man whose lace cuffs brushed my arms looked nothing like Ian, but he also had none of Percy's frigid restraint. He quirked an eyebrow when he caught me gazing at him.

"No, I'm not all right. Chauvelin was threatening me," I said. I had no need to raise my voice above a whisper. In the narrow space behind the potted plant, Percy's hard body pressed me against the wall.

"With what?"

"He has proof, or says he has proof, that Armand has been helping the League of the Scarlet Pimpernel. If I won't help him find the Pimpernel—tonight, at Lord Grenville's ball—he will have Armand arrested and executed for treason." Marguerite's renewed fear pounded at my temples. My voice shook, and the rest of me, too.

"Ah," he said. "I thought it must be something like that. Fear not, my dear. No harm will come to your brother. I give you my word."

He sounded sincere. And he hadn't dismissed my implied offer of a partnership out of hand. Taking heart, I asked, "What should I do? Chauvelin has a vicious streak. If I say I know nothing, he'll probably arrest Armand out of spite, to teach me a lesson. Can I equivocate, do you think?"

Percy ran a finger down my cheek. "If you must. But whatever you do, don't tell him the truth. He'll be livid when he finds out, but it will buy us some time."

"Time for what?" Marguerite interjected.

He smiled. "Why, to enlist the help of the Scarlet Pimpernel, my dear."

The corridors remained deserted. The strains of Glück sounded from inside the hall. Great crystal chandeliers cast gleaming reflections off polished wood. A dangling dracaena frond tickled my ear. Percy stared deep into my eyes, as Ian had during that elastic minute in Jeb's office. I could think of nothing but his closeness, his body. Why had I ever believed I disliked him?

He took a step toward me, boxing me in. My fingers brushed his satin coat, stroked a pearl button. Quivers of desire flashed through me. Pressed between the wall and Percy, I blushed from head to toe, like a girl at her first adult party. Every nerve ending tingled, and the silk and lace of the *Directoire* gown did nothing to conceal my reaction. Or his, if it came to that.

When he moved back, I fought disappointment. The Percy of the book didn't relent toward Marguerite for hundreds of pages, and Ian and I had every reason to resist each other.

Although he didn't *look* resistant.

In a husky growl, he said, "Oh, the hell with it!" And as swiftly as he'd dragged me behind the dracaena, he pulled me into his arms and kissed me.

A small sound rose in my throat. Protest? Pleasure? I couldn't tell. The passion in that kiss poured over the barriers separating me from Marguerite. My lips parted in response to the pressure of his mouth. His tongue made sensuous circles against my own. Somewhere, Marguerite cast a blue glow of amazement. Then we again became one person, lost to our surroundings. Floating in a sea of sensation bounded by Percy's body wrapped around my own, I pressed against him, wanting more.

A fingernail traced the row of tiny buttons along my spine, setting off tremors that ran from head to heels. Percy's hands tangled in my curls, threatening to pull them loose from their big black bow. The corridor felt like a sauna. Desire swept me away.

Until, adrift on waves of sensuality, I sensed a dark spot emerge from the depths and solidify into a horrid thought.

No one's kissing me.

Percy loved Marguerite. He was her husband, not mine. I'd become my worst nightmare, a female version of my father.

Or Ian loved Marguerite, who was beautiful and charming. That made more sense than him kissing me. He disliked me. I didn't like him, either.

Right, Nina. I hate him so much I melted into his arms. He might dislike me, but I couldn't dislike him one-tenth as much as I'd believed.

I pushed at Percy's chest. He raised his head, looking shaken, his impassivity no more than a memory. Marguerite and I, coalescing into our unique selves, stared at him, speechless.

«*Pardi,*» she said. «Even before, it was never like that.»

«No.» I wanted to apologize for kissing her husband, but I had no words to explain the mixed regret and envy I felt.

From the top of the stairs, I heard a door open. Footsteps sounded in the corridor, a single pair of booted feet. Percy stepped out from behind the dracaena and extended his arm. "Shall we, my dear? Lord Grenville awaits." The smooth voice quivered, the husky tone not completely subdued. Grenville had a rolled Scottish r.

When I held out my hand, he lifted it and brushed my fingers across his lips. "Courage, *mignonne,*" he said. "We're in this together." His eyes bored into me, as if he sought to convey a message only I would understand. And he'd called me *mignonne*—sweetheart—an expression Percy never used.

My spirits rose, and I smiled at him. "Together," I said.

9. Lord Grenville's Ball

Lord Grenville planned to hold his ball at the Foreign Office, where he served as Britain's equivalent of the secretary of state. Thanks to the crush of sedan chairs and carriages carrying the invited guests, it would take at least an hour to traverse the short distance from Covent Garden. When I suggested, with a certain mischief, that we could walk and arrive in half the time, Marguerite let out a howl of protest that would have burst my eardrums if uttered aloud. In some places, looks *are* everything.

On the whole, though, I found her more amenable to my schemes than before. I gave Percy credit for her shift in mood—or if not hers, mine.

Since we would soon be surrounded by others, I forced myself to stop mooning over the kiss and tried to engage her in a discussion of how best to thwart Chauvelin.

«Percy will take care of it,» she said with a blithe unconcern that I found almost ludicrous after her earlier refusal to talk to him. «He gave his word.»

So he had, although agreeing to an alliance didn't mean that I intended to step back while he reaped the glory. But given that the chances of convincing Marguerite to take matters into her own hands rather than rely on some guy, however gorgeous and manly, hovered somewhere below zero, I wasted no time in refuting this.

«Of course,» I said instead. «He did suggest we could help him by slowing Chauvelin down, though.»

Despite Marguerite's conviction that women shouldn't do much besides look pretty, she was quick-witted. She grasped the big point right away. «How? Chauvelin doesn't need us. With the information he showed us, he can find the Pimpernel without our help. It sounds like a test: prove your loyalty or Armand dies. We'll fail that test if we try to slow him down or misdirect him.»

«You're right,» I said. I should have figured that out for myself. «He can send his men to spy on Sir Andrew and Lord Tony. But the opposite is true, too. We don't need him.»

Marguerite gasped. «And let Armand die? Never!»

«No,» I said. «Of course not. Percy will save Armand. He gave his word. But think, Marguerite. Percy is a man of honor. Chauvelin is not. He lied to you before, and he's lying now. Why should he keep his promise to release Armand? He's more likely to kill them both: Armand *and* the Scarlet Pimpernel. And blame you, the beast, as he did before.»

Marguerite shuddered. «Oh, *Sainte Vierge*. I couldn't live with myself. What options do we have?»

The million-dollar question. To which I did not have an answer. I let my half-formed ideas tumble out, using Marguerite as a sounding board. «Percy wants time to warn the Scarlet Pimpernel. That means we must pretend to look for the Pimpernel while staying out of Percy's way—and keeping Chauvelin away from both of them, which is the hard part.»

So far, so good. Of course, Percy and the Pimpernel, being the same person, always traveled together, but Marguerite didn't know that, and at the moment it didn't matter. Tomorrow she would learn the truth, and I could lay off the obfuscation. Hallelujah!

More important, keeping Chauvelin away from Percy and the Scarlet Pimpernel met my objectives for the game. Armand's fate didn't bother me. No student played him, so most likely the computer had created him. I didn't share any of that with Marguerite.

«We can make up a story,» I suggested. «Tell Chauvelin we've discovered that the Pimpernel will be in the garden at midnight, say.»

Marguerite pondered this. «We'll have to pick someplace deserted.»

«Not really. It would distract Chauvelin big time if we sent him chasing off after an idle fop or two. Still, we don't want him hurting anyone, and he might. He is *such* a weasel.»

Marguerite sat up straighter. I could almost see her ears perk. «You called him that before. What is it, this weasel?»

Our partnership had strengthened the connection between us, but not to the point where I had perfect command of French. So I envisioned a weasel.

«Ah,» she said. «*Une belette.* You have reason. It is the eyes, so small and mean.»

«And that narrow face. And the way he rubs his hands.» The man gave me the willies. I shoved his image out of my mind and focused on our problem. «Suppose we tell him the Pimpernel plans to attend Lady S's rout, or Lord M's hunting party, two or three days hence.»

«Which Lady S?» My fellow conspirator needed a bit of training in nonliteral thinking—unless I'd lost my ability to communicate clearly since entering the game, which, given how many weird ideas I had to juggle at once, wouldn't surprise me.

I explained. «We should pick an initial that would fit several people. The League wouldn't tell everyone in town where it planned to meet, would it? It's supposed to be a secret organization.»

She got it then. «Let's say S's party. That would be the same as G's ball, so it would sound right, and if you count first names, there are at least six S's, male and female, giving parties between now and Thursday.»

«S's party,» I said. «That sounds good. Let's say that. And if we do find out something specific about tonight, we'll tell Percy. He can warn whoever's at the real meeting place that Chauvelin is after him.»

«Yes! What an adventure!» In my mind, Marguerite's blue eyes sparkled and the red-gold curls danced.

With a pang of angst, I realized that I would never, in my own body, look that beautiful. For one insanely jealous moment, I battled the urge to tear the sensors from my head and run home. Obviously, Percy had kissed Marguerite, not me.

Before I could do anything drastic, the sedan chair stopped moving and Percy's face appeared at the window. We had reached the Foreign Office.

Lord Grenville's ball was, as they said in those days, a squeeze—therefore a huge success. Marguerite and I emerged from the sedan chair to take the arm of George, Prince of Wales. At thirty, Prinny already tipped the scales at an unhealthy weight. His corset creaked. I strove not to giggle.

Marguerite accompanied the prince up an enormous staircase while Percy sauntered a few paces behind. A dozen men in uniforms manned trumpets, like something out of

Ivanhoe. The fanfare was for the prince; we just profited from the association.

As we entered the ballroom, a chubby man in elaborate livery, including a powdered wig, pounded the floor with his staff and announced, "His Royal Highness, the Prince of Wales. Sir Percival Blakeney, Lady Blakeney." Everything stopped. The prince waved to the crowd, and in response the musicians started up again while we were bowing and curtseying to the host and hostess.

The Foreign Office teemed with hundreds of guests, besatined and bejeweled and generally decked to the nines. Only Marguerite sported a *Directoire* gown, and it drew oohs and ahs wherever she passed. Amid the glorious colors, Chauvelin's funereal black stood out like a fly in Vichyssoise. He managed an oily bow when Lord Grenville, looking as though someone had pulled out his teeth with pincers, dragged him forward for an introduction to the prince. As foreign secretary, Grenville had had no choice but to invite the French ambassador, and once Chauvelin had the bad manners to accept, the host couldn't snub his guest. Some jobs are tough.

I forgot about my jealousy. The ball was a historian's dream; and watching the prince say rude things to Chauvelin, who didn't dare reply in kind, raised my spirits faster than the champagne. Percy reveled in spouting a most ridiculous poem to everyone we met:

> *They seek him here, they seek him there,*
> *Those Frenchies seek him everywhere.*
> *Is he in heaven, or is he in hell?*
> *That demmed, elusive Pimpernel.*

Every time the Weasel heard it, he looked more sour. I concealed my grin behind my fan. Very useful things, fans. I hadn't truly appreciated them until that night.

But the best part came within five minutes of our entry. Percy trotted off to land his poem on another willing victim, leaving Marguerite holding the prince's arm. Lord Grenville, with a sigh of relief, escaped from Chauvelin. Then, before the Weasel passed out of whisper range, Grenville gathered to his bosom, so to speak, Madame la Comtesse de Tournay, rigid and upright in solid black. I recalled that her husband was trapped in France, and she wanted to solicit the prince's help—as though Robespierre and his goons gave a hoot for what the Prince of Wales thought of them. Sir Andrew and Lord Tony had assured her that the Comte de Tournay was the Scarlet Pimpernel's next rescue project. She'd have done better to place her faith in them. But one could see why she might hedge her bets.

"Oh, dear," the prince murmured in Marguerite's ear, "she looks very virtuous."

Marguerite made a flirtatious comment about virtue in women having appeal only when lost. I left her to it. She didn't need my help to keep the prince in line.

And that's when it got good. With great pomp and circumstance, the prince informed the haughty lady, "Every compatriot of Lady Blakeney's is doubly welcome for her sake … her friends are our friends … her enemies the enemies of England." Patting Suzanne on the head, he added, "Charming, charming." He extended a hand to Marguerite. "You will give this lovely émigrée the benefit of your friendship, will you not, Lady Blakeney?"

The expression on the comtesse's proud face was priceless. Disdain for Marguerite warred with ingrained respect for royalty till I thought the old bat would choke. I was laughing too hard to speak when Marguerite swept Suzanne into a hug and bore her off, her mother's frigid words of approval hanging like icicles in the air behind them.

❁

A short time later, Percy and I strolled through the rooms—
he as suave and impervious as ever. On the surface, the kiss
at the opera house meant no more to him than the incident
with the fish pond.

His savoir-faire far exceeded mine. Searing flashes of
memory threatened to send my self-control to the bottom
of the ocean.

I forced myself to concentrate on the present, to stop
thinking about the kiss. Marguerite and I had a plan. I had
sketched out the broad strokes with Percy, and he agreed that
the scheme should work. My job was to implement it, not to
moon over kisses, however spectacular. If Ian and I deflected
Chauvelin, both of us should win. I could live with that.
Especially if it led to more kisses…

Nina, stop that!

A white-wigged lackey approached, bowed until his nose
brushed his knee, and announced that the Prince of Wales
awaited Sir Percy Blakeney in the room set aside for gambling.
Percy dropped my arm and with a murmured apology went to
answer his ruler's summons.

He hadn't left the room before Chauvelin's voice oozed
into my right ear. "Look over there," the voice said.

Across the room, I saw Lord Hastings slip a piece of paper
to Sir Andrew Ffoulkes. Sir Andrew tucked the note into his
sleeve.

"Find out what that note says," Chauvelin went on.
"Discover the identity of the Scarlet Pimpernel, *Citoyenne*, and
share that information with me. If you do, I will give you your
brother's letter tomorrow. He will live. A happy ending. Fail
me, and he dies."

His threat tumbled Marguerite into full-scale panic. Our conversation in the sedan chair blanked from her mind. Visions of Armand—bound, suffering, dead—tormented her.

Yesterday, her fear would have pushed her into control of our shared body and shut me in the background. Today, my earlier work paid off. I managed to hang on.

"You speak nonsense," I told Chauvelin, since Marguerite could not respond. "Sir Andrew's note may have nothing to do with the Scarlet Pimpernel."

Chauvelin rubbed his weasel hands together. "You had better hope, *Citoyenne,* that it does. If I leave this ball without learning the true identity of France's greatest enemy, your brother will pay the price."

I gripped my lace skirts, as Marguerite had done at the opera house. "How do you expect me to learn the contents of a private note?"

"You're an *actress.* Bring me the note, or tell me what it says, within the hour. Or be prepared to hold a memorial service for your brother."

Marguerite cowered in the back of my mind. I swore at him under my breath. As I watched him slink away, anger cast a reddish veil across my vision. How dare he manipulate her this way!

His absence, and my fury, revived Marguerite. With her support guaranteed, I chased Andrew into the anteroom where he had gone, according to the book, to read his note and destroy it. Chauvelin watched from the sidelines, a derisive smirk twisting his mouth.

As Marguerite and I entered the anteroom, Andrew thrust a piece of paper into his pocket. His welcoming smile seemed forced.

Up to this point, the general line of the story, except for my interludes with Percy, had proceeded according to plan. Andrew had followed the script by taking his note to the anteroom rather than a location not mentioned in the original novel. The other students, too, had stuck to the baroness's plot. I had my suspicions of David, but I couldn't prove that he had any influence on Chauvelin. Which might mean that only Ian and I had escaped our characters enough to operate independently within the game.

My spirits soared. The contest would be a cakewalk, in that case.

The clear demands of her role brought Marguerite's inner actress to the surface. In the novel, she'd excelled at this point, so I left the task of intercepting Andrew's note to her. With the grace that had no doubt earned her standing ovations on the Paris stage, she raised one hand to her forehead and swooned. Andrew caught her in mid-fall. Gentleman did such things in those days.

"You're ill." Concern roughened his voice as he lowered her into a chair. "Sit here while I fetch Percy."

"No, no." Marguerite opened her eyes. "Stay with me, please. I'll be fine in a moment. I just need to rest. The ballroom's so hot it made me dizzy." She lowered her lids once more, watching him through her lashes.

I braced myself. According to the book, Andrew was supposed to pull out the note, glance at it, then hold it to the candle that stood on a nearby table. As the smoke rose, Marguerite would leap to her feet, snatch the paper from his hand, and produce a flattering if false story about his cleverness in helping her overcome her faintness while she memorized the half-burned words.

None of that happened. Instead, Suzanne dashed into the room and upended the plot in a swirl of silk skirts. The table next to me went flying, together with the fruit basket and silver candelabra it held, including the very candle with which Andrew was supposed to burn his note. He yelled in surprise and, hopping from one foot to the other like one of Marguerite's beloved turkeys, stamped on a small flame that licked at the Aubusson carpet. I sprang to my feet, startled into abandoning my pretense of weakness. My chair crashed to the floor behind me.

As if summoned by the noise, Tony ran in and threw up both hands. "Marguerite, my God, are you all right?"

Marguerite cursed in French. I kicked a rolling apple and stomped on a handy grape. How could I have underestimated my fellow-students like that? The three of them had indeed found a way to take charge of their characters. *And* they were working together. Most likely, they had set up this situation in advance. Andrew had stuck to the script to give me a false sense of security. It had worked, too.

Well, I could think on my feet as well as they. I beckoned them in. Suzanne poured water from a nearby vase onto the candle flame, giving Andrew a chance to stop his firefighter routine. The three of them clustered around me.

"I'm fine now," I whispered. "I was hiding from Chauvelin. I swear, the man has more arms than an octopus. I've been dodging him ever since Percy went off to play hazard with the prince."

They looked skeptical, as well they should, since they had no illusions as to what Marguerite was doing in that room. I produced an elaborate shudder appropriate to the Comédie Française. "Don't leave me alone with him, if you love me. *Pardi*, he seems to believe I will sell my virtue for a word of French. And I a married woman!"

Suzanne reacted first. Clapping her hands against her cheeks, she cried, "*Ma chère*, we will not desert you. That dreadful man! Andrew, you must escort her to the ballroom."

He extended his arm, but as I stepped toward him, a familiar drawl interrupted our developing scene. "La, my dear," Percy said. "And here a little bird told me that you needed my assistance. Little birds can be so contrary, don't y'know?"

"Percy!" My exclamation echoed Andrew's and Tony's. I ran forward and clasped my husband's hand. In the background, Chauvelin lurked.

"Dearest," I said to Percy, to shore up the fibs I'd been telling. "'Twas nothing. An absence of gentlemanly behavior in one who should be old enough to behave better."

I cast a minatory glare over my shoulder, in case the un-gentleman in question missed the point, and took pleasure in watching him slither away once more. With Chauvelin dispatched for the moment, I curtseyed to Andrew. "Percy will escort me. I would not tear you away from *ma petite* Suzanne. Especially when the minuet is about to begin."

I placed my hand on Percy's arm. He graced me with his most elegant bow. "I should be honored, m'lady. It has not slipped your mind, I hope, that I find the minuet rather tedious."

Marguerite, languishing inside my head, sighed. «No problem,» I told her. «I'll handle it.» And with a girlish enthusiasm drawn straight from her playbook, I said, "But for *me*, Percy? You will dance with me, won't you? I would be so disappointed if you did not."

His lips twitched, and I knew I had won. As he escorted me to the ballroom, I kept a wary eye out for Chauvelin, but he had gone to ground in his weasel hole for the moment, leaving me to enjoy my dance (the quadrille, it turned out, not the minuet) with Percy.

Marguerite alternated between puzzle and panic. I did my best to reassure her. But I myself felt as tightly wound as the clock we passed in the hall, aware that I'd reached a crisis point.

I'd tell Chauvelin the story Marguerite and I had constructed, but would it do me any good?

I could pretend I had learned the story from Andrew's note, although I couldn't tell how much of the scene in the anteroom Chauvelin had witnessed. And even if misdirection, by itself, counted as thwarting David—which it might not, because he too had no doubts as to the true identity of the Scarlet Pimpernel—Suzanne and Andrew and Tony could claim just as much credit as Ian and me. Which left me wondering if I was wasting my time.

I muttered as much of this stew of fears and frustrations as I could squeeze past the computer into Percy's ear while we were dancing, although the quadrille is not the waltz: we had about two seconds each time we held hands before the dance separated us once more. He proposed that I decoy Chauvelin anyway, so when the quadrille ended, I gave him Marguerite's best curtsey and went off to negotiate the details with her.

We had to retreat to the "retiring room" set aside for ladies, as Chauvelin had re-emerged from his burrow. I tripped over him skulking in the corridor as I left the ballroom, but a quick shimmy behind a rotund duchess won me the refuge I sought.

«Seems to me we have two choices,» I began, once the ladies' room door closed behind us. «Make up a time and place for a meeting here, or stick with the S's party story. Which one will cause Chauvelin more trouble?»

«S's party,» Marguerite said. «If we set a meeting here, Chauvelin will have his answer by the end of the night. Use S's party, and he'll waste almost a week wangling more invitations and checking each place for the Pimpernel before he realizes we led him astray. But we need to explain why the Pimpernel didn't come to the ball as he said he would.»

«All is discovered. Fly?» I suggested. Tension made me giddy.

Marguerite frowned, and the maid who'd been heading our way with a towel scurried away. «Don't be silly,» Marguerite said. «Who talks like that?»

«Sorry.» I had to stop letting my weird sense of humor get the better of me. Although I was playing a game, Marguerite saw Armand's plight as deadly serious. I would alienate her if I didn't rein in the bad jokes. «Suppose we say the Pimpernel heard at the last minute that his enemies would be here? From the way Grenville carried on earlier, I doubt he expected to entertain Chauvelin.»

Marguerite nodded. «Yes, good. So the meeting has been moved to S's party. Won't Chauvelin writhe to think he has to attend yet another society function?»

Glad to see her spirits rise, I joined in her laughter. «Won't he, though? Horrid man. Shall I tell him, or you?»

«You.» She smiled, and the maid ventured to hand her the towel. «You did a great job with Suzanne.»

«My pleasure,» I said. Which was true: I was enjoying myself to the hilt. The twists to the plot had raised the stakes in the game, and Marguerite was fast becoming the best friend I'd never had in middle school. With a thrill of anticipation, I washed my hands, gave the used towel back to the maid, pasted suitable reluctance on my face, and went off to throw a well-earned monkey wrench into the Weasel's schemes.

I found him propping up the wall opposite the ladies' room doorway. High-society matrons subjected him to their lorgnettes as they went by, but Chauvelin ignored them. I walked past him, beckoning with my fan, and heard his heels clicking on the parquet behind me. I stopped in a more or less deserted corridor near the stairwell. Chauvelin almost ran into me. I watched him put out a hand to steady himself. A tiny victory, unintended but welcome. Anything to keep him off-balance!

"I saw the note," I said, glancing over my shoulder as though afraid of pursuit. "The Pimpernel's plans changed. Someone warned him, and he stayed away. He reset the meeting for S's party. Soon, I assume, but the message didn't say when."

The Weasel rubbed his hands together, becoming more melodrama villain by the minute. "And how was it signed?"

I shuffled my feet until he repeated the question, then hung my head and whispered, "It wasn't signed. There was a symbol, in one corner, of a five-petaled flower."

"The Scarlet Pimpernel." Chauvelin stroked his forefinger along my cheek. "You've done well, my dear. S's party. My, my. Lord S or Lady S?"

I shrugged to indicate my ignorance of S's gender. My palm itched to slap him. Sure, his actions supported the lies I'd told in the anteroom, but that didn't mean I welcomed his attentions. In the book, Chauvelin had no romantic interest in Marguerite. He merely manipulated her to serve his political goals. Sexy professor in disguise or not, this joker had no right to paw me. So to counteract what my mother called "ideas," I trod on his toe.

"Oh, forgive me," I said, meaning nothing of the sort. "How clumsy! You will give me Armand's letter now?" I scooted back a few inches and let Marguerite's fear show. He'd promised to hand the letter over tomorrow, but I didn't believe he had any such plans. Might as well put him on the spot right away.

In the back of my brain, Marguerite was cheering. «Good! Tread on him again!»

Chauvelin was not cheering. Marguerite in that dress was too enchanting for her own good. Perhaps I should have insisted on a nun's habit.

«And miss out on Percy's kiss?» Marguerite asked. «Not for a dozen leering Chauvelins!»

I had to agree. I asked for the letter again, keeping a good couple of feet between me and Chauvelin and "accidentally" smacking him with my fan whenever he got too close.

After a while, Monsieur Ooze gave up. "Oh, I'll send you your brother's letter." He sounded, for once, more disgruntled than sinister. "When I catch the Scarlet Pimpernel, here or in France."

"Tomorrow. You promised," I reminded him.

He scowled. "Not tomorrow. After S's party."

Marguerite freaked again at the thought of postponement. «We should have changed the time for tonight!»

«No,» I reassured her. «You were right. We delay him much longer this way, and he doesn't need the letter to arrest Armand. Our job is to slow him down, so Percy can find the Scarlet Pimpernel.»

"Soon then." I curtseyed to Chauvelin. "Otherwise, I'll ask Percy to remind you." I stared at his limp cravat until his cheeks reddened, then did an end run around him and headed back to the ballroom. Marguerite and I had completed our task.

As I moved into the main entryway, I checked the grandfather clock that stood in the hall. It was half past ten. I could have sworn we'd arrived at the Foreign Office years ago.

For the first time that evening, I felt my heart rate slow to normal. Briefly closing my eyes, I released a long breath. The big scene was behind me. I'd fulfilled Plan A (don't give Chauvelin any information he can use to trap Percy) and Plan

B (ally with Ian). Surely that was enough to qualify as a win, despite the troubling partnership demonstrated by Suzanne, Andrew, and Tony.

Time to check in with Percy.

10. The Crossing

EXCEPT THAT PERCY WAS NOWHERE TO BE FOUND. I searched the ballroom, the library, the supper room, the garden. I poked my head into the room set aside for games of chance, earning a chorus of invitations to join various tables and confer good fortune on more than one inebriated gentleman, but not one sight of a certain blond heartthrob did I catch. In fact, I saw *no* blond heartthrobs: Andrew and Tony, as well as Percy, appeared to have vanished into the Avalon mists.

Where had they gone? In retrospect, I can't believe how long I waited for the truth to dawn. In my defense, I can cite only that my mental horizons were still bounded by Baroness Orczy's novel. Her plot required the whole group of us—Andrew, Suzanne, Tony, Chauvelin, Percy, and myself—to hang around the Grenvilles' ball until one in the morning, so the men must be around somewhere, even though I saw none of them but Chauvelin, his funereal black unmistakable as he passed among the throng.

Marguerite sent the occasional muttered comment, most of them expressing mild confusion at my insistence on prolonging the search. She didn't resist, just went into a kind of doze.

In due course, I ran into Suzanne, looking as befuddled as I felt. "Where are they?" I demanded.

She didn't ask which "they" I had in mind. Good. That meant I was talking to my fellow-student, not Mademoiselle de Tournay. "Not a clue," she said. A worried frown creased her perfect brow. "I danced the cotillion with Andrew, then Percy signaled to him—not long after you slipped out—and I haven't seen either of them since. Or Tony, although he disappeared earlier, during the quadrille. I've checked everywhere."

"Me, too." I subjected an unoffending Dresden shepherdess, adorning the mantelpiece behind Suzanne's head, to a glower that would have left her shivering in her shoes were she not made of china. "You don't think they fell foul of Chauvelin?"

"The three of them? It seems unlikely."

I agreed that it did. Marguerite had woken up and was pounding at my brain, shooting questions and proposing options. I tried to ignore her and focus on Suzanne, but Marguerite didn't make it easy. "Let's go round the rooms again," I suggested after a bit. Since she'd been urging exactly that, Marguerite calmed down.

But Suzanne and I together had no more success than we'd enjoyed alone. I had reached the point of worrying that Percy must be lying in an alley somewhere, injured if not dead, when a liveried lackey approached me with a silver tray. On the tray lay a folded note addressed to "Lady Blakeney." I snatched it and tore it open, ripping a corner of the paper in my haste.

"Careful," Suzanne said. She pressed against my arm, trying to peer into the folds.

Taking a deep breath, I spread the paper open and moved toward the closest candelabra, holding the note so Suzanne could read the text without difficulty—other than the challenge of following Copperplate handwriting scratched in water-logged ink with a quill pen and rife with eighteenth-century "make it up as you go" spelling and capitalization rules, that is.

The signature caught my attention first. No statement of love or farewell, not even a first name, just the single word "Blakeney." And above that, three sentences that lit a spark of fury that threatened to consume me. Cleared of its old-fashioned orthography, the note said: "Madam, Business calls me to the North until Wednesday next. Sir Andrew has agreed to accompany me. The coachman will convey you home. Blakeney."

"*Nom d'un nom.*" Suzanne smacked her fan against a nearby cabinet. "They've done a bunk. Dumped us women here while they go off and play the hero. Of all the…" She finished with a word in French that had Marguerite clapping her hands over our ears.

"Exactly." I turned the note over in my hands, tempted to tear it into shreds and feed it to the fire. I didn't, though. I needed it as evidence, to wave in Percy's face before I used his guts for garters.

Marguerite said, «I do not understand. Percy often travels to the North with Andrew. I went there once; it was dull. Why fuss so?»

Instead of answering, I fixed my gaze on Suzanne. "Come to Blakeney Manor tomorrow, *chérie*. Maman will agree, will she not, since the prince has approved our friendship?"

Suzanne's hands, clenched into fists that threatened to snap the ivory sticks of her fan, relaxed. She nodded. "Indeed, Marguerite, an excellent idea. We can count only on each other, it seems, for the next ten days."

Satisfied, I kissed her on both cheeks and took my leave of the Grenvilles, thanking them profusely on Percy's behalf as well as my own. Suzanne had understood my unspoken message: the men have betrayed us; we must work together to salvage our chances of winning the game. And she had agreed. Tomorrow, we would head for France.

Where I would extract maximum pleasure from spiking Ian Campbell's guns.

Two hours later, when I descended from Percy's luxurious coach onto the driveway of Blakeney Manor, I was still livid. I stomped up the stairs, tripped over the hem of the *Directoire* gown as I marched through the door, and had to fight to muster a few pleasant words to greet the butler and Louise, Marguerite's maid.

Marguerite couldn't grasp what made me so angry even after I explained as best I could. Marguerite, in fact, was the only reason I had returned to Blakeney Manor as commanded by Percy—that and the convenience of the manor as a place for negotiating with Suzanne. Here—tomorrow morning, according to Baroness Orczy's plot—Marguerite was supposed to stumble over a signet ring that would clue her in to her husband's secret identity and reveal that Chauvelin had manipulated her into betraying her own husband, sentencing Percy to a swift and brutal death. Until that happened, I had no hope of convincing her to pursue him to France—or even that he had gone to France, not to the North. So here we were, ready to stumble on cue.

Somehow I survived the undressing ceremony with Louise. I rallied long enough to tell her that the dress had almost caused a riot, which pleased her. I let her brush out my hair and wrap me in another exquisite negligee. But it wasn't until she curtseyed and departed, the pile of gold lace and cream satin cradled in her arms, that I stopped hyperventilating and managed to draw the first complete breath since I discovered Percy missing.

By then, the clock had struck two. I should have been sleeping, but my fury remained too raw. The whole way from London, I had brooded over Ian's betrayal and my own stupidity in trusting him. And why, when all was said and done? Because he kissed me. What a dolt!

Because he kissed me and called me *mignonne,* I believed he had accepted my offer of an alliance. I told him my plans. I took his advice. I deceived Chauvelin. And I'd no sooner finished lying to Chauvelin than I found out that he, Andrew, and, most likely, Tony had sallied forth from the Foreign Office, heading for France. He didn't even have the common decency to admit what he was doing—to say goodbye in person!—let alone to keep me in the loop.

And I should have expected nothing less. I had never, ever liked him. He teased me and tormented me and called me Ninel. So what if his kiss made me weak at the knees? I was a scholar, dammit, and I would act like one. I pummeled Marguerite's feather pillows to prove it.

A scholar. Through a haze, like fog, I heard a memory of my father's voice, introducing me to one after another of the slinky fashion models he liked to date. Interchangeable lovelies, few of them older than I am now. What didn't alter was his description of me—the smart daughter, the one with no looks.

Sparrow. I'd forgotten he was the one who came up with the name: "Brown hair and brown eyes, she looks like a bird." Nessa used it only as a joke. My stomach lurched. I felt sick. I could play Marguerite for the rest of my life, but inside I was Sparrow, and that wouldn't change.

And Sparrow had believed she could win over Percy. No, face it: Ian. How could a smart woman behave like such a fool?

The next morning, Mr.—more likely, Monsieur, if I thought about it—Alphonse had plenty of cause for complaint about her ladyship's failure to do justice to his lovely breakfast. Leaving the brioche half-eaten on the table, I carried a cup of coffee to the terrace and contemplated the mists that obscured yesterday's sunshine. With Marguerite's help I'd managed to find a plain muslin dress that required only three or four petticoats and a small hoop. It had a bright blue sash and a linen fichu that crossed over and tucked into the low neckline. She looked as lovely as the Dresden statuette that had garnered my ire the night before and seemed unconcerned by her husband's absence. Then I remembered she was anticipating a visit from her best friend.

Whose plans for the meeting differed completely from hers. I wondered how Marguerite would cope when she realized what Suzanne and I had in mind.

The coffee warmed my hands and smelled wonderful. I sipped it, gazing into the mists. Marguerite hummed and thought of Suzanne, while I entertained dark thoughts about Percy. Where was that duplicitous skunk by now? Gliding over the water on the yacht I'd seen in Dover, I supposed. It would take hours to cross the English Channel in a sailboat.

More than twelve hours? I had no idea. In the somewhat more balanced state brought on by a night's sleep, I recognized that Percy had probably wanted to improve his chances of rescuing Armand by getting a jump on Chauvelin. I understood that. What I could not forgive was being left out in the cold with Suzanne.

Something moved amid the rosebushes. «What's that?» Marguerite asked.

«I don't know.» I leaned forward to get a better view. Farther into the gardens, I saw a flash. Light? Reflection? I couldn't tell. I heard a distant rustling, a squawk, then silence. Puzzled, I turned Marguerite toward the house.

It always annoys me when heroines in novels run blindly and alone into dark alleys at midnight. I tend to throw such books into a corner and stomp on them. So I assure you that I did not race into the garden to investigate the shrubbery. Instead I sent a couple of footmen, who returned within twenty minutes to assure me that nothing and no one threatened the peace of Blakeney Manor.

"Maybe one of the dogs got out, m'lady," the strapping lad I knew as Charles told me. I've seen enough skeptical expressions in my time to guess he believed I'd invented the whole thing. He didn't dare say that, though.

He could be right, even so. "Maybe," I said, then dismissed them and thought no more about it.

Marguerite bubbled with anticipation of Suzanne's arrival. As minutes turned into hours, I chewed my lip, wondering if my visitor would show up. Perhaps she'd had second thoughts about allying with me. In that case, I would have to get Marguerite to France on my own.

When we passed Percy's study and saw the door unlocked, I went in, determined to scoop up his brass signet ring with the scarlet pimpernel on it. Marguerite protested, but I was adamant. Until she learned her husband's secret identity, the computer would refuse to let me talk about him freely. Not only did I need her cooperation if I were ever to cross the Channel, but the clamp on my tongue threatened to drive me mad. A few more days of lockdown, and the servants would be wrapping me in a straitjacket and chaining me to a post.

We roamed around the study for quite a while, Marguerite grousing the whole time, before we stumbled over the ring hidden in the carpet. I'd read the book and almost missed it; goodness knows how she found it on her own.

Still, we got there in the end. I showed her the ring. «It's true, then?» she asked. «Percy *is* the Scarlet Pimpernel?»

Images tumbled around in her head. Anomalies noted but ignored, events reassessed in the light of this new information, memories of a time when her husband hadn't worked so hard to conceal the truth from her. The discovery of the ring opened her eyes, changing her feelings toward Percy in an instant.

In my view, the story went downhill from here. Reading about Marguerite dropping the beloved brother like a hot potato and moaning about her willingness to die for the man she'd just spent 150 pages spurning had always tried my patience to the hilt. It was the main reason I'd written her off as a birdbrain. Listening to it at a time when the only interaction I wanted with her husband involved a large kettle and a truckload of boiling oil fit my definition of a nightmare.

But since I couldn't expect her to absorb such a massive shift of perspective in a flash, I had to hope she'd get over it soon. Meanwhile, as she came to grips with reality, I pocketed the ring. In a computer game, you can't tell what might come in handy, and if nothing else, it would keep the servants from finding it.

I spared a minute to admire the leather-and-wood austerity of Percy's private sanctum, the neatly stacked rolls of paper, the maps of France pinned to the wall, and the portrait of his beautiful but—according to the baroness—mentally unstable mother that hung over the fireplace. You could see where he got his looks. My twenty-first-century sensibility also grasped why he might have a problem with women he loved revealing deep and hidden flaws. But I didn't share this idea with Marguerite. She had enough on her plate.

Briefly I wondered if the woman in the portrait *had* been mentally unstable, as distinct from unhappy or the survivor of some emotional trauma. The eighteenth century had a blanket conception of mental illness, and treatment options were nothing short of barbaric. Percy's mom can't have led an easy life, even though her husband took her abroad to more forgiving lands and doted on her, according to the baroness.

A glimpse of the clock above Percy's desk reminded me that his valet would soon return with the key. We had no more to do here. I pushed Marguerite out of the room, reminding her that Suzanne had promised to arrive any minute.

Although by then, I was entertaining doubts about Suzanne. Surely she would have reached the manor already if she intended to visit.

Still, I figured I should give her a few more hours before pulling the plug. Which meant I needed to find something for Marguerite to do while we waited. As we reached the front hall, I saw through the half-open door that the mist had cleared. «Shall we gather some flowers?» I suggested. «The drawing room could use a bit of color.» Marguerite, still preoccupied, emitted a haze of agreement, so we went off to enjoy the beautiful day.

The footman who'd provided assurances about the runaway dog produced a pair of shears and a basket on request. He offered to accompany me as far as the rose garden, but I refused. I'd be in sight of the house, they hadn't found anything threatening when they searched, and I needed solitude to brood over the possibility that Suzanne, too, had done a bunk. So, accepting a bonnet in lieu of a parasol, I picked up the basket and shears and stepped out into the sunshine.

The rose garden beckoned, and I took a moment on first walking into it to drop the things I was carrying, sit by the side of the fish pond, and run my fingers through the gleaming water. A carp appeared right underneath my hand, and startled, I laughed.

Something rustled in the hedges. My laughter faded, and I looked around, trying to identify the presence I sensed but couldn't see.

Running feet alerted me to danger. Before I could jump up, strong hands closed around my neck and squeezed. For the first time in my life, I fainted.

My temples were pounding. My throat ached, and the moisture had drained from my mouth. My tongue felt fuzzy and thick. I couldn't move my hands or feet, and odd lumps poked my body, which hurt from the top of my head to my toes. But the worst part was not being able to think. An ice pick in my head speared every wispy idea that went by, then tossed it out of the way even as I reached for it. I had no sense of Marguerite.

Liquid touched my lips, cool and refreshing, but before I could react I drifted away again. This happened several times: me coming to, noticing pain, half-choking on liquid, slipping back into unconsciousness. Each time I awoke, I felt worse, but on one occasion I surfaced enough to open my eyes and keep them open.

I tried to focus. The world swooped up and down in enormous curves that made me want to burrow my head under a stack of pillows and stay there forever.

After another indeterminate while, I realized that the dips and swoops meant I was on a boat. Sure enough, when I dragged myself to my knees—with a yelp of protest, because my wrists ached—I looked out the porthole and saw great white-capped waves. It was dark, the waves lit only by moonlight. I sank back, doing my best to muster thought against the incessant pounding in my head.

This shouldn't have happened. When nothing else could get through the storm in my brain, that thought came strong and clear. I struggled to recall the events of—the day before? I'd lost track—the hours since I had left London. But I couldn't make sense of the jumbled pictures in my head: a dog in the rosebushes wrestled with Marguerite's bonnet while I waved a pair of shears above my head and Percy laughed at me from the fishpond. I was losing it, big time.

Where *was* Marguerite, anyway? Had she vanished when the simulation changed course, because she no longer had any baroness-scripted lines to say?

And how did any of that translate into me on a boat heading God knows where, rope burns on my wrists, a bruised throat, and my head in agony?

When I could, I staggered to the door and found it locked. No surprise there, since no one knocks a person out and abducts her only to let her walk away at the first opportunity.

Head whirling, I turned around. Other than the filthy mattress I'd been lying on when I awoke, the room contained a table and three chairs, bolted into the floor. I staggered to the closest seat and sank onto it, palms pressed against my aching brow.

Chauvelin! The name burst through the fog that enwrapped me. Realizing in a rush how I'd ended up on the boat, I could have kicked myself for my obliviousness. Since Marguerite had no other enemies, it seemed obvious, even in my incapacitated state, that Chauvelin had kidnapped me.

Although what he wanted remained unclear. Even a twister like Chauvelin couldn't have decided that *Marguerite* operated in the dark as the Scarlet Pimpernel. And despite his leching at Lord

Grenville's ball, I rather doubted that he had kidnapped me to satisfy his lust, like the villain in some ridiculous bodice-ripping romance. (Yes, I do read something besides French revolutionary history.) If he had, he would soon learn to appreciate the salutary effects of a hatpin in strategic parts of his anatomy.

I had reached this point in my deliberations—if we can call them that, given the mental fog that kept me squinting at the porthole like an old-time sailor on a drunken spree—when a key twisted in the lock and Chauvelin himself arrived, trailed by a thug who looked too big and beefy for the porcelain teapot and cups he balanced on a wooden tray. The thug, burdened with a major five o'clock shadow and in sad need of a bath, sloshed the tea as he dumped the tray on the table in front of me. I slid to the far corner. My involuntary travels had already stained and crumpled the muslin dress, and my prospects for obtaining a change of clothes seemed poor at best.

The thug produced a grisly grin at having forced me to move, then slouched out of the room in response to a curt command from his master. I narrowed my eyes, searching for signs of flamboyant David in Chauvelin's huddled form. Better to negotiate with my professor than a malicious French agent. But no hint of scholar shone through that guise.

Chauvelin waved his hand at the table. Alone with my enemy, exhausted and anxious, I watched and waited. Surely he didn't expect me to play the society hostess under these circumstances!

In fact, he did hesitate for a moment, until something in my expression alerted him that I wasn't in an amiable mood. "Please," he said with exaggerated politeness. "Have some tea. It will remove the taste of the laudanum."

Opiates, huh. No wonder I felt fuzzy. Suspicion swept through me, and I decided to play the lady after all. I poured a cup and handed it to him. "You first."

Between the bruises on my throat and general dehydration, my voice croaked like the raven Chauvelin often resembled. At least Marguerite hadn't retreated so far that I'd lost her native fluency in French.

Chauvelin laughed as though I'd given him a present. "Dear lady," he said. "You don't think I'm trying to poison you, I hope?"

He sipped the tea. When he didn't keel over, I poured another cup for myself and drank it. My mouth eased back toward normal, and some of the lightheadedness retreated. If only my thoughts would settle into a coherent pattern.

"Apparently not," I said, once it became clear that we would both remain conscious. "What *are* you trying to do?"

He guffawed once more, as if he'd brought me here to serve as his personal jester. "Why, to catch the Scarlet Pimpernel." He waved at my battered appearance, then patted me in an anything but avuncular fashion. "Sir Percy. So lovely a prisoner, how can he resist?"

I wiped the patted hand against my skirt in the most ostentatious fashion I could manage. Renewed longing for a hatpin mingled with shock. The Scarlet Pimpernel. Sir Percy. Despite everything the five of us students had done, Chauvelin had ignored the red herring of S's party and set off on Percy's trail. The lovely prisoner line, I assumed, meant that he intended to use me as bait. To catch the Scarlet Pimpernel. Percy.

Little did Chauvelin know that perfidious Percy gave not a hoot for me and my fate. He had left for France without a backward glance. And he deserved to lose, the swine, after the fast one he'd pulled on Suzanne and me.

Befuddled as I felt, I recognized the folly of pointing out to Chauvelin that Percy had no use for me. If the Weasel believed he'd made a mistake, he might kill me on the spot. Then I would be the loser, and Percy's chances of winning would only improve. Whereas if I played my cards right, while Percy walked into Chauvelin's trap, I might find a way to walk out.

Chauvelin was still cackling into his tea, too sure of his own cleverness to exhibit any concern over my silence. My aching head and the lingering effects of laudanum inhibited my ability to develop a comprehensive plan, but I mustered enough presence of mind to clasp my hands together and plead in Marguerite's overwrought style. "Oh, Monsieur," I cried, "you cannot be so great a villain! To use me to trap the man I love above all others!"

I nearly choked on that last phrase, as you can imagine, but it had the desired effect. Chauvelin curled his lip and straightened, physically separating himself as he regarded me with the scorn powerful, chauvinist men reserve for weeping women. With luck, he would underestimate me from now on.

He stood and headed for the door, tray in hand. Not until he reached it did he turn to deliver his parting shot. "We reach Calais in an hour, m'lady. Then we will see what Sir Percy does. Somehow I think he will not want to leave you in my tender care." I responded by letting my fear and confusion show and gripping my hands until the fingertips turned red, and he departed, still cackling.

As I heard the key turn in the lock once more, I dropped my head onto my arms, drained of emotion and brain power both. Whimpers rose unbidden to my throat. Chauvelin had, willy-nilly, solved my problem of how to get Marguerite to France. And his decision to use me as bait rather than execute me on the spot had given me another chance. But when the time came, would I have the strength to escape?

11. Le Chat Gris

THEY DIDN'T DRUG ME TO GET ME OFF THE BOAT, WHICH I guess counted as an improvement. Chauvelin's henchmen bound my hands in front of me, more gently this time and with cloth rather than rope in response to a barked order from their leader. They bound my feet, too, then the man who'd brought the tea threw me over one massive shoulder as though I were a mail sack and headed for the side of the ship. There he dumped me into a large basket and lowered me into a dinghy.

Deprived of Marguerite's support, I coped by closing my eyes, clutching my elbows, and trying not to think about what would happen if the rope broke. It helped that I lacked the energy to sit upright. I couldn't see much beyond the sides of the basket.

Chauvelin joined us, and the dinghy started for shore, which gradually became visible through the gray dawn light. The whole way there, I prayed that he hadn't noticed my fear. He had enough advantage over me without finding out I hated heights.

More than ever, I wished Marguerite would return. Ironic, when I'd disliked her only a few days ago. My present uncomfortable circumstances didn't give me much appreciation for irony, though.

No one spoke to me during the short trip, for which I extended silent thanks. Propped against the side of the dinghy, I shivered in the morning breeze and looked everywhere but at Chauvelin. The harbor hadn't much to recommend it. No graceful *Day Dream* indicated Percy's proximity. Chauvelin had miscalculated, most likely, and Percy had come ashore at a point other than Calais. Which could interfere with my escape plans. I tried to care about the prospect of losing, but even the small rush of emotion I had managed on the boat had dissolved into a vague melancholia. What happened next didn't matter, since I had no control over it anyway.

Fishing boats dotted the bay, tattered and dingy. Their half-starved crews appeared oblivious to the concept of barbers or dentists. Everywhere, people's clothes hung ragged over bare arms and legs. Many wore the tricolor cockade on red woolen hats and wooden sabots on their feet. The women seemed tougher and surlier than the men.

The fishermen shouted to one another in a guttural patois I could not understand. The muslin dress, however crumpled and dirty, must have struck them as suspiciously fine, for those who spared the dinghy a glance scowled as though one bound *aristo* might single-handedly undermine the revolution. A big tattooed fellow—dressed like the rest in cropped trousers, grungy shirt hanging over his pants, and cockaded hat leaning off to the right of his grizzled head—favored me with a glare ferocious enough to pierce even my despondency. I shifted my gaze to the rolling waves, chilled to encounter such hatred. When I glanced up again, I saw his companion tugging on his sleeve to get his attention. But the tattooed man remained fixated on us as the oars propelled us toward shore.

The dinghy scraped the pier, and one henchman passed me off to another before I'd had time to decide whether throwing myself into the water would do anything other than soak the muslin dress and give me a choice between drowning and freezing. With my hands and feet bound I couldn't swim, so on the whole the odds of escape appeared slim against those of a humiliating rescue by Chauvelin's men. I might as well hang on and hope for a better opportunity.

My personal brute slung me over his shoulder again and headed for a rundown inn at the far end of the street. *Le Chat Gris,* the sign said, although the weathered animal swinging in the wind didn't much resemble a cat, even a gray one. Chauvelin doused the innkeeper's objections by waving his official tricolor scarf around and muttering threats. These eventually led to my landing on my bottom in what the innkeeper's wife euphemistically called the "upstairs room."

Room, my back teeth. Three-sided closet with curtain, and a half-shredded curtain at that. The "room" resembled a cupboard set into the side of the wall. Although the horrid straw pallet in one corner did suggest that the innkeeper rented it out to unsuspecting guests. Ugh!

The loft, however, had one advantage over a real room: I could hear—and, through the shredded curtain, see—much of what went on in the dining room, set at an angle beneath me.

The henchman unfastened my bonds, grinned hideously through a split lip, and thumped down the stairs. Through the rips in the curtain I saw him station himself near the door.

They'd untied me. I couldn't escape yet, but I could move. Create a diversion, and I might have a chance. At the thought, my melancholia lifted. Determination took its place.

The innkeeper handed me a hunk of dry bread and a cup of something he called wine. It tasted like a cross between salad dressing and cough syrup and had the kick of a dead engine, but I chose not to complain. Better cough syrup than water, in a place like that.

If I dipped the bread in the vinegar and let it sit for a bit, it tasted like something only a year or so old. My various woes and pains kept me from feeling hungry, but determination triumphed. I needed energy to get myself out of this mess. So I ate the food and didn't fuss, certain that no one would care if I did. On the contrary, shutting me up would probably make Chauvelin's day.

I guessed that Chauvelin had scared the innkeeper into producing a better meal for himself when the smell of beef stew and onions rose from the room below. Maybe he thought he was torturing me. If he did, I hope it gave him pleasure, because he was wrong—about the food, anyway. Wondering what he had up his sleeve kept me on tenterhooks.

Marguerite hadn't re-emerged. Her disappearance worried me a good deal, even though I had my doubts as to how useful she'd be in a crisis like this. But alone or not, I couldn't sit around and throw up my hands in despair. *Le Chat Gris* didn't run to anything as bourgeois as clocks, and it wouldn't have helped if it had, since I had no idea how much time had passed since I left Blakeney Manor. Even so, Chauvelin had stated his intent to use Marguerite as bait, so it behooved me to get my act together and find a way out of the inn before he followed through on his threats.

If only I didn't feel like overcooked pasta or one of Chauvelin's starchless cravats.

I needed time to recover. But where? The mattress in the corner looked as though it played host to an entire colony of parasites—worse than the one on the boat. In desperation, I leaned my head against the wall and shut my eyes.

The strangest thing happened. Because I was semi-drugged and exhausted, because I'd just confronted my fear of heights once more, because I felt abandoned and angry, or in response to some combination of these things—I could never afterward decide—the fog that had surrounded me since I awoke on the boat cleared in a most unexpected way, dumping me back in the playground where Nessa had pushed me off the monkey bars so many years ago. I felt smaller, younger. The pattern of my thoughts changed, as though I had again become the child I was that day. I couldn't have faked it if I'd tried; I hadn't seen the world that way in eighteen years. At the same time, as if through a movie camera, my adult self watched the six-year-old from a great distance.

The child I'd become concentrated on getting to the top of the metal dome in front of her. My tongue stuck out as I grasped each bar, stretched my legs to cover each enormous step. Nessa, two years older, had scaled the dome with ease and already straddled the ladder that ran between identical half-spheres. I felt no fear, even though I'd already climbed higher, proportional to my size, than the box of Percy's carriage. Behind me I heard adults talking—my parents. Their words held no interest for me.

With great pride, I joined Nessa on the horizontal ladder. The metal bars felt slick under my hands, but by carefully judging each gap I managed to get across the five rungs separating me from my sister. The moment I reached her, my mother's voice rose in a shriek of rage. Startled, I missed my footing and tumbled over the side. Nessa grabbed the wrist closest to her, shouting, "Daddy, Daddy," but he was too busy screaming at my mother to notice. Terrified, sobbing, I caught the ladder with my free hand and hung on for what seemed like forever.

No one came. The park was deserted except for the four of us. Nessa's yells and my wails rose in intensity, but neither parent paid any attention. My arms grew heavier, then heavier still. Nessa can't have been much better off. Even a skinny little sister packs a considerable weight when you're holding on to her for dear life with one arm and trying with the other to keep yourself balanced on a metal ladder seven feet from the ground.

I let go. The extra weight was more than Nessa could support. She lost her grip and I fell with a horrible whump onto the cedar chips below. I could hear Nessa scrambling off the bars, but what filled my vision was blue sky speckled with dancing lights. The fall knocked the air out of my lungs and I gasped for breath, not injured so much as shocked and sore. Fog swirled around my senses as I fought to stay conscious— as it had ever since in moments of extreme stress.

Now I knew why I feared heights. And why I believed the bottom would drop out of my world if I trusted a man. Because my father left that day and didn't look back. He didn't stop to find out what had happened to his daughters. By the time my mother reached me, he was already in the car. I didn't see him again for eight months.

Time passed in long, lazy spirals, spinning me in and out of various states that a clinician would call dissociation but to me felt like something out of science fiction. How had I forgotten that? Twisted it as I had? Remembered Nessa as pushing me when she'd done nothing of the sort? No one else had cared enough to help me, and I'd ended up blaming my sister for something that was in no way her fault. And my father, as always, walked off scot-free.

Tears ran down my cheeks. Tears I'd never dared shed, because they would not bring him back or make him love me. I missed him.

Not my real father. He'd been … not present, exactly, but around at irregular intervals, charming and careless. Henry VIII, the multi-married man whore. As I grew older, I learned what to expect. Not to count on him, mostly. He was easy to despise, sometimes fun to be around, impossible to love.

So no, I didn't miss my father. But the *illusion* of a father who was strong and caring and dependable—that I missed with such aching intensity that for eighteen years I hadn't allowed myself to remember the day the dream shattered.

The lightheadedness I'd experienced in the boat cabin returned. I felt detached from reality, as if floating in space. From a great distance I heard Chauvelin slurping.

The noise irritated me into action. Furious energy ran through my veins, dispelling the lingering effects of laudanum. I didn't need Percy, or Ian, or whatever he called himself. I'd fought my own battles since childhood. I could fight them here, too. Chauvelin was one more obstacle to overcome.

The bread and cough syrup kicked in, and I began to search Marguerite's pockets. Nothing presented itself other than a ribbon, which I used to tie Percy's pimpernel ring around my neck, in case I had to make a run for it and lost the thing.

The room beneath me fell silent. No more slurping. No more sounds of any description. I glanced through the holes in the curtain and found Chauvelin missing.

He returned to the dining room while I was assessing my chances of making a bolt for the door. For a moment, despite the description that I—even in my pathetic condition—vaguely recalled from the original novel, I didn't recognize him. He had donned the black cassock and flat hat traditional for a French priest.

Bizarre. Percy adopted disguises to get past the local authorities and avoid capture, but what Chauvelin thought he was doing in that getup escaped me.

Beneath the energy sparked by anger, I sensed fatigue lurking. He'd better give me an opportunity soon, or I'd end up in a heap on the floor.

Not bothering to play his priest's role to the hilt by saying grace, Chauvelin sat down at the table, spooned something into a bowl, and resumed his slurping. He poured a glass of cough syrup, broke off some bread, and looked like he planned to settle in for a while. Because my loft hid one section of the dining room and the door that must lead to the kitchen (or where had Chauvelin's food come from?), I could see only the back of his head.

A commotion started at the inn door. The brute on duty left, and another, even more villainous man replaced him. Not more than five minutes passed before I heard someone bellowing, "God Save the King," at the top of his lungs. Another of Baroness Orczy's more absurd plot points, but it raised my spirits as nothing else could have.

I was not dead yet. Percy had accepted Chauvelin's lure.

He sauntered into that wretched, broken-down inn looking as though he'd just left the races at Newmarket—sixteen-caped driving coat, leather breeches, spotless cravat, and immaculately coiffed blond hair. For a wild moment, I fought the temptation to throw myself down the stairs and into his arms.

As if the swine had not deceived and abandoned me in London. *Honestly, Nina, can't you ever use that brain?*

I inched closer to the stairs, plotting how to take advantage of the distraction his arrival had caused. The henchman had lost interest in me and was staring at Percy the way kids stare at exotic animals in the zoo. Meanwhile, Chauvelin had doubled over. From the choking sounds emanating from him, I deduced that the food he'd been swallowing when Percy strolled into the room had gone down the wrong pipe. As Chauvelin sputtered and gasped, Percy pounded his enemy's back, apologizing.

"Good thing you weren't wearing laymen's clothes, what?" he said. "That cravat of yours would sag even more after you covered it in stew. Really, I had no notion you were in holy orders, but demme if it isn't a good thing after all."

Chauvelin couldn't muster speech, but he raised his head, I assume to glare at his tormentor. He sat kitty-corner below me, and thanks to the hat, I couldn't see his face. While he focused on Percy, I reached the top stair.

Percy turned to the henchman. "Ask Madame Brogard if she has anything that will help, there's a good chap." He offered the first part in French, in the most atrocious accent I'd ever heard. The thug slouched toward the far side of the room.

"Actually, I saw her out front," Percy told him. The thug slouched in the other direction.

The slouching took a long time, during which Percy continued to taunt his adversary with his usual good humor. As the thug left, I heard Chauvelin recover enough to sputter, "And how is Lady Blakeney?"

Like he didn't know. I supposed this was his opening gambit, since it would do him no good to capture me, then keep it a secret. With the thug gone and Chauvelin preoccupied, I began my silent descent, sliding from stair to stair on my bottom and trying not to draw attention to myself. Weak-kneed or not, I had to make my move or I'd be lost. Adrenaline and anger would substitute for stamina.

"Quite well, I'm sure," Percy said with elaborate unconcern. "She's hosting her annual water party tonight."

So it was Wednesday. I'd lost forty-eight hours, thanks to Chauvelin, but I had no time to worry about that.

Chauvelin leaned back in his chair. I froze in place. "I think not," he announced—striving, I guess, to match Percy's unflappability. "In fact, she is in France. It seems she prefers my company to yours."

Percy's mask of indifference cracked. He leaned across the table and hauled Chauvelin to his feet by the simple expedient of placing both hands under his chin. "You lie," he said.

I couldn't hope for a better opportunity than this. From somewhere I mustered the strength to stand, took a deep breath, and rushed down the stairs. My breath escaped in a whoosh as I reached the bottom. My knees gave way, and I grabbed at the banister for support. Staggering, I glanced over my shoulder at Percy. His hands tightened around Chauvelin's throat. The Frenchman went limp in his grasp.

I opened my mouth, prepared to tell him what I thought of him, but Percy intervened. He dropped Chauvelin where he stood, caught me round the waist, and kissed me, hard. Two strides brought us to the kitchen door that I hadn't been able to see from my loft. As he set me down, he said, "Run, darling, if you can. There are guards out front, but I have a man in the kitchen. He'll help you."

Darling? Who was he kidding?

"Yes," I said. No point in arguing, since I had no breath. And Chauvelin wouldn't remain unconscious for long. I could ponder Percy's motives later. He'd given me my opportunity to escape, and escape I would. I picked up my skirts in both hands and dashed for the outside, hoping to reach it before I fell down. Behind me, Chauvelin groaned.

As I hurried through the door, I heard Percy's familiar drawl. "Deepest apologies, m'dear fellow, for my shocking lack of restraint. But I have to say, her ladyship seems rather less eager to accompany you than you thought."

❁

The dining room and loft had left much to be desired by way of sanitation, but compared to the kitchen they looked like the Ritz. The innkeeper's wife stood next to a filthy counter, her arms immersed up to the elbows in a large glazed sink. She stared at me as I raced by. I caught a glimpse of red out of the corner of my eye, glanced in that direction, and immediately wished I hadn't.

Wood crashed against tile as the thug Percy had sent to request help for Chauvelin knocked over the bench that stood on the far side of the table. My escape had recalled him to his duties. So much for Percy's man in the kitchen.

"My favorite carafe, you clumsy oaf!" Madame Brogard smacked the thug around the head with her dishtowel. I'd have cheered if I'd had a breath to spare.

But I didn't, so with the thirty seconds or so this interlude gained me, I lifted my skirts almost to my knees, fled into the yard, and ran.

Not fast enough, alas. Behind me, a door slammed onto the wall and wooden shoes pounded against the ground. Within moments, the thug had grabbed me round the waist and lifted me half off my feet. His other hand clamped over my mouth. I thrashed like a maniac trying to break free. "Stop, Marguerite, it's Andrew," the thug said in English into my ear.

Andrew? I twisted to get a better view of the scarred, dirty face. It was Andrew, bearing no resemblance to the brocaded dandy who'd messed up my schemes at Lord Grenville's ball.

He grinned at my stupefaction and said, "Can you run farther? Percy wants us out of here before Chauvelin has time to realize how you got past me."

Could I trust him? I doubted it, but again I lacked breath and time to argue. I let him catch my hand and drag me into the darkness. Within moments I stumbled, and he picked me up. By then I had just enough strength to put my hand on his shoulder. Independent as I am, I didn't make a peep of protest.

12. Cottage, Near Calais

THREE FIELDS AND A DOZEN DITCHES LATER, ANDREW PUT me down, placed a finger against my lips, and whistled. Clouds had covered the moon, so I strained to see him amid the shadows. I heard a whicker. Hot horse breath touched my cheek as a velvet nose prodded my shoulder. Andrew tossed me onto the pommel and vaulted into the saddle behind me.

What was it with these people? I stared at the ground below and told myself I would *not* get dizzy. Marguerite flashed past my thoughts, but before I could acknowledge her, she disappeared. I was alone with Percy's questionable lieutenant and an enormous horse.

And a troop of soldiers making enough noise to raise the dead. My acrophobia faded, chased off by a deeper fear. As Andrew, one arm at a respectful distance around my waist, sent the horse cantering along the muddy path that substituted for a road, I clung to his jacket. Staying on the horse required whatever energy I retained.

Time again lost its meaning. "How did you find me?" I asked at one point, but Andrew shook his head.

"Later," he said. So I sat in silence, afraid of pursuit but relieved that we seemed to have outrun Chauvelin's men, trying to recover my strength while the horse negotiated an infinite number of fields and spinneys.

Troubling questions spun through my brain. Percy had abandoned me in London, then shown up to rescue me in Calais. Why? Or was I fooling myself again, and he'd come after Chauvelin, with no notion of helping me escape? Still, he hadn't left me in Chauvelin's grip, which would have been easy enough to do and would have helped him win the game. Instead, he'd sacrificed himself, or so it appeared.

Trust him? Not trust him? The other questions boiled down to those two alternatives, but in the end I couldn't decide. I still resented being dumped. And I lacked sufficient information to put Percy's behavior in context. We might be allies still, or enemies (but then why call me darling?). The only thing I couldn't deny was that, for some reason of his own, Percy had chosen to offer me another chance at the game.

The ride went on, and on. At last I saw ahead of us what looked like a one-room hut. The clouds obscured much of the view, but every so often a breeze blew them apart for a while before they closed in again. In one such moment, I noticed that the farm appeared deserted: no lights, tumbledown shutters, not much equipment. One scrawny chicken huddled in a bush, its head tucked under its wing. Its fellows had probably gone to neighboring farms—or neighboring stewpots. Almost everything in Calais had this desolate air, as though the revolution had dealt the death blow to a land already sucked dry.

Andrew made an odd call, like a sea bird's, three times in succession. No one answered. He touched a finger to my lips again, but I had no intention of talking. Chauvelin had had plenty of time to react to my escape, and since Baroness

Orczy's plot ended in Calais, I had no way to predict what might happen from here on. The changes introduced by our group had set us off on a new adventure.

I examined the house. It looked empty, but it could be a trap. Or Andrew could be playing a side game of his own, turning my apparent escape into a second captivity. I had to stop forgetting that he and Tony had as much cause as Percy to play the rest of us false, whatever loyalty Baroness Orczy had written into their characters. For that matter, I wouldn't put it past Suzanne to have agreed to come to Blakeney Manor to lull me into procrastinating while she donned men's clothes and made a mad dash for the coast. She hadn't fulfilled her promise to visit, after all. She could be waiting in the hut, ready to provide whatever assistance Andrew required.

The horse stopped a good distance from the cottage. Andrew helped me slide to the ground and dismounted. The long ride had had one benefit: it had restored the starch to my knees. My head and throat still hurt, but the effects of the laudanum had dissipated and the morning's raw pain had subsided into a dull ache. I felt no worse than a person recovering from the flu.

"Stay here," Andrew said, pressing the reins into my hand. The horse put its head down and began munching. Like Percy, Andrew was tall, and his horse well built and powerful. At my best, I doubted I could have held it if it took a notion into its head to stroll off, so I hoped it had no such plans.

Andrew disappeared into cloud-covered darkness, although for an instant a gust of wind revealed him silhouetted against the door. Apparently his investigation satisfied him, for he soon returned, took the reins from me, and led the animal toward the side of the house while I slogged along behind.

As we reached the back wall, Andrew stopped and caught my wrist. "I have to tend to the horse," he whispered. "Inside you'll find clothes Percy left for you, soap and water and everything you need. Change quickly. Others of the League will join us here."

I opened my mouth to ask whether Percy would be one of them, then realized Andrew knew no more than I did and shut it again. As I turned toward the door, Andrew pulled me back. "No fire," he said in the same quiet voice. "No light."

A warning I didn't need. The shutters had as many holes as Madame Brogard's curtain, and light beaming from a deserted farmhouse would alert half the neighborhood. But we had enough trouble on our hands without me wasting time arguing, so as Andrew led the horse to a lean-to attached to the side of the cottage, I opened the door and went in.

I found a single room, not spacious but reasonably clean, suggesting Percy's fine hand at work. No Suzanne. No other person, in fact. Half a dozen straw pallets lay around the walls, and a curtain closed off one end of the room. If anyone had left washing supplies and new clothes, I thought they would put them behind the curtain, so I checked there first. I saw a small pile of men's garments, a cracked china basin, a clean towel, and, best of all, a bar of soap and a hairbrush. I desperately needed a bath, but that would have to wait. As fast as I could, I stripped off the ruined muslin dress, washed my hands and face and as much else as I could reach, and patted water on my hair. Then I picked up the boy's clothes and tried to figure out how they went together.

I'd mastered the undergarments, stockings, and shirt and was working on fastening the breeches when I heard footsteps crossing the threshold. Wary, I peeked around the corner of the curtain, but it was only Andrew, returned from rubbing down his horse.

"I'm here," I said. "I'll be out in a moment." I buttoned the breeches and added the waistcoat and jacket but left the neck of the shirt open. After Percy's rude remarks to Chauvelin, I didn't think he needed an opportunity to comment on my inability to tie a cravat.

If Percy appeared. I seemed incapable of keeping two logical thoughts together for as long as it took for the next one to form.

Hairbrush in hand, I pushed back the curtain and joined Andrew at the large picnic-style table at one side of the room. He had pulled out a set of plates from somewhere and was doling out portions of bread that put the rusks at *Le Chat Gris* to shame, accompanied by a rather delicious-smelling cheese, cups, and a flask of wine that I would have laid odds did not taste like cough syrup. He looked up as I entered.

"What am I going to do with this?" I croaked, pointing at the waist-length curls. "Should I cut it?"

"God, no," Andrew said. "Percy would have my head. We'll tie it up."

Well, it was true, men in those days wore their hair long, easily down between their shoulder blades, tied back with a ribbon at the nape of the neck. I thought Andrew was dreaming if he believed Marguerite's hair would tie up as he expected, but since I much preferred not to cut it, I walked to the bench that jutted out next to the unused fireplace, sat down, and started to brush.

Vaguely I recalled a story about my great-grandmother, who'd contracted rheumatic fever as a girl. In those days, the treatment included not catching a chill, so the doctor had forbidden her ever to shampoo her hair again. Family legend said she'd kept it clean by brushing it through silk a hundred times a day. The whole thing sounded like a complete crock, but with no other alternatives, I decided I might as well give it a try, even though my linen petticoat might not have the same qualities as silk.

Brushing left me plenty of time to think. Andrew had ducked behind the curtain to change, and my croak didn't work above a whisper, which scuttled any hope of conversation. I did try to corral my random thoughts into some kind of order, but too much had happened too fast, with so many zigs and zags that I couldn't make sense of it. Andrew couldn't be planning to betray me if he expected the League to arrive en masse; Percy could be either friend or enemy; Marguerite had vanished; and despite my fears, Suzanne had not appeared. How could one poor, tired brain process such a welter of inconsistencies?

As it turned out, the brushing didn't remove much by way of dirt, but it did leave Marguerite's hair more manageable. Meanwhile, Andrew had re-emerged a changed man—not yet the London fop, but an action hero in tan shirt and leather breeches and waistcoat. No wonder Suzanne was infatuated. He didn't look half-bad. Not quite as heart-stopping as Percy, but definitely not bad.

The adrenaline had worn off while I sat brushing my hair, to the point where I struggled to keep my eyes open. But with forty-eight hours largely unaccounted for and a renegade husband perhaps in thrall to Chauvelin, I forced myself to stay awake long enough to pump Andrew for information.

"Percy got away," Andrew assured me when I asked whether Chauvelin had captured Percy in my stead. "He planned that diversion. I went out the back with you while he dashed off in the other direction. He should arrive soon. We have the Comte de Tournay stashed in a fisherman's hut a few miles down the coast from *Le Chat Gris*. If Chauvelin hadn't kidnapped you, Percy would have left Hastings and Bathurst to get the comte onto his yacht while he distracted the troops."

"He *planned* it? Did Chauvelin send him a message, saying he had captured me?"

"No. We saw you in the harbor. On the dinghy as he was bringing you in. Percy hit the roof. I had to haul on his arm to stop him diving into the water and grabbing you away. It was his own fault. I told him he shouldn't have left you in London."

Hair fell into my eyes as I shook my head. His words evoked an image in my mind—the harbor, someone tugging on a sleeve—but I couldn't place it. While puzzling over the reference, I picked up a black ribbon Andrew had left on the table and used it to tie back Marguerite's mane.

"Why did you?" I asked. The bunk they'd done from Grenville's ball still stung. "Suzanne and I were ready to murder the pair of you. Not to mention Tony."

"Tony? Tony had nothing to do with it. As for us, I'll let Percy explain. It was his idea, not mine." Andrew kicked a handy piece of kindling. "Have you seen Suzanne? I'm worried sick that Chauvelin grabbed her, too."

I felt my brow crease as I added this information to the whirling mass of disconnected facts that populated my mind. Tony had nothing to do with it? Where had he gone, then, since he left the ball at about the same time? "I haven't seen Suzanne since I entered the carriage. She said she would come to Blakeney Manor the next day, but she didn't. I thought she'd had second thoughts about allying with me. Could Chauvelin have intercepted her on the road? But her family wouldn't allow her to travel alone."

When his face lost its color, I wished, too late, that I'd kept my dire speculations to myself. "It's possible." His voice sounded strangled. "I asked Tony to stay in London, to watch over her. To bring her here, if he sees an opportunity. And I hope he does. I thought her safe with her family, but if Chauvelin can kidnap you, why not her? We should stay together."

"Tony left before you did," I said. "I don't know where he went."

Andrew swore and smacked the table. By then, I'd had it. I collapsed on one of the pallets.

Hooves in the yard woke me. Across the width of the cottage, my eyes caught Andrew's. Fearful, I sat up.

We remained in darkness, although the clouds had cleared. My eyes had long since adjusted to the dim light. So when I looked beyond Andrew's head and saw, through the broken shutters, the eyes of the tattooed fisherman from the dockside, I hadn't the slightest doubt of what I was seeing.

"What is it?" Andrew said when I emitted the loudest croak I'd managed yet.

"At the window." I gulped for air. "He's gone now. A man I saw in Calais."

The cottage had only one door, a serious design flaw. "Behind the curtain," Andrew said, but before I could do more than struggle to my knees, the door opened, and the fisherman walked into the room. I blinked. He wore the ragged clothing and the wooden shoes, but he'd taken off the red hat and the scars. He was rubbing his face with a cloth as he came in, smudging the tattoos painted on his cheeks. It was Percy.

Percy. Andrew tugging on his sleeve. The pair of them, disguised, in the harbor at Calais, watching Chauvelin convey me in the dinghy from the boat to *Le Chat Gris*. Just as Andrew had said. And here I'd believed the tattooed fisherman's fixed stare meant that he hated me.

"You? You nearly gave me a heart attack!" It came out in a hoarse whisper, but in any case, I never got an answer. He took one look at me and burst out laughing.

"Sink me, Madam, don't you make a fine boy!" Before I could respond, he turned to Andrew. "My horse is grazing in the yard. Can you see to it before Hastings and Bathurst scare it off?"

"Of course, Percy." Andrew pulled the door shut behind him and went, I suppose, to look after the horse.

Something else I never found out, because the moment he left, the adrenaline surged again. I sprang to my feet. "I don't know whether to hug you or smack you! What possessed you to run off and leave me in London? I thought we were partners!"

"We are, love, we are." Percy caught me in his arms, whirling me around and kissing me as though he'd expected never to see me again. His hands roamed everywhere. Those wonderful fingers caressed the bare skin over my spine until I purred with joy. When I had time to notice, I found myself sitting on his knee, shirt unbuttoned halfway to the waist.

"My darling," he said in Ian's husky voice. The r in "darling" was definitely his. He took my face in both hands and rubbed his thumbs against my cheeks. His eyes glowed dark with passion. "My darling, when I saw you in Chauvelin's grasp…" He let the sentence die unfinished while he kissed me all over again.

After a bit, we came down to earth. I was composing my ruffled mind, intending to probe again for the explanation he hadn't given, when Ian offered it unasked. Watching him pick his words with care, I guessed that, whereas I was operating without benefit of Marguerite, Percy remained very much in the picture.

"I miscalculated," he admitted. "I wanted to outpace Chauvelin, and that meant riding to Dover. I thought you and Suzanne would slow us down."

"Well, that's true," I interjected. "I can't ride worth a darn. Maybe she can, but not me."

He grinned at that. "Ever the honest broker. But I miscalculated by believing that Chauvelin wouldn't bother you women if you remained in England. If you weren't rescuing Armand and weren't getting in the way of him trying to catch the Scarlet Pimpernel, why wouldn't he leave you alone? My mistake, as I realized when I saw you in Calais harbor." His palm caressed my cheek. "You looked pathetic, *mignonne*. Chauvelin's lucky I didn't do a lot worse than throttle him. It's not easy playing the bloody hero."

"You were being chivalrous." I should have realized that sooner. Sir Percy Blakeney was an eighteenth-century gentleman. Naturally, he believed it incumbent on him to do the dirty work while protecting the women in his life.

He blushed. "Yes. Forgive me?"

My answer surprised even me. "I suppose." I kissed him. "Thanks for helping me escape that hellhole in Calais."

A discreet knock on the door heralded the return of Sir Andrew, Lord Hastings and Lord Bathurst in tow. Percy hurriedly rebuttoned my shirt to something approaching decency. He caressed the bruises left on my throat from my encounter with Chauvelin's men in the rose garden, and I heard him mutter something unprintable and quite uncharacteristic regarding Chauvelin's canine parentage and probable fate.

"What's this?" His long fingers tugged at the ribbon.

I pulled out the ring and showed it to him. "I found it in your study. I brought it with me so the servants wouldn't see it. Do you want it back?"

He peeled the ribbon over my head. "Good lord, woman, you roamed over half of France with a piece of jewelry marking you as the Scarlet Pimpernel tied around your neck? Suppose Chauvelin had found it?"

"I didn't have it round my neck then. It was in my pocket."

Percy groaned and tossed the ring over his shoulder. "Here, Andrew, keep it, will you? In case something goes wrong."

Being gentlemen, the members of the League turned their backs while I tucked in my shirttails. Except Percy, who treated me to the full force of his heavy-lidded stare. At any moment I expected him to pull out his quizzing glass.

"No cravat," he said with the wicked grin he usually saved for Chauvelin.

"I know my limits," I told him with dignity. "You can tie it for me in the morning."

He loved that. I could tell by the smirk.

13. Marles-les-Mines

THE NEXT FEW HOURS PASSED IN A BLUR. THROTTLING, kidnapping, unwanted opiates, ghosts from the past, a mad dash through French fields at night, and general hysteria took their toll. At some time during the night, I felt a long body next to mine. Strong arms enfolded me, and a man's voice whispered in my ear. Or maybe that was just a pleasant dream.

By the time I awoke, I found no one in the room but Percy, who stood at the table peering at a large piece of paper. The scruffy clothes that had formed part of his disguise last night had given way to dark broadcloth and white linen, which he wore with an unconscious elegance that seemed quite out of character for a provincial gentleman.

Hard as I tried, I couldn't reach Marguerite. Retiring behind the curtain, I made an effort to provoke her with images of herself in boys' clothes, but it didn't work. With a sigh, I focused on restoring what sartorial splendor I could without the aid of a mirror, then returned with a folded cravat in my hand. The red curls again tumbled past my waist. I doubted many people would see me as a man.

I held one strand out to Percy. "I could cut it," I offered, as I had with Andrew. My voice felt scratchy, but it had improved since the night before.

Even that dreadful suggestion didn't revive Marguerite. It got a rise out of her husband, though. His head jerked up from what I identified as a map of northern France. "Over my dead body," he said. "Give me the brush and I'll take care of it."

I handed him both brush and cravat. He dropped the necktie on the table and picked up a small black pouch. Into this, he brushed, folded, and pushed the recalcitrant curls to create something that resembled a bag wig. I suppose the lack of shampoo helped by flattening the mop into something stuffable, but from the reflection I saw in the window, it looked more like a ballerina bun than any ponytail ever seen on a man.

"Don't worry," Percy told me. "You're supposed to be a young law student from Calais, traveling to Paris to resume your studies, so no one will think it odd if you wear your hair in a rather old-fashioned style."

I thanked him. His long-fingered, capable hands had already picked up the cravat, and in no time he'd wound it around my neck. "A young man of limited means," he said meditatively. "Nothing too complex. A simple bow, I think." And presto, a simple bow appeared.

"Good." His thumb brushed my bruised throat, less sore than before. "They won't even see that you don't have an Adam's apple."

Just what separated Percy's creation from Chauvelin's often-mocked endeavors still wasn't clear to me, but when one man is twitting another over the other's limp cravat, a smart post-Freudian woman doesn't ask too many questions, if you know what I mean.

Nonetheless, it seemed to me that he had missed an important point. "I may look like a young man," I asked, "but what good will it do if I can't ride a horse?"

"Blast. You can't, of course." He tapped the map— reconsidering his plans, I assumed, in light of my reminder.

As he pondered, I searched through as many of Marguerite's memories as I could access to verify that I'd told the truth. At best, I saw a few pictures of her on a sidesaddle. And to make use of those, I'd first need to find whatever sharp stick would prod her back to life.

A disturbing thought occurred to me. If I didn't revive her soon, what would happen to my French?

"Certainly not astride," I said. "Unless you want to spend most of the journey picking me off the ground."

"Hmm." Percy examined me from head to toe, then stripped off the cravat he'd tied a minute ago. "Excuse me." He went out in the yard and soon returned with the necktie covered in blood.

"That's not yours, is it?" I asked, horrified, although I couldn't imagine an alternative. Percy would skewer himself before he harmed a horse.

"The chicken." He must have noticed my instinctive cringe because he added, "It's still alive."

As alive as anything was in this computer-generated world. The thought calmed my nerves enough that I managed not to make faces as he wrapped the bloody cloth around the upper part of my right arm. He unbuttoned the top fastener on the shirt and mussed my bagged hair, then ripped a matching hole in the jacket I'd not yet put on.

"Bullet wound?" I strove to match his dispassionate interest.

His mouth quirked—so much for my attempts to sound casual. "Swords, I think, darling. We don't want anyone probing it for leftover weaponry, and you young men are devils for a duel. The honor of some hussy in Calais cost you the use of your right arm and your ability to ride. Dreadful, isn't it?"

"I've become the vicomte!" I laughed. The silly bantam already seemed years away. "So I ride with you?"

He bent forward and kissed me quickly. "You're a trouper, sweetheart. Yes, you ride with me."

The three League members charged through the door in a group, flocking around their leader and the map. I stood off to one side and munched bread and cheese, admiring the sight of Percy in action. It amazed me to see him flip back and forth as he did between languid society idiot and this focused, intense man, but as I watched him, I began to understand something I'd only glimpsed while reading the book. Each side of his personality played off the other. The intricate schemes to foil the masters of Madame la Guillotine were also, in their way, a type of game, a series of magical mirrors that confused and deceived, just as his entire foppish portrayal misled his peers into underestimating and dismissing him. So many facets, interacting and reflecting—little wonder that Baroness Orczy and many since her had fallen in love with her creation.

The news was mixed. The League had succeeded, despite Chauvelin's interference, in spiriting Monsieur le Comte de Tournay de Basserive onto Percy's yacht, the *Day Dream*, for imminent reunion with the comte's grateful family. But Armand had not reached the rendezvous point, thanks to orders issued by that same Chauvelin as soon as the French agent arrived in Calais. He had lost his grip on me and failed to capture Percy, but he had secured another hostage to bait his trap once more. Also, Tony and Suzanne remained unaccounted for, although no evidence suggested that Chauvelin held them, too.

"They'd better both be in London," Andrew said, "with Tony guarding Suzanne as ordered. Or he's going to need a damned good explanation why not."

"She'll be fine, old man," Percy said. "Sink me if she's not." Andrew slumped onto a handy bench, his face grim. I guessed he did not feel reassured. I wouldn't have, in his shoes.

Percy pulled a penknife from his pocket and sharpened a quill, preparatory to marking up the map. "Meanwhile, we have our task cut out for us here. Brogard, the innkeeper at *Le Chat Gris,* told me that Chauvelin has ordered Armand conveyed to Paris."

"Do you trust Brogard?" Bathurst interjected, saving me from having to ask.

"Within limits." Percy dipped the quill in the ink pot next to him. "He hasn't betrayed us so far." He touched the map with a fingertip. "I'd like to intercept the carriage long before Paris. If something goes wrong, we'll have time to consider new plans. Here, at Marles-les-Mines, we will make our first attempt."

The quill circled a tiny blob on the map, not a city or even a town, to judge from the size of the surrounding blobs. "Hastings, you took the earlier watch, did you not?"

Hastings, a dark-haired young man of medium height, nodded.

"Chauvelin has no reason to haunt Calais now," Percy said. "He'll be eager to draw us into a new trap, using Armand as his lure. So you should have no trouble circling back and collecting the rest of the League." His quill stabbed the map. "Meet us here by sundown. There's an abandoned church not far from the village. But take care. It's not likely, but Chauvelin may have left troops to monitor Père Blanchard's hut."

"I'll go with him," Bathhurst said, "unless you need me here. I had several hours' sleep while waiting in the woods."

Percy nodded. The two young men started to leave, but at the door Hastings turned back. "And if something goes wrong? How do we reach you?"

"Make sure one of you is free at all times," Percy answered after a pause. "If the other goes missing, no heroics. Send for help right away. To our men near Calais, if you can, and to us, if not."

"Agreed," Hastings said. A few minutes later, we heard their horses in the yard.

"And we three?" Andrew asked as the door closed behind them.

"Ah." Percy tapped the map. "We ride for Marles-les-Mines to reconnoiter the territory." He glanced my way, a certain mischief in his eyes. "Ready, m'dear?"

Tackling an enormous horse with Percy's arm around my waist, while I leaned back against him, faint from my "injury," proved bearable, even pleasant. Riding astride in this way felt much more secure than sitting sideways in front of Andrew, although by the time we reached our destination several hours later, my legs and spine ached. When Percy signaled a halt at a small country inn that far outstripped *Le Chat Gris* in terms of comfort and hospitality, my muscles cramped. The ostler took the horse off to the stables, and I trudged into the inn on Percy's arm, the "injury" doing double duty, as it were. So far, Chauvelin and his troops had played least-in-sight.

A few respectful "Citizens," not to mention a fat purse slipped into the innkeeper's hand, secured us a private room. Percy sent Andrew off to investigate the church and the general layout and lowered the bar on the door.

For the first time since leaving Blakeney Manor, we were alone. But alone in an entirely different way. My stomach churned with anxiety. I sat on the bed, one foot bent underneath the opposing knee, uncertain what to say.

I understood what Percy wanted and that he had every reason, after the way I'd responded, yesterday and at the opera house, to believe that I shared his desire. (He was right.) But although he saw me as his wife, I wasn't. I'd lost contact with Marguerite, and Percy was inscrutable by design, an enigma throughout his many novels. Not to mention Marguerite's husband.

Then there was Ian. I didn't know him either. Half the time I couldn't tell him from Percy. For the moment, we were allies, but only a fool would forget that if I lost this contest, his chances of winning improved, and vice versa. Or that a computer had created and maintained the room where we sat. I prided myself on being a modern woman. I could entertain the idea of sleeping with him, but not here, inside the game, with Jeb and his staff monitoring every move.

Use your head, Nina. Within the last week, you've loved him and hated him and put him out of your mind. Don't careen from one emotion to another—like Mom, like Marguerite. You're a scholar. Act like one.

Percy came to sit beside me. His hand brushed my cheek. "You don't want this, *mignonne?*" Disappointment tinged his voice. "We may not have another opportunity for days."

Mignonne. The word he'd used at the opera house. My skin tingled, as it had when he kissed me behind the dracaena. I wrapped my unraveling logic around me like a cloak.

"I don't know." I caught the hand that strayed from my cheek to my ear. "How alone are we, really?"

He raised my clasped hand to his lips. "As alone as we need to be, I swear. Is that the only thing that concerns you?"

It wasn't. I had other questions I couldn't ask, including about stuff like safety. I had contraceptive implants that were supposed to last years, so I didn't worry about pregnancy. Still, I knew the rules for twenty-first-century sex—and though I doubted Ian had contracted AIDS, it paid to be careful. But explain to an eighteenth-century gentleman why he should use protection while making love to his wife? It would take diplomatic skills greater than I could muster to pull that one off. So I focused on my many reasons to question his sincerity. "Who are you, behind the mask?"

His face relaxed into that dazzling movie-star smile. "The man who loves you, darling."

He *loved* me? My jaw dropped open. But while I stared at him, shocked, Marguerite surged out of nowhere, as if summoned to life by his declaration, and ran her fingers through Percy's hair. "So you forgive me at last?" she asked in French. "Ah, how happy you make me."

"Forgive you? I am the one who needs forgiveness." Percy's husky voice left me in no doubt as to who was speaking. I'd heard that voice on the drive home from Dover, at the opera house and the ball, in the cottage last night. The same voice that moments ago had murmured *mignonne*.

Not to me, though. To Marguerite.

Distrust crushed my attempts at dispassionate analysis with the subtlety of a buffalo stampede. I reached to shove him away, only to find that I couldn't lift a hand. Marguerite's resurgence had tossed me into the background again. When I struggled, briars worthy of the Sleeping Beauty's castle shot up around me. I tugged in vain at the brambles.

In the nick of time, the cavalry arrived in the shape of Andrew, knocking at the door. Percy cursed and went to answer it. I could hear muttering—some of it Marguerite's. But her frustration created a distraction that made it possible for me to shove myself to the forefront again.

Where I fumed. At myself more than at them. Despite my self-talk about remaining analytical, I'd stood by while Ian Campbell duped me *again*. No, not duped. He loved Marguerite. When would I get that through my head?

My dad's lessons stuck. No man picks brains over beauty. Remember that, Sparrow.

By the time Percy closed the door and turned back to me, I was shoving my shirt into my trousers the way an impatient magician might stuff a recalcitrant rabbit into a top hat. In response to my anger and Marguerite's frustration, Percy lifted my hand, pressing a kiss into my palm. My stomach, to my great annoyance, tightened.

"Sorry, sweetheart," he said. "Duty calls."

No need to admit that I saw the interruption as a godsend. "I understand," I answered. His cheek pressed against the heel of my hand. "We should go. Andrew's waiting."

I told myself the incident meant nothing. But in my heart of hearts, even I recognized that something fundamental had changed. I just refused to put a name to it. Then.

14. Taproom, Marles-les-Mines

PERCY AND I DECIDED THAT THE LAW STUDENT COULD afford to dispense with the blood and have his "injury" covered by a fresh bandage, although there wasn't much we could do about the ripped jacket and stained shirt. He sacrificed another cravat to wrap the pretend wound anew and restored my hair to neatness, then we went downstairs.

We found Andrew in the taproom, a tankard of ale at his elbow and a bowl of chicken soup steaming on the table before him. Percy ordered two more of the same, raising an eyebrow at me as a sturdy young waitress plunked the tankard into my hand.

"Don't get her tipsy," Andrew said when the girl had gone. He meant me.

"She has to drink something," Percy answered, also referring to me. "Who knows what's in the water, and wine won't keep her any more sober than beer." We spoke French, to stay in character. I noticed that the atrocious accent Percy had displayed in Dover had given way to near-native fluency. Marguerite came off her silken cloud long enough to mark the oddity of that. I sensed her purring—he loves me, he *loves* me! The whole situation made me want to throw up.

«Don't you feel silly now for insulting his accent at the Fisherman's Rest?» I asked.

«Aren't *you* grumpy today?» Her wide, startled eyes glowed azure blue in my mind.

No kidding. And because he loved her, not me. Imagine that.

I sensed no response to my sarcasm. And I did feel kind of guilty for taking it out on her. It wasn't her fault that Ian preferred her to me. «I'm sorry,» I said, to make up for my ill humor. «I know you love Percy, but I feel like a third wheel. I might as well have stayed home!»

«Then I wouldn't have met you, and that would be sad.»

Which reminded me that I'd missed her, too. «Yes,» I said. «Not knowing you would indeed be sad.»

The men had yet to decide whether I could handle one beer. Marguerite had nothing to contribute. My link with her, although stronger, didn't reach far.

"I'll be careful. With Chauvelin on the loose, you can count on that." I stared at their tankards. "Worry about yourselves."

Percy didn't bother to conceal his amusement as he looked me up and down. "Either one of us could drink you under the table, m'dear."

He had a point. They were both nine inches taller than me and proportionally heavier. I spread my hands in acknowledgment. "True. But I swear, I can manage a beer."

He treated me to his half-smile, dropped the topic, and turned to Andrew. "What did you find out, old chap?"

Sir Andrew ran his hand over his head, disarranging the brown wig he'd donned over hair almost as golden as Percy's.

He patted it back into place. "Rumors that a troop detachment will arrive before dark. Otherwise I'd not have disturbed you. No mention of Armand—nor Chauvelin, for that matter—but a courier representing the Committee of Public Safety asked the local blacksmith about the best places to stay."

"Committee of Public Safety. Which employs Chauvelin as its agent, when he's not pretending to be a diplomat. You did right to interrupt us." Percy gazed at me, his expression unreadable, then swigged ale and wiped his mouth on the shabby but clean napkin the sturdy waitress had supplied on request. I wondered what he wasn't saying, even though no gentleman would raise such a topic in public. Did he recognize the uncertainty as mine? Did he revel in the memory of Marguerite's response? Or had our conflicting impulses confused him?

To conceal my relief at escaping the awkward situation in the inn bedroom, I concentrated on my soup. It emitted a fragrant smell of parsley and broth, with feather-light dumplings and a few carrots thrown in for good measure. It also contained a surprising amount of chicken. Percy must have tipped the waitress well.

Quite different from *Le Chat Gris,* thank goodness.

"Faith," Andrew said, "we can assume the committee has other agents, but it seems a bit of a coincidence that one would travel here at the very moment when we know Chauvelin plans to convey Armand to Paris."

Percy leaned back, tapping his fingers against the tabletop. He hadn't touched his soup. "We've preceded him, if he's sending couriers. That's a blessing. We have time to intercept him. Have the men reached the church?"

"Not yet," Andrew said. "Within the hour, I'll wager."

"Could Chauvelin take a different route to Paris?" I asked, since that possibility seemed to have eluded them.

"Not likely," Percy said. "That is, he could, but it would take him twice as long and defeat his purpose. We want Armand, and Chauvelin wants us."

Which pretty much summed up the situation, I thought.

For the hour that remained before twilight, Percy and Andrew amused themselves by strolling the village in various disguises, scouring for further news of Chauvelin. As sundown approached, they resumed their lawyer suits and we set off for the abandoned church, carrying packets of the ever-present bread and cheese supplied by the obliging innkeeper.

We handed the packets to Hastings and the three League associates he had recruited from the forces left in Calais. They had arrived not long before, carrying the very information that Percy and Andrew had sought throughout the afternoon. The four young men fell on the food as Oliver Twist did on his gruel, but between bites they shared what they had learned.

"The coach is about an hour behind us," Hastings said. "Heavily guarded, as you would expect. Chauvelin isn't traveling with it, but he has at least a dozen troops assigned there, including two riding inside."

"Good work," Percy said. In an hour, the countryside would be pitch black; the church clock had struck eight some time ago. "How fast is the coach traveling?"

"Not fast," one of the younger men said. "Five miles an hour, perhaps. It's an old-fashioned rig, and not well sprung."

"Sink me, we may have him, then." Percy clapped the younger man's shoulder. "How do you feel about becoming a highwayman, Philip?"

Philip waved a pistol in the air to indicate his enthusiasm for the role, and Percy laughed.

Over the next half-hour, Lord Bathurst's contingent of four straggled in. Percy nodded a greeting to each man as he entered. "Ah, John," he announced, as Bathurst himself came through the door, the last of that quartet. "I have a mission for you. Please escort Lady Blakeney back to the inn and keep an eye on her."

"Excuse me?" I said. "Keep an eye on me? You must be joking!"

Percy drew me off to one side. "Now don't fly into a miff, m'dear. I meant nothing derogatory by it. Can't drag you with me into a crowd of French soldiers, what? The demmed fellows don't shoot that well. They might aim at one of us and hit you by mistake."

He was right. Since I couldn't ride by myself, I'd slow them down. Even so, the male superiority rankled. "They might aim at me and shoot one of you by mistake," I told him.

Percy, unmoved, chucked me under the chin. "Precisely, Madam. So please accompany Lord Bathurst to the inn and protect us all."

Grumbling, I accepted the inevitable. At first Percy insisted I stay in the private room, but Lord Bathurst convinced him we could serve the League better if we took seats on opposite sides of the taproom and mined whatever gossip we could. I doubted the inn at Marles-les-Mines had a thriving social life at the best of times, never mind on a Thursday night, but hanging out in the taproom had more appeal than staying in a bedroom by myself without even a book to read. Besides, I felt sorry for Bathurst, stuck wife-sitting when he'd rather be off getting shot with his buddies.

"Very well," Percy said at last. "Sit in a dark corner, though, Madam, and don't invite trouble."

"Yes, Percy." It came out as a snarl.

Percy bent over my hand and said to Bathurst, "Godspeed, my friend. I think you're going to need it." To me, he added, "Don't hurt him, darling."

Bathurst guffawed, the swine. Gathering what remained of my dignity, I turned my back on them and walked away.

I'd reached the church doors when the realization struck me. Guns. Shooting. If something went wrong, Percy and Andrew might die. I spun on my heel and ran across the room, threw my arms around his neck, and kissed him. "Take care of yourself, please."

He pulled me close and whispered in my ear, "Don't worry, *mignonne*. I'll be back in an hour."

Bathurst waited at the entrance. As I walked with him to the village, my lips tingled from that kiss.

Fifteen minutes later, Bathurst and I entered the taproom. As ordered, I retreated to a dark corner. Bathurst, who'd decked himself out as a local farmer in loose shirt and baggy cotton pants, lounged in full view at the far side of the room. In a village this size, everyone would know he didn't belong in Marles-les-Mines, but like the other members of the League, he had taken great care with his disguise and could hope to convince the locals that he lived somewhere nearby.

The waitress brought another tankard, which I planned to nurse throughout the evening. Apart from any implied promise to Percy, I had no desire to end up with my reasoning ability impaired, or even hung-over tomorrow morning. I needed to keep my wits about me to stay one step ahead of David.

Lord Bathurst showed less restraint, although I saw no sign that he was really drunk as distinct from pretending to be.

As Percy had said, any member of the League could put me under the table and remain standing. The eighteenth century was not an abstemious age.

Nothing much happened for the first hour. I sipped ale at a snail's pace and allowed the waitress to bring me more soup, not because I wanted it but because I needed a reason to hang around. The other patrons ignored me, lured by the jocular exchange between Bathurst and several worthies gathered round the fireplace. I'd just about decided I'd be better off upstairs when I saw Chauvelin.

He came alone, and at first he didn't notice me, even after Bathurst shot me an unnecessary warning glance. I slid farther into my dark corner and waited.

Something alerted him. I don't know what. My sitting alone in the shadows may have struck him as odd, or maybe his network of spies tipped him off to my presence before he entered the inn. Either way, as Bathurst watched in alarm, Chauvelin crossed the room, oblivious to the group by the fire, and settled onto the vacant bench at my table.

"Good evening," he said with the smarmy courtesy that always made me contemplate violence.

Marguerite woke from her haze, radiating panic. «Hush,» I said to her. «He can't do anything dreadful here. Bathurst's watching out for us, and you'll break my concentration if you keep thinking fear at me. Relax. I'll handle it.»

She didn't buy it. Who would, in her shoes? But she did pull back and leave me in charge. Not so far that I lost access to her French, fortunately.

Chauvelin went on. "The innkeeper tells me you are a young law student returning to the University of Paris." He beckoned to the waitress, who brought a flask of wine and two pottery cups. "And injured. Not seriously, I trust." He raised the flask. "Would you care for wine?"

I shook my head, and he said, "No, I see you have ale. Pray excuse my clumsiness."

When I didn't reply, he went on. "I am Armand Chauvelin, special representative of the republican government in Paris. It is my duty to investigate strangers to the area."

In a pig's eye. But I kept mum. The more I said, the easier he'd find it to identify me.

Lord Bathurst had relaxed in his corner near the fire and resumed his casual questioning of the local farmers. From time to time, he shot quick, anxious glances my way.

Undeterred by my silence, Chauvelin raised the candle sitting at the far end of the table and surveyed my face. "The strangest thing, resemblances. When I saw you sitting here, in the dark, I thought you would look like an English friend of mine. Now I perceive an even more curious and striking similarity to that English friend's wife. But here you are," he swept a hand through the air, marking the distance from my head to my waist, "clearly a man. Perhaps you have relatives among the St. Just family?"

So much for keeping mum. He *had* guessed my identity before he joined me. I retreated, metaphorically, to my next line of defense. "Not to my knowledge," I said. "They call me Pierre Dupont. My family lives near Calais."

"Stranger and stranger," Chauvelin remarked. "Even your voice reminds me of Marguerite St. Just. She has a remarkable speaking voice, you know. Quite unique."

"The actress?" I tried to imitate Percy's imperturbability. "She'd have to, wouldn't she? But I heard she married an Englishman, so I suppose she has turned her back on our republic."

Chauvelin lowered the candle and leaned back. "Really, Lady Blakeney, what do you take me for?"

The answer I'd have liked to give to that question would not have advanced our discussion in any direction other than the schoolyard, so I searched for something more appropriate. No doubt Percy would have found some brilliant one-liner, but I made no claim to my husband's brand of savoir-faire. "What do you want, Chauvelin?" I asked.

"Why, dear lady, surely you know that?" So long as he wasn't waving the candle in my face, I had the advantage: I caught his every fleeting expression, whereas he had to guess at mine. Right then he was gloating, which I admit troubled me quite a bit.

He shifted in his seat, and the candle flame caught his face from a different angle. The curve of Chauvelin's lips, the angle of his cheekbones, evoked an unexpected resemblance to David. The flash of recognition set off a chain of impressions in my brain—less thoughts than a series of subconscious insights that crystallized in that instant. The process we call intuition, which is in fact the lightning-fast processing of mental images.

I had noticed that Ian and Percy had become almost interchangeable. However superficial my past acquaintance with Ian, I couldn't avoid noticing that he had revealed a previously hidden swashbuckling side during the simulation. I also realized that in the last week I had become more like Marguerite. My concealed Nessa, if you like, had emerged. I enjoyed the dressing up, the parties, the flirting. I valued my skills as an academic, but I had come to understand that I didn't need to exclude other areas of life.

But if Ian and I benefited from incorporating the less-explored parts of our personalities, where did that leave David? His part required him to channel a manipulative fanatic. And if Chauvelin represented David's shadow self, David would have to deal with consequences much more severe than those the rest of us faced. I felt a fleeting sense of empathy for him.

That moment of compassion raised another question: did I want to work with Chauvelin? I could write a different dissertation. Having lived as Marguerite, having experienced Chauvelin's twisted loyalties secondhand, I no longer needed to study how revolutionaries thought. I could move on.

This whole line of reasoning flashed through my mind in an instant. Marguerite jumped up and down, demanding to know what was happening. I brushed her off, knowing I couldn't explain. «Hush. I have to listen to Chauvelin.»

"I want the Scarlet Pimpernel," Chauvelin declared. "Sir Percy, as you know very well. You've disappointed me so far, but with your brother's life at stake, you must realize the value of cooperation. What is this Englishman to you, compared to the interests of the country that mothered you and now requires your aid?"

A fine speech—total tommyrot, of course, but grandiloquent enough to set off some major scene chewing. If Percy and the League were doing their job, Armand's life would not be at stake for long, but I felt certain Chauvelin had more than one means of causing trouble. My stomach clenched at the thought. "What do you want from me?" I asked.

Marguerite's terror grew. «Steady,» I told her. «Bathurst won't let him hurt us. We're distracting him. While he's here threatening us, he can't chase Percy, can he?»

Chauvelin produced his weasel smile. "Why, dear lady, you might choose to leave this inn and accompany me to the place where my troops are holding your brother."

Yeah, right. If I had bats in the belfry, maybe. "I don't think my husband would like that." My voice trembled. I cursed silently, wishing I'd been able to hide my fear. The memory of my last captivity at his hands lingered.

Bathurst ordered another round for his farmer friends. "My best sheep," I heard him boast, "sold for a pretty price, and off-season, too. Drink up, *mes amis.*" He waved at Chauvelin.

"Won't you join us, *Citoyen?* And celebrate a poor man's good fortune in these hard times?"

Chauvelin shuddered. "Not tonight, Citizens. I have business for the republic."

A chorus of groans greeted this statement. The company had become quite merry, lubricated by toasts to Bathurst's imaginary sheep, and they took some persuading before they gave Chauvelin up as a bad job and went back to their mutual admiration society.

I'd hoped that in the hubbub of conversation, Chauvelin would overlook my anxiety. No such luck, I discovered. Instead, he ogled me as he had on the boat.

"So, Lady Blakeney," he said, smooth as butter, "the most beautiful, most *radiant* actress in Paris so fears her cold Englishman that she will allow her only brother to perish on the guillotine?"

My flash of empathy flickered, then died. Furious, I leaned forward and glared at him. "Have you forgotten what I told you at the opera house? I think you'll use me to trap the Scarlet Pimpernel, then kill Armand anyway—me, too, if I stand in your way. So save your breath. I'm not *choosing* to go anywhere with you, and I don't see any of your private army, so stop trying to manipulate me."

I never found out how he would have replied to my challenge. As he opened his mouth to answer, Percy smacked him on the shoulder with sufficient force to send his forehead cracking against the table. Marguerite jumped up and cheered. I echoed her mental «Huzzah!»

"Sink me," Percy drawled in English, "if I don't humbly beg your pardon, Monsieur Chauvelin. Demmed clumsy of me, don't you know?"

He had changed into his usual London garb and again exhibited the magnificence he had brought into *Le Chat Gris.*

The faces of Bathurst's drinking companions almost sent me into hysterics. If they'd looked up to find King Louis XVI waltzing into the inn, I doubted they would look more stunned. And why not? If anything like Percy in full fop mode had ever entered their ken, I'd buy shares in the Brooklyn Bridge and call them a sound investment.

Chauvelin's normally sallow complexion had turned green, but he recovered enough not to protest when Percy slumped into the seat next to me and poured wine into the unused pottery cup.

"Ale, m'dear?" My husband raised one elegant eyebrow.

I sighed. "It's warm, Percy. I don't even like it." I tipped the tankard toward him, so that he could see for himself that I had drunk less than a quarter of the contents.

France's special representative ignored this brief marital interchange. "I was discussing her brother's probable fate with Lady Blakeney," he said. "I thought she might like to visit him. With me, *naturellement.*"

You had to give Chauvelin credit: he had guts, given Percy's reaction the last time he tried a line like that.

«What?» Marguerite asked. «What did Percy do?»

Her eager questions reminded me that she'd missed the whole scene at the inn in Calais. «Throttled him.» Despite my mixed feelings about Percy, I glowed at the memory. «Within an inch of his life.» Her satisfaction heartened me. The sister of my dreams, sharing my every thought.

But not the love of her husband. I had to remember that.

Chauvelin flinched when Percy raised a languid hand, but tonight my husband relaxed against the wall and said, "Lud, Sir, Lady Blakeney does as she pleases. She don't need my permission." He regarded his adversary through guileless eyes. "Perhaps 'twas your company she sought to avoid." His blue gaze fixed on Chauvelin's neckline, where the cravat, wine-spattered since its wearer's encounter with Percy's hand, hung pathetically, any starch it might have contained completely dissolved.

One point for Percy. The dyspeptic expression that afflicted Chauvelin whenever he encountered my husband strengthened. He looked as though someone had stolen his cup and returned it full of vinegar. "I find it difficult to believe that Lady Blakeney, so fond of her brother that all Paris used to talk of it, now cares nothing for his welfare."

Marguerite wailed. I squashed her and settled back to enjoy the spectacle. Under other circumstances, I would have defended myself, but watching Percy handle Chauvelin gave me the kind of unalloyed pleasure that life seldom offers.

"Odd's fish, man," he said, "do you imagine I whip her? No, no, no, 'tis not the style in English high society."

The way he stressed "English" turned the bland statement into an insult to Chauvelin's entire nation. Chauvelin's mouth pinched in response. I expected another barb, but instead he treated us to a frigid bow. "I see I'm wasting my time, Sir Percy. Please excuse me. Lady Blakeney, I bid you good night."

The minute he left the room, Percy turned to me, the action hero once more. "Upstairs, Madam, and change. We ride before he has a chance to gather his troops."

"But what happened? Did you rescue Armand?"

"No time," Percy said. "Make haste, m'dear. I'll tell you the whole on the road."

He had a gift for getting to the heart of things. As I sped out the door and up the stairs, I saw him join Bathurst and the group by the fire.

15. Northeastern France

WHEN I REACHED THE PRIVATE ROOM, I DISCOVERED PERCY had chosen to restore me to womanhood. No reason not to revert to my natural state, since Chauvelin had pierced my male disguise with such ease, but I nonetheless regarded the pile of female clothing with some trepidation. Percy must have secured it before entering the taproom. He did have a remarkable head on his shoulders.

Marguerite greeted the change with enthusiasm. The pile included a striped woolen skirt and plain cotton blouse, sabots for my feet, and a white head cloth that would conceal the too memorable red-gold hair.

It was the skirt that bothered me. Floor-length dresses had complicated my escape from Chauvelin, and I did not look forward to abandoning my convenient breeches and boots. Percy had been both emphatic and convincing about our need to hurry, however, so I decided not to keep him waiting any longer than necessary.

Peasant skirts, I found, ran shorter than those of a noblewoman like Lady Blakeney. Mucking out stalls and chasing chickens require a certain freedom of movement. Resigned, I took a quick glance at the mirror, decided that I looked like the veriest farmer's wife, and dashed down the stairs.

I found only Lord Bathurst, who caught my arm and directed me toward the stable yard. An unusually tall farmer straddled the back of a sturdy plow horse. Recognizing him under the dirt, I grinned. Percy's baggy shirt and pants looked even shabbier than Bathurst's. He tended to take his disguises to the limit, as evinced by the tattoos he'd sported in Calais. Since I suspected that histrionic streak contributed in part to his success, I forbore from teasing him and allowed Bathurst to help me onto the pillion mounted behind his back. It amused me that Marguerite, the actress, had without realizing it married so instinctive an actor.

The riding astride had left Pierre Dupont rather sore. In that respect, my new persona had distinct advantages. I wrapped my arms around Percy's waist and settled in for the journey.

We stopped first at the abandoned church.

"We'll meet in Vitry-sur-Artois," Percy said, circling a new location on the map. His pen traced the line of the road. "It's another village, slightly larger, here to the southeast." Marguerite had never heard of it.

In turn, the League members checked the map, nodded, and faded into the woods. Percy and I were alone for the first time since we'd left the private room at the inn.

He lifted me back onto the pillion and stood watching me for a moment, hands on my waist. "What happened?" I asked once more. "Did something go wrong?"

"No time," he said again. "We have to get out of the area before Chauvelin decides to initiate a search." He placed one foot in the stirrup.

"Can't you at least tell me why Armand is not here?"

I ducked as his other foot swung over my head. Percy adjusted his position in the saddle. The horse had reached a trot when he spoke over his shoulder. "The coach came by right on schedule. Our men stopped it, but they found only soldiers inside. Chauvelin duped us. Either Armand was never there, or they removed him before reaching Marles-les-Mines."

Marguerite freaked at that. As we rode into the woods, my head resting on Percy's broad back, I had to work full-time to keep her from screaming.

In Vitry-sur-Artois, the League met in a decrepit barn. Deserted farmhouses, abandoned churches, tumbledown barns—revolutionary France became more unappealing by the minute. Admittedly, the aristocrats who served the numerous kings named Louis had not distinguished themselves by public service and concern for the poor, but so far the alternative didn't strike me as much of an improvement.

Or Jeb's staff had taken a few liberties with the historical record. I kept forgetting the world that surrounded me wasn't real.

Nine pairs of eyes met mine as I looked around. The League of the Scarlet Pimpernel—minus Tony, charged with guarding Suzanne in London. I set my historical speculations aside for later contemplation and returned my attention to the present.

Marguerite was fading again. I hoped to find a way to rally her before she disappeared altogether, but Chauvelin's pursuit left me with few opportunities to plan.

"Andrew identified the coach," Percy said for the benefit of Bathurst and me, who had missed the rescue attempt. "The one supposedly carrying Armand. He and Hastings posed as ostlers and loosened a strap in the right leader's harness."

"How did you know where it would break?" I asked.

"We didn't," Andrew answered. "But we thought it would happen somewhere near Marles-les-Mines."

Percy picked up his story again. "I sent everyone to string themselves out along the road. After a couple of miles, the strap tore free. The right leader shook his head, and that upset the left one. Then Andrew and Hastings spooked the horses further by dashing out in front of them."

"Dressed as highwaymen," Hastings put in. "That was my favorite part."

Percy pretended to cuff him. "Young ruffian. After that, it was easy. The noise brought the rest of the League to the scene, and they distracted the troops while Hastings rode around to the far side of the coach."

"Only problem was," Andrew said, "that we didn't find Armand, just a couple of terrified infantrymen. Country boys pressed into service."

Hastings chuckled. "You should have seen their faces. They dived under the seat, didn't even try to reason with me. Lily-livered poltroons."

"Goodness," I said. "What a dreadful pair of cowards. And you waving a pistol and wearing a mask. If only they'd realized you were friendly!"

"*Touché.*" Laughing, Hastings saluted me. "Anyway, I called to Andrew, he got everyone together, and the whole lot of us dashed off down the road, leaving the troops to report to Chauvelin. Tony will be livid when he finds out he missed this job. Where is he, anyway?"

"Collecting Suzanne from England," Andrew said. When Percy raised an eyebrow at him, Andrew blushed. "To keep her safe from Chauvelin," he added.

"In France?" Percy asked.

"With us. I sent him a message before we left for Marles-les-Mines. They should arrive today or tomorrow." Andrew sounded defensive. From what he'd told me at the cottage, I guessed that he and Percy had engaged in this argument before they rode off, leaving Suzanne and me at Lord Grenville's ball.

I thought of mentioning my abduction, then decided not to take sides. Indeed, I could only guess whether Suzanne was safer with us or with her family: both options seemed risky, for different reasons. Having realized that I could write a decent dissertation even if I chose not to work with David, I no longer cared so much whether I won the game, so Suzanne's presence or absence didn't affect me in that sense. But we were friends in normal life, so I admitted to some curiosity regarding her fate.

Percy watched Andrew for a moment, then shrugged. "As you wish. If we can protect Suzanne better than her parents, bring her here, by all means. But I hope you're right about the timing. We could use Tony's help." I heard Andrew sigh with relief.

Percy refocused his attention on the larger group. "In the interim, we need to retrieve Armand. This Chauvelin is becoming a bloody nuisance. Too demmed clever by half. Where's the map?"

Lord Bathurst gave him the map, folded to show the circle surrounding Marles-les-Mines. Percy spread it out on a handy manger filled with moldy straw.

"They started here." He pointed to Calais. "We know they had Armand then, and they've had little more than a day to hide him. We go back to Calais and fan out. Everywhere within a day's ride."

"That's a lot of ground, Percy," Hastings said.

"Yes." Percy placed a foot on the manger, touched his thumbnail to his mouth, and pondered the map. "We can work in circles, close to town at first, and cast about for information. Then, when we know which way they went, we can move in force."

He would have made a formidable general. The League nodded as though they shared a single head and listened as he divided them into pairs, each with its assigned territory.

My return to *Le Chat Gris* did not fill me with joy—or the Brogards either, as best I could tell. You'd have had a hard time figuring out whose spirits rose higher when it turned out that Percy had no intention of staying there. Under normal circumstances, he would board his yacht, but the *Day Dream* had not yet returned from England. Although he complained quite a bit, I didn't mind. Any impulse he might have felt to bundle me on board and leave me there died unborn, which in my opinion definitely constituted the lesser evil. I enjoyed the game, even at its filthy worst, more than sitting around a boat waiting for Chauvelin to waylay me again.

Although the first twenty-four hours did leave me wondering if Percy had pulled another fast one on me. He escorted Marguerite to a peasant hut outside Calais, while he tore off back to town to supervise the hunt for Armand. I glared at his receding back until he disappeared behind a haystack, cursing his chivalrous instincts and vowing to plot an escape route, just in case.

Our host family consisted of a wizened but hardy old woman with a round apple-cheeked face, a couple of sons in their twenties, and the older son's wife. Unlike most of Calais's inhabitants, they greeted us with a serene hospitality that quite touched me after so much surliness. That we looked like peasants ourselves probably helped.

The disguise did have one disadvantage. When I begged the young wife for a bath, you would have thought I'd suggested stringing the family's only cow up by the heels.

"A bath?" The young woman regarded me with awestruck eyes. "You mean, wash yourself all over?"

"My hair, especially." I pulled the kerchief from my head and let the limp strands fall free. I held one up for her inspection. "Look how dirty it is. We slept in a stable last night."

"'Twill take an age to dry," she said, doubt in every line of her face.

"Yes. You will not mind if I sit for a while by the stove, in return for helping you with supper later?"

"You could do that," she said. "Come with me, and I'll wash it under the pump, but we can't give you a bath, for we have no tub to put it in."

It sounded better than nothing, so I followed her to the yard. The whole way, I could hear her muttering, "Wash herself all over? Whoever *heard* of such a thing? Why, she'd catch her death."

I knelt under the pump. While she fetched soap and produced a lather of sorts, I said, "Doesn't anyone ever take a full bath?"

Marguerite roused herself long enough to scold. «Of course not,» she said. «They're peasants! Leave off, before she chatters about you to everyone she knows!»

She had a point, although her poke in the ribs would have worked better before I'd said anything. The damage was done.

The young woman—Jeanne, it turned out—wet my hair and worked lather into it. "Well," she said in answer to my question, "I did hear that Farmer Gilbert, over near Les

Roches, took a full bath on Michaelmas last. He didn't see Christmas, 'twas said."

"No one else?" I gasped as she pushed my head under the pump and doused me in cold water.

When I came up sputtering, I found her staring thoughtfully at the henhouse. "No," she said. "Can't think of a one."

«See?» Marguerite muttered. «What did I tell you?»

«Fine, fine, I'll take care of it.» A square of linen lay draped over the pump handle, the closest the family had to a towel. I wrapped Marguerite's hair in it, bent over from the waist, and squeezed. "Thank goodness you stopped me, then," I said. "How foolish you must think me."

Jeanne gave me a radiant smile of pure relief, revealing a missing tooth. "'Twas the funniest thing I'd ever heard. A fine lady you might be, talking like that."

"That's rich. A fine lady, is it? And my man a fine gentleman, I suppose. Riding off on that misbegotten excuse for a carthorse." The towel had absorbed as much moisture as it could hold, so I gave Marguerite's hair a final twist and let it fall. Handing the towel to Jeanne, I headed for the kitchen. "If you can find this fine lady a comb, she can braid her hair before she helps you stir the porridge."

That amused her no end. Marguerite, too, I was pleased to note. She hadn't had much fun since I showed up, poor thing.

Percy returned the next evening, regaling me with stories of the League's search for Armand. And in the morning he invited me, again dressed as a boy, to accompany him as far as the fisherman's hut that the League used as a base. Good choice: it saved me from having to stalk him unseen or roam the French countryside searching for him.

If Ian had any influence on him, of course, Percy had figured out that I'd cause twice as much trouble left to my own devices. In that sense, inviting me to stay where he could keep an eye on me worked for both of us.

So off we trotted, heading for Calais, sustenance in the form of bread and cheese and a flagon of cider enclosed in our saddlebags. About three-quarters of the way to the coast, we veered west, reaching the shore a few miles from the port. Another battered hut, this one distinguished by fishing nets slung from the rocks and traps piled by the door—it reminded me of last year's vacation in Maine, except that no one would rent this lonely shack. But it was secluded and nondescript, the perfect combination for our current needs. We moved in.

And there we stayed, hour upon weary hour. Man, the search was dull. The sea cut off any northern retreat, but that left three other directions to cover. A coach could travel only on roads, which limited the options to four or five, but after the mishap at Marles-les-Mines, Percy refused to take anything for granted. Chauvelin might have conveyed his prisoner on horseback or even on foot—he could have doubled back or stayed in the area the whole time. That meant the League had to search every copse and hut and fisherman's boat (without the owners' knowledge) until their chief felt satisfied they had left no stone unturned.

I'd just about decided that a person *could* die of boredom when trouble arrived with its dog and a bone. To be specific, Tony appeared—alone, with bad news. The day after I escaped from Calais, Chauvelin had sent his men after Suzanne. She had disappeared from the garden at Lady Sanford's house, right in the middle of the evening fireworks celebration, and no one had seen her since. Whether Chauvelin had brought her to France, imprisoned her somewhere in England, or simply disposed of her, her frantic family had not succeeded in discovering. The Comte de Tournay, Tony said, was beside himself: if he had only eluded pursuit and accompanied his family in the first place, no rapscallion would have dared assault his beloved daughter. Which was complete nonsense, but one had to make allowances for a father's battered dignity.

Not to mention Andrew's. Watching him turn red and pace, I imagined he might explode from berating Tony. Andrew held Tony responsible for Suzanne's welfare. Which made even less sense than the comte blaming himself. Tony had no more ability than the rest of us to predict Chauvelin's next move. If anyone bore the blame, I suspected Marguerite and I had as much claim as anyone: had we not invented the "S's party" story? It was just like Chauvelin to twist the knife by grabbing Suzanne from a celebration hosted by a Lady S.

I had no chance to mention S or her party, and I doubt it would have done much good if I had. Andrew had temporarily yielded the floor to Tony, yelling back that he lacked both second sight and the ability to spirit Suzanne away by magic. What did Andrew take him for?

Tony's protests fell on the proverbial deaf ears. Andrew refused to listen to reason.

But where *was* Suzanne? Chauvelin had not mentioned her in the taproom, and I saw no reason for him to capture her unless he planned to wave her in front of us as bait. To lure Andrew into turning against Percy, perhaps. In his current mood, Andrew might well fall for such a ploy.

Maybe Chauvelin had killed Suzanne, with the intent of fomenting distrust between Andrew and Tony and creating opportunities to attack us one by one. But that plan wouldn't work either, unless he told us she was dead.

While I considered these points, Andrew and Tony continued to shout at each other. I opened my mouth to intervene, but Percy beat me to it. Clamping one heavy hand on Tony's shoulder and the other on Andrew's, he let out a roar that must have rattled windows in Paris. The two of them stopped spitting and stared openmouthed at their normally imperturbable leader.

"Right," Percy said, in the most no-nonsense voice I'd ever heard him use. "Sit, both of you, and shut up. Unless you *want* to do Chauvelin's work for him."

"You, too, Marguerite," he added without looking at me. I dropped onto a pile of sacks and hugged my knees, curious to discover what he had in mind. I had to be listening to Ian, since "shut up" didn't sound like an expression Percy would use.

Andrew and Tony sat on rough piles of coats arrayed on opposite sides of the hut, where they could practice fierce-ogre expressions to their hearts' content. Percy ignored the byplay and joined me on the sacks. "Look," he said, in the same authoritative tone, "it's a contest, we know that. Us against Chauvelin. He'd like to make it each of us against the others. Why else did he kidnap Marguerite? Or Suzanne. He breaks our unity, he wins. If we stick together, *we* win. It's a variation on the prisoner's dilemma. He's doing his best to convince us that one or two of us can succeed by betraying the rest. But if the five of us defeat him together, we can dictate our own terms. We rewrite the rules of the game."

I have to admit, I was impressed. Not only that Ian had managed to get so much past the computer by recasting it as relevant to our present situation, but also that he'd figured out the basic flaw in David's scheme. That was more than I had done, despite obsessing over every detail.

The prisoner's dilemma. As soon as he said it, I realized he was right. In the prisoner's dilemma scenario, players do best if they cooperate, but the rules of the game make people believe that they will profit most from betrayal. Just like this game, where David had set the situation up to convince us that we should fight one another for his approval, when in fact he wanted all five of us to fail. If we stuck together and treated Chauvelin (that is, David) as our common adversary, we would make his job ten times more difficult.

No wonder Ian had accepted my offer of an alliance. I'd thought in selfish terms: how to strengthen my own position against Andrew, Suzanne, and Tony. But he'd seen farther, into the logic of the game itself. I had misjudged him, and over something much more serious than his having a crush on Marguerite. I felt a new respect for him, as well as a huge sense of relief. If Andrew and Tony accepted Ian's argument, I could stop fearing a knife in my back.

"You're right," I said. I'd have liked to keep the surprise out of my voice, but I didn't quite manage. Percy's eyes flashed amusement as he turned his head in my direction.

Andrew leaned against the wall, his eyes narrowed in contemplation. Tony burst out laughing. "That prick," he said. "Demme if you haven't called his number, Percy. He would love to set us to squabbling." He crossed the room, his hand extended to Andrew. "What are the odds that Chauvelin has your beloved stashed in a nearby inn, waiting for you to hare off and rescue her? Let's show him we aren't such easy prey!"

Percy winked at me, and I inhaled the first full breath I'd taken since Tony walked in. No need to suggest the alternative: that Chauvelin had killed Suzanne in London.

Percy escorted me back to the farmhouse that night, then left to pursue a fresh trail, promising to return within hours. Hastings remained as guard. I didn't protest: the prospect of a long slog through the Calais night didn't hold much appeal, plus the delay gave me time to bring Marguerite up to date. But stars came and went without signaling Percy's reappearance. Worried that I might have underestimated his danger, I headed into the courtyard for a quick consultation with Hastings. We were exchanging forceful suggestions as to how best to proceed when Percy rode in.

"Why are you not asleep, m'dear?" He carried no quizzing glass in his yeoman's garb, but I had no difficulty imagining him wielding it at me.

"You promised to come back ages ago," I said.

"You missed me. Charming." His languid tone grated on my nerves, already raw from fussing over his safety—to no purpose, as it turned out. His dismissal of my concerns reminded me of the bad old days, before I pushed him in the fish pond, and I remembered only later that Percy acted this way when he wanted to divert questions. I was plotting how to dump his head under the pump when he spoke to Hastings. "Good job, Edward. You kept her out of trouble."

«Men!» I said to Marguerite. And with that, I ran into the hut and left Percy and Hastings congratulating each other on saving me from the nonexistent dangers posed by Jeanne's farm. I retired to my assigned pallet, where I tossed and turned, trying to sleep. In the end, I must have succeeded, because dawn arrived without my seeing it happen. Percy had left again, as I soon discovered, although Hastings emerged from a barn, yawning and tucking in his shirt, moments after I finished washing my face.

Around noon, Lord Bathurst brought the news that the League was ready to move. While he tipped Jeanne's family liberally and accepted the onion pies they pressed on him, I collected my spare kerchief and said goodbye. We walked across a field and ducked behind another barn, where we found the League in its many disguises drinking beer, munching on sausage and bread, and trading jokes. The men jumped to their feet and bowed when I arrived.

"Thank you, m'dear." Percy took the pie I held out. Hoping he had recovered from yesterday's wayward mood, I settled at his side. The pies were wonderful, still warm, with the caramel taste and tempting aroma of well-cooked onions.

"What have you found out?" I asked.

"Ffoulkes and Hastings tracked Armand down." Percy swallowed beer. "Six soldiers, more or less, rode off the day we left the area and cut across fields in the direction of the Paris road."

"Armand was with them? You're sure?" I took another bite of pie.

"We asked at least ten people," Andrew said. "They agreed that one member of the group wasn't in uniform and always rode in the middle."

"Also," Hastings added, "when we got a description, it matched Armand's, although most of our informants couldn't confirm more than dark hair and eyes, which fits about three-quarters of the French population."

"We tracked them to the Paris road." Andrew wiped his mouth on the towel that had wrapped my onion pie. "A little too coincidental, don't you think?"

"Indeed. Good work, both of you. We'll go after them." Percy twisted his head. "And the *Day Dream*?"

"I left her anchored in a cove. She can't be seen from Calais," Tony said.

Percy regarded me, mischief in his face. His eyes, crinkled at the corners, had the same shape as Ian's. "You wouldn't send me off to wait there, would you?" I asked.

The gleam in his eyes gave way to open laughter. "Don't worry, m'dear. I'm not letting you out of my sight. Who else could get kidnapped in the middle of Surrey?"

"Oh, how unfair! As if it were my fault!"

As I pulled my feet under me, ready to storm off into the woods, Percy caught me in his arms. His voice shaded into tenderness as he whispered in my ear, "Apologies, darling. And if that nasty little man touches you again, I won't be held accountable for my actions."

My eyes locked with his. It was Ian speaking, and he meant every word. A thrill shot through me. I couldn't shake the sensation that we were no longer talking about the game.

"That way, Madam." Percy pointed at a nearby copse.

Grimacing, I took the pile of boy's clothes he handed me and worked my way through the bushes. Compared to my latest guise, the fisherman's lad had dressed like a fashion plate. I had to look like complete riffraff, with Marguerite's hair piled under a dirty red hat with a tricolor cockade and the ugliest pair of slippers you ever saw on my feet. The shirt hung loose enough to cover the anatomy of a dozen females, and the pants ended in ragged cuffs just below the knee. Quite a bit more ragged after I dragged myself out of the shrubbery. I was glad I had no mirror to hand. Poor Marguerite was palpitating at the whole idea.

«You can't dress like that,» she kept muttering. «It's indecent.»

«Do stop!» I told her when my patience gave out. «It's no fun for me, looking like something the cat dragged in. I am trying to make sure no one associates this character with you!» It didn't reconcile her, exactly, but it did shut her up.

Percy tied a red scarf around my neck to complete the outfit, then jerked his head in the direction of the rough wagon he proposed to drive. "In you go, darling," he said. "Look as if you hadn't two brains to rub together."

I sprawled on the sacks that lined the cart and did my best imitation of the village idiot, which sent Percy into gales of laughter.

All went reasonably well till we reached Bully-les-Mines, although time dragged. Percy's taciturn farmer barely exchanged two words with Andrew, sitting on the box next to him, never mind with the slack-jawed youth huddled among the sacks and barely within hearing distance. Reading wasn't an option. How I missed my books!

Daydreaming worked for a while, as did cloud animal detection and sleeping, but as the cart rumbled its unhurried way along the same road we had already traveled twice, I became increasingly, agonizingly bored.

Marguerite refused to talk to me, even when I prodded her. I worried about offending her until I realized she'd sunk into gloom worrying about Armand.

Poor Armand. He was the object of our extended journey, yet we seemed to be farther from rescuing him than ever.

And what of Suzanne? None of the searches had turned up any sign of her. Not on this side of the Channel. More and more, it seemed likely that Chauvelin had gotten rid of her when he had the chance. For bait to work, you have to let the prey know where it is, but we had received no communications from our least-favorite Frenchman.

Unless he wanted to keep us on tenterhooks. That sounded like him.

Somewhere around Norrent-Fontes it started to rain: a steady drizzle that worsened with each mile we traveled. The *Day Dream* looked better by the minute.

At Bully-les-Mines, the road forked. The cart turned left without hesitation.

"Do you know where you're going, then?" I heard Andrew ask. "Which way they took Armand?"

"Where we're going, yes," Percy said. "Which way Armand went, no. We need to find out, and that's best done by daylight, which we won't have much longer. The others will meet us at our destination; I told them how to get there before we left."

I twisted in my seat. "Are we stopping? Hallelujah!" Receiving no response beyond a quick smile, I huddled deeper into the sack that provided my only protection against the rain. Even an abandoned barn would be better than this.

16. Woodland Refuge

THE ROAD PERCY CHOSE WOUND AMONG WOODS FOR SOME time before the trees parted to reveal a small, jewel-like park with a brick house right in its center. After so much desolation and decay, the manicured grass and pristine paint struck me with special force. Fairy-tale colors glowed against the grayness of the surrounding landscape.

The wagon pulled to a stop before a barn ten times as well repaired as any that I'd seen since leaving Richmond. A young League member I didn't know by name came out and held the barn door. The horse raised its dragging head as we approached food and shelter, almost breaking into a trot.

Sir Andrew jumped down as the wagon drew to a halt and began unbuckling the animal from the shafts. His companion was already ladling oats into a feedbag. Percy walked around to the back of the wagon and regarded my bruised, damp state with compassion.

"Welcome, m'lady," he said with a good approximation of a court bow that contrasted sharply with his rain-drenched peasant clothes. He extended his hand. "Let's go inside."

Sack clutched around my shoulders, I scooted toward the tailgate.

After so many hours in the jouncing wagon, my feet had gone to sleep. My knees buckled the instant I hit the ground.

"Steady." Percy caught me. "Are you all right?"

Blood rushed to my toes in ripples of pain. "I will be," I said. "I have pins and needles." As my circulation returned, I began to take baby steps, then normal ones.

We worked our way to the back of the house, where Percy, to my astonishment, pulled a key from his pocket and opened the door. He must have been waiting for my reaction, because at my raised eyebrows his face lightened until he resembled nothing so much as a young boy caught in some prank.

"It belongs to me," he said. "I often stay here on my way to Paris. It's a safe place to keep supplies. Clothing, for example."

"This house? It belongs to you?" No wonder it looked different from everything around it. From what I'd seen, Percy took great care of his possessions. Of course, he could afford to.

He pushed the door open and stood back, ushering me in. In the small hallway that separated door from kitchen, I turned to face him. "But won't the French look for you here?"

Long fingers traced the line of my cheek. "They never have. Officially, my caretaker has confiscated it. He's a loyal revolutionary, on the surface. But my father plucked him out of the gutter forty years ago, gave him an education, set him up in business, and made it possible for him to marry. Jacques would do anything for my family. If we leave at first light, no one will know. There are so many confiscated estates around here that the central government can't keep track of every one."

It seemed risky, but I knew from the books that Percy had a reckless streak, however carefully he laid his plans. "It runs in the family then," I said out loud, "the need to help others. I hope Jacques doesn't betray your trust."

Percy shrugged. "He won't. You'll see for yourself when you meet him tomorrow. Come, Madam, upstairs with you. We need to find you some dry clothes."

His eyes widened. I had removed the sack and hung it on a peg. "Immediately," he added.

I looked down. The heavy linen had absorbed three hours' rain and now resembled nothing so much as a wet T-shirt, revealing my peasant-boy persona as a complete fiction. "Oops!"

I peeled the linen away from my skin, which didn't improve things a bit. At least Percy seemed to enjoy the sight.

The League would arrive any minute. With no time to waste, I darted up the stairs. Once safely at the top, I stared, astonished. Mellow wood doors opened to either side of a cream hallway. I explored each room in turn until I found one that could belong to Marguerite. She felt listless and faint, off in her own world.

I sensed no familiarity with the house. That puzzled me, especially after I found a dresser and a wardrobe, door ajar and full of women's clothes, in the room I had chosen. Dripping water on what looked like a priceless Oriental carpet, I surveyed the white paint and delicate brass moldings and wondered what I'd stepped into. Even the bed had lace-edged sheets and pillowcases, as though someone expected visitors at any moment. A pile of eighteenth-century linen—what I wouldn't give for a Turkish bath towel!—that reminded me of dishcloths stood next to a china basin near the window.

What was going on here? Where had the women's clothes come from, if Marguerite didn't know the house?

Baroness Orczy had never mentioned a mistress. Still, she was anything but forthright when it came to sex. Marguerite and Percy had been estranged for a year, and a mistress might explain his coldness when I first entered the simulation.

It sickened me. Did *every* man cheat? Memories of my father prickled like thistles in my mind. Sending silent sympathy to Marguerite, I stripped off the soaked outfit, dumped it in a heap near the fireplace, and ran a towel across my body with short, angry strokes. After wrapping a second towel about me from breast to thighs, I turned my attention to my hair. The red hat had absorbed much of the moisture, keeping the long curls from being drenched. I had braided and tied them when Percy entered the room.

Dusk was settling in. The skies slowly cleared, and sunset glowed red on the horizon. Percy stood, his hand resting on the doorjamb, his eyes fixed on my face. The sight of him— tall and strong and, without the artificial air he often wore, amazingly handsome—stopped me in my tracks. In my state of undress, I felt acutely vulnerable. I shot glances around the room, looking for a robe—anything to cover my nakedness.

The wardrobe contained a silk peignoir. I grabbed it, hoping that my concentration on the clothes would hide my confusion from Percy.

Percy, who had betrayed Marguerite in this enameled snuff box of a house. Or had he? I had to find out. I owed her that much. She was the one he loved, not me.

He held out a hand. I evaded it and pointed at the open wardrobe. "Whose clothes are those?" My voice quivered. Blame my father and the bimbos.

Percy's blue eyes widened. I had the impression I could see clear into their depths. "What, those? I bought them for you. Have you forgotten, Madam? We intended to spend our honeymoon here."

Hearing the edge in his voice, Marguerite winced. No need to ask what happened to that plan: her major screw-up with the

Marquis de St. Cyr had jettisoned any hopes for a honeymoon. No wonder she had no familiarity with the house.

My breath escaped in a rush. "Oh," I said. I'd created a chimera. "I thought…"

I never finished the sentence. "For Pete's sake!" Percy slammed his fist on the table. A vase teetered, and he caught it by the rim. Water sloshed, and an orange aster sailed through the air.

No, not Percy. That had to be Ian talking, because Percy would never use such an expression. And he wasn't done. "What do I have to do to convince you, woman? I'm not a bloody saint, but I think I can handle common decency, which does not—let me repeat, *not*—include shagging one woman while telling another I love her!" He marched out of the room, leaving me staring at the shut door.

Where did *that* come from? We'd never been lovers, not even friends. But he wouldn't talk to Marguerite that way, would he?

She didn't think so, either. «Go after him,» she said. «Apologize.»

Apologize? Why?

I remembered the kiss at the opera house, his assurances that he had my back, the look in his eyes in that room in Marles-les-Mines just before he'd declared his love—for Marguerite, I'd thought. Could I have read him wrong? It wouldn't be the first time I'd misjudged. As I mentioned before, romance has always remained something of a mystery to me.

But Ian Campbell, behind that façade of his, in love with Nina the Analytical? I *had* to be kidding myself. Didn't I?

Marguerite insisted otherwise. Called me a narrow-minded bookworm and a lot of rude things in French that boiled down to having my head in the clouds instead of focusing on what was in front of my nose (I didn't say she avoided clichés). After

untold minutes of abuse, I agreed she might have a point. Wrapping the peignoir more securely around me, I took a deep breath and went after Ian.

The door opened onto a dressing room, about the size of a walk-in closet. I found him sitting on a small camp bed, staring out the window, his chin propped on his hands. The room was otherwise empty except for a washstand with bowl, basin, and hand towel and one of those contraptions that holds a suit of men's clothes. The camp bed had no sheets, and the room was cold.

I sat behind him on the bed and put my arms around him. "I'm sorry," I said into his ear.

He reached back, scooping me onto his lap, and said softly, his Scots accent more pronounced than usual, "Can you not bring yourself to trust me?"

"It's new to me, trusting a man. Inside I'm terrified. And not knowing who I'm talking to half the time doesn't help." I explained, briefly, about my father's casual attitude toward commitment.

He kissed my nose. "I never guessed. And here I thought it was me you hated."

When I shook my head, he stood up and headed for the bedroom, still holding me. "Let's get you somewhere where you won't freeze."

"I'm not too heavy?"

He stopped in the doorway, his face alight with laughter. "You're joking. A wee thing like you?"

I subsided, embarrassed at how much I was enjoying the helpless maiden act, and he carried me to the bed, kicking the door shut behind him. He placed me on the mattress, then lay down beside me.

"There's more," I said, determined to come clean—or as clean as the computer permitted.

"Is there now?" he asked. "Go on." Picking my words carefully—the computer balked at "monkey bars," for example—I told him about the day my father left.

"And I blamed the whole thing on my sister," I finished. "Isn't that terrible? I was so jealous of her, growing up beautiful when everyone compared me to a sparrow. Until I came here, I didn't consider how life looked to her. I expect she suffered as much as I did."

I stopped, nervous, but it made no sense to hold back. If he was going to take offense, better he do it before I let whatever was between us go farther.

"You thought I hated you," I said. "But I was sure *you* hated me. Because you shut down every conversation. And you kept teasing me."

He produced Percy's rueful smile. "Ah, my abominable sense of humor. But really, love, didn't you notice that I was trying to get your attention?"

I felt stupid. When he explained it, it made perfect sense. "No, I can be unbelievably dense about stuff like that." My throat started to ache. "My dad made it so clear that I was not good enough, not pretty enough, for him. Why would you like me?"

He placed a finger under my chin and turned my head toward him. "Why would I like you? You're beautiful, desirable, smart. Why wouldn't I like you?"

I lifted one strand of Marguerite's hair. "Well, of course, I'm beautiful *now*."

"You're gorgeous always, love." He grinned. "Even in elf leggings." I smacked his shoulder, not hard. Why argue with his delusions? "And I swear, on my mother's grave—mind, the old dear's not dead yet, so she'll show up and scrag me if I lie—"

I giggled. I couldn't help it. A big man like that, worried about his mother?

"You can laugh," he said. "Fearsome she is, the pint-sized darling. But I digress. I swear that whatever happens, I will *not* go off and get involved with someone else unless you and I first agree that we're through. Got it?"

"Got it," I said, and pulled him toward me. As I sank into his kiss, I forgot my fears. Forgot everything, in fact, except the touch of his hands, his mouth. I'm sure you can guess where things went from there.

When we joined the League, I expected to intercept a few knowing looks, but Percy's men saved their ribbing for one another. In our absence they'd raided the larder. A fire blazed merrily in the hearth. Jars of preserves—meat, vegetables, fruit—covered the table, now completely surrounded by young men waving forks and trading stories like the kids in Harry Potter movies. Lord Tony handed each of us a plate and a glass, and we took over the settle near the fire. Only Andrew stood apart from the crowd, pacing from shuttered window to table and back, as if he could retrieve Suzanne by digging a path with his feet. Giddy over my brand-new connection with Ian, I felt a sharp pang of sympathy for him.

On the whole, though, I felt better than I had in days. Cozy and warm, I pressed my back against Percy's side, relishing the food in front of me and the lavender smell of clean clothes. I quashed the inner voice that worried about Suzanne, insisting we would find her trail tomorrow. Wrapped in a brown wool gown that I'd found in the wardrobe, my hair braided, and soft leather slippers on my feet, I snuggled into the arm tucked around my waist and picked at Lord Tony's offering.

A humming energy filled me. The cart ride, although painful and boring, hadn't required any exertion, and for the

last ten days I'd lived on an emotional roller-coaster. I felt tired and exhilarated at the same time. Even after I handed my plate to Percy, who deposited it somewhere on a shelf near the fireplace, and relaxed against his shoulder, I could not repress the odd urge to … do what? Jump up? Dance? Shout out my frustrations like a primal therapy client?

At the table the young men jostled, raising glasses and, as usual, trading jokes. In our corner, Percy and I sat wrapped in a cocoon of silence. I tipped my head back to see his face, and he pulled me onto his lap. "Yes, Madam?"

"I'm starting to understand you," I said—quietly, so the others wouldn't hear. He raised an eyebrow.

"You're a gambler at heart, Percy. You love this life—the danger, the challenge." My roving fingers caressed his shirt, not the rough cotton he'd worn as a farmer but his own fine linen.

"'Tis true," he admitted. "I enjoy the chase. Life at home seems tame in comparison to outwitting Chauvelin, don't you think?"

I did, and said so. Despite the stress and discomfort so prevalent in revolutionary France, I didn't look forward to the ease and familiarity of Cambridge. Life in the game was exciting, and my developing relationship with Ian kept the tension bubbling in ways that were both pleasurable and frustrating. The eighteenth century operated at a slower pace, with different standards—narrower than ours in some ways yet broader in others. No Internet or e-mail, no telephones, no airplanes or railway trains, no telegrams, radio, television, or movies. No mass transportation other than the stagecoach, which traveled at a rocketing five miles an hour. I understood, in ways I hadn't before, how Percy could roam around France largely undetected, despite having Chauvelin and most of the French army on his tail. By the time anyone could send a letter or ride for help, the Scarlet Pimpernel had moved on. And most people had no idea what he looked like. I was encountering the full range of life that would become my dissertation, that explained my grandmother and Marguerite, and I longed to experience every facet of it.

Some members of the League cleared the table while the others spread pallets on the floor. Hastings said, "Is there anything else we need to discuss tonight, Percy?"

The shoulder behind me shifted, as though Percy was shaking his head. "I'm for bed." Two fingers pinched my midsection. "Well, m'lady?"

I felt relaxed and comfortable there. Still, a night in a real bed had become an event not to be missed. I let Percy usher me up the stairs.

17. Douai

WE DID, INDEED, LEAVE AT DAYBREAK. WHEN I DESCENDED
the stairs in the brown dress, a hooded cloak over my arm and
memories of the night before adding a spring to my step, I
found Percy in riding clothes, sitting at the kitchen table and
talking with a man who turned out to be Jacques, the caretaker
and nominal owner of Percy's cottage. My fears that he would
turn us in disappeared the moment I saw him. About fifty
years old, he had a sturdy body and a warm, open expression.
Devotion glowed in his eyes. As I moved about, cutting bread
and meat for sandwiches, I could hear Percy urging Jacques to
protect himself first.

"Go to your daughter," he said. "The house will survive.
What will happen to you and your family if the republicans
find out we were here? It's useful for me to have a safe place
to stay, but the situation has deteriorated since we made our
arrangement. At any moment, England could declare war on
France."

But Jacques shook his head stubbornly, no matter how
often Percy repeated himself. "I'd have nothing without your
father—and you, milor'. The republicans don't suspect me,
and life itself is dangerous these days."

I placed a plate of sandwiches on the table between them. "Please, eat."

"No, Madame," Jacques said with a smile. "Thank you, but I will eat later. Go quickly, before the Jacobins come." He turned to Percy. "Do not fear, milor'. Next time you need me, I will be here."

"You could come with me." Percy crinkled his brow. "But we're heading into danger, not away. Perhaps on our return."

Jacques slapped the table. "Into danger, is it? And you with a beautiful wife to care for? Leave her with me! She will be safe with my Marie."

Percy's expression of concern vanished. He shot me a wicked glance.

Not more teasing!

But when he spoke to the caretaker, his voice was quite serious. "I left her safe in Richmond, Jacques, but I'd not landed in Calais before an agent of the Committee of Public Safety abducted her and brought her here. She stays with me." He touched Jacques's arm. "But you, my friend, will send for us if need be. Agreed?"

"Yes, yes." The caretaker began gathering plates. "If necessary, I will send for you. Be off now, and Godspeed."

At Percy's nod, I packed up the food, wrapped Marguerite's warm cloak around my shoulders, and said goodbye to Jacques.

By the time we reached the yard, Lord Tony was waiting, reins in hand. The horse carried a pillion, similar to the one on which I'd ridden from Marles-les-Mines but of better quality.

"We are bourgeois today," Percy said. "Shopkeepers from Lille, heading for Douai on business. Where, rumor has it, Chauvelin has stashed Armand." He mounted the horse with his usual grace, and Lord Tony lifted me onto the pillion. My arms closed around Percy's waist.

"Do we have a plan?" I asked. Facing the back of his neck made it difficult to converse, although not as difficult as riding in yesterday's wagon.

"We collect information," he said. "Then we can plan."

❁

The rest of the League met us in a copse not far from the Douai walls. "Chauvelin suspects you're nearby," Hastings said by way of greeting. "He's doubled the guard on the main gate. He's hunting for trouble."

"Any sign of Suzanne?" Percy asked. Hastings shook his head. I gritted my teeth. The more time passed without our finding her, the worse things looked for Suzanne.

"Chauvelin's not using her as bait, then," Percy replied. "Or not yet. And of course, he suspects we're nearby. He's holding on to Armand to lure us. We need to let him think he's succeeded."

I didn't like the sound of that.

Until Percy revealed the details. Then I hated every word.

"You plan to negotiate an exchange, then walk right up to him? In the middle of the town square? He'll haul you off in chains before you pass the gates!" Fury edged my voice. *You'd put your head in a noose? Sacrifice yourself right after I decide to trust you?*

His men echoed my objections. "Egad" and "Lud, Percy, have you lost your mind?" and "Sink me" filled an air swiftly turning blue with far less printable expressions.

Percy waited until we ran out of complaints before he deigned to explain. "True, my friends, but we are running out of time. Let Chauvelin reach Paris, and we have to work twice as hard. He wants to pick us off one by one. Only a concerted effort will stop him. We must rescue Armand—and Suzanne, if he has her."

"And when he's captured *you*?" I demanded. "What then?"

"Lud, my dear," he said, with his most irritating smile. "Your concern is touching, but I have no intention of letting him capture me."

A sound like a growl escaped me. My hands clamped to my hips like a washer woman's, but Percy treated me to the raised eyebrow and observed the group with the dispassionate gaze of a schoolmaster, while we tried to make sense of his contradictory statements.

Sir Andrew got it first. "A feint. You'll station men among the crowd and try to grab Armand before Chauvelin can grab you. I don't know, Percy; it's awfully risky. We'd need split-second timing and the devil's own luck to pull it off."

As soon as the words left his mouth, I realized not only that he was right, but that the plan appealed to Percy for exactly that reason. A gambler, I'd called him last night, and he hadn't contradicted me. He loved this dangerous game, pitting his wits against an opponent and winning against great odds. The more danger, the better he liked it, and what could top beating Chauvelin on his home ground?

«Marguerite!» I wailed. «Say something!»

She didn't respond. Panicked at the prospect of losing Percy as well as Armand, she dug herself into a hole inside my head and refused every urging to make herself visible. I'd have dragged her out bodily, but she had no body. And under the circumstances, I felt tempted to beg her to make room for me.

I forced my voice to steady long enough to ask, "Couldn't you lure Chauvelin outside the walls? Your chances would be better with an ambush in the woods."

"He'd leave Armand cooped up." Percy shook his head. "Suzanne, too."

Suzanne. Yes, Suzanne was the problem. Recapturing Armand would annoy Chauvelin, but it paled in importance next to freeing Suzanne (assuming Chauvelin held her). No fellow-student played Marguerite's beloved brother. No real harm would come to Armand, whether we rescued him or not. But if we wanted to resolve the prisoner's dilemma, we could not afford to abandon Suzanne.

Percy was still talking. "No, we must go to Douai, then take Chauvelin by surprise inside the town." He waved his hand at me, then at Andrew. "Only the three of us will enter the town as people he can identify. The others will be in disguise."

He tapped each man in turn, assigning him a task, before returning his attention to Andrew. "You, my friend, have the most difficult part. I rely on you to negotiate the exchange with Chauvelin. Let's hope he has enough sense to realize that he has nothing to gain from holding you as yet another hostage. And sound him out about Suzanne while you're there. His silence bothers me."

Andrew's look of grim determination intensified at the mention of Suzanne. "Me too. He made sure we knew he had Armand. Why has he said nothing about her? If he's laid so much as a fingernail on her…"

He let the sentence trail off, leaving Chauvelin's fate dire but unnamed. I rubbed my palm with my thumb as I sought words that would dissuade Percy from his current scheme. I felt convinced that other options existed, but not one presented itself to my troubled brain. Chauvelin held Armand—and possibly Suzanne. Nina at her most analytical could not imagine her enemy doing anything so flat-out dumb as wandering into an ambush in the woods with his hostages in tow.

Which left the flat-out dumb moves to Percy, whose present plan sounded more foolhardy than brave. For a while, I hoped the League would override him, but the members had sworn obedience to him, their chief. When he insisted, their objections died down.

Sick at heart, I turned to study the trees, biting my lip. Emotional fog swirled around me. Abandonment, I told myself—fear of being left by someone I care about. *No, by someone I love.*

Love? Where did that come from? I remembered last night, how special I'd felt, how cherished. But I didn't trust that feeling, not with loss looming over me. Teetering on the brink of disaster, for once I welcomed the fog.

The massive walls loomed over us as we rode through the Porte de Valenciennes into Douai. Water surrounded the town, so we had to cross into it by bridge, then pass through one of those huge stone medieval double gates to enter. At the moment, the gates stood open, although soldiers eyed everyone who came in: carts piled high with goods being carried to market, a few horses, peasants on foot. The crowd milled and pushed like ants clambering over sugar. Respectably clad in our bourgeois garb, we attracted no particular attention, but in my head, I could hear the gates clang shut at Chauvelin's command.

Percy looked back and said, "Courage, darling." My arms refused to release their death grip on his waist.

The horse clopped placidly down the Rue de Valenciennes. Neat gabled houses—inns? shops?—pressed in from either side. My heartbeat accelerated, and I took several deep breaths. Hyperventilating wouldn't help.

We dismounted at the edge of the square. At first, I could see nothing but people: hundreds of people pressing against stalls and hawking wares. We wended our way through the crowd, stopping from time to time to examine an object at one makeshift shop or another. Although I didn't identify any familiar faces, I felt a teensy bit comforted by the knowledge that the League members, in various combinations of disguises they had worn earlier in the week, blended in with the locals attending the market. A group in the corner broke out in song: "Ça Ira." Tony must love that. Then I saw an arm wave and recognized the pattern on the sleeve: he was leading the chorus.

As we reached the far end, the mob cleared, leaving a wide circle between itself and the uniformed men stationed there. Andrew's negotiations had succeeded. Armand was waiting, surrounded by a small group of soldiers, perhaps eight or ten. Chauvelin, dressed in his usual matte black, stood nearby, rubbing his weasel hands together. I tried to think of a good line of argument to use with him, but nothing came to mind. Even at the opera house, he'd resisted Marguerite's appeals. My hand on Percy's arm, we walked at an unhurried pace toward the troops.

A few feet from the soldiers, Percy stepped in front of me. Off to the right, I saw that Tony had abandoned his choir in favor of lounging in the vicinity. He was impersonating an artisan, with a loose shirt belted low on the waist and brown homespun trousers tucked into his boots. When I caught sight of him, he was alternating between studying his fingernails and gaping at a plump brunette leaning out of a window on the opposite side of the street. Chauvelin gave no evidence of having noticed him—nor he Chauvelin, for that matter.

The special representative had other things on his mind. Percy, to be specific, although he addressed his first remarks to me. "Well, well, Lady Blakeney. At last, you show some concern for your brother's safety. I had almost given up on that vaunted devotion of yours."

He had a nerve. Even Marguerite, catatonic from fear, mustered a flicker of indignation in response to Chauvelin's latest insults.

The muscles in Percy's back tensed, but he reached out and drew me forward. "Quite right, of course," he said smoothly. "Must be eager to see Armand, what?"

Eager didn't begin to describe what I felt. Marguerite might wail and weep, but I was every bit as scared. Still, that was a cue if I'd ever heard one, so I dragged my feet past the soldiers and greeted the brother Marguerite loved.

I had seen Armand only briefly, at the beginning of the simulation when he said goodbye to his sister and she confided how unhappy her marriage had become. The slender, dark-haired young man before me looked strained, already thinner, more careworn. Not wrinkled, of course—he was much too young for that—but definitely less innocent.

«Marguerite,» I said as fiercely as I could. «Come out of there and greet Armand!»

Her head cleared the edge of the hole.

«Now!» I said. «We're in bad enough shape as it is, without me making some ridiculous mistake. Please! I need you.»

She managed to pull herself together. I retreated as they hugged and kissed on both cheeks and spouted effusive versions of "How are you, my darling?" and hugged again until Chauvelin had had enough and ordered the soldiers to haul Armand away from his sister. The men complied with unnecessary gusto, although they didn't go far, stationing themselves about a foot behind Chauvelin. Marguerite again dropped from view, and I scuttled back to stand beside Percy, just outside the military presence.

"So." Chauvelin rubbed his weasel hands together once more and gloated. "Everything begins to go my way. First, the lovely Suzanne de Tournay falls into my hands."

A roar from the crowd interrupted him, and a scuffle broke out in one corner. I guessed that Andrew had overheard, and other members of the League were restraining him.

Chauvelin checked himself for a mere moment before continuing. "And today the great Scarlet Pimpernel delivers himself into my grasp. Robespierre will appoint me to the Committee of Public Safety without delay."

Oh, dear, he *would* say something like that. The corner of Percy's mouth twitched, and I knew he was about to let fly some outrageous remark. Chauvelin would lose his temper, and we'd fall even further into the soup—if that were possible.

Before I could decide whether to pinch Percy or step on his foot, he gave his most elaborate court bow and said, voice slightly muffled, "Your servant, Mon-soo-er Chambertin. Always happy to aid the murdering masses, what?"

I should have kicked him. Chauvelin went purple. He couldn't even talk, just dragged at the often-mocked cravat and gasped for air.

Percy straightened, pulling into himself the way a cougar does as it poises to spring. Amid the milling of the crowd—responding to the sounds of confrontation, I guessed, for they couldn't have understood a word of the conversation, conducted in English—eight familiar faces popped up, two of them directly behind Armand.

Chauvelin shrieked, "Seize him!" Percy whirled, picked me up, and threw me toward Lord Tony, who had grabbed the reins of the nearest horse from its astonished owner. Tony tossed me onto the pommel, sprang into the saddle, and sent the horse racing down the nearest side street. Behind us, I heard Chauvelin shout in French, "Leave them! *He's* the one I want." I twisted in Tony's hold, trying to peer over his shoulder and nearly managing to knock myself off the horse, but I could see nothing but a swarm of uniforms, Percy's blond head in the middle.

Not for an instant did I fear that I might fall. I thought only of Percy.

Three hours later, the nine remaining members of the League broke through a window in the confiscated Couvent des Clarisses and settled into an empty cell. Two left at once to discover what they could, and another pair stood guard, meaning in this case that they lolled around in the street outside and pretended they had no place to go.

Revolutionaries had stripped the convent of everything the Poor Clares had once owned, even the furniture. Andrew dispatched another pair of men to procure simple food and straw for bedding, although no one felt much like eating or sleeping.

You could have cut the atmosphere in the room, as they say, with a knife. We hadn't rescued Armand or Suzanne. Instead, we'd lost Percy. Just as I'd predicted.

I'd much rather have been wrong. Chauvelin's scheme to pick us off one by one was working—too well. Once I would have welcomed that development, but my original goal had changed. Ian had convinced me that the five of us should join forces. I couldn't turn my back on him. Whatever the others decided, I had to go after him.

I glanced at Sir Andrew, promoted overnight from chief lieutenant to man in charge. If you could call it that. Andrew looked like someone hit by lightning. Whenever my pacing brought me within range, I heard him muttering his beloved's name. His hands clenched and released, as if he were imagining throttling Chauvelin the way Percy had in the Calais inn.

That was the one small spot of calm in a roiling sea: Chauvelin *had* confirmed that he held Suzanne. He hadn't killed her. If we could find her, we could rescue her. He'd keep her in the same place as Armand, wouldn't he, or if not there, then with Percy? Even Chauvelin couldn't stash people in umpteen different locations, surely. He didn't have unlimited resources.

Meanwhile, muttering and fantasy throttling would not help us. What could we do? My skirts shushed round my feet as I paced back and forth, ignoring the three depressed young men who sat chin in hand or exchanged the occasional quiet word in corners. Too distraught for tears, I walked to the window and stared at the street, empty of everyone but the pair of League guards. The brisk October air, chilled further by the convent's stone walls, set me shivering despite Marguerite's cloak, which I clutched with both hands to keep the hysteria at bay. Marguerite herself hadn't emerged from her hole since the troops dragged her away from Armand. Instead, she emitted radiating waves of panic.

We had to get Percy back. But how? My mind felt as blank as a fresh sheet of paper. No, not blank. Hideous images of Percy bound in a tumbrel, of the guillotine and headless corpses, whirled inside my brain, crowding out every potential solution. In my anxiety, I lost my sense of playing a game. My surroundings, the threat, Percy's capture—everything felt real. Images of the night before haunted me. How safe I'd felt as he cradled me in his arms, how warm, how intimate our contact. Tears I refused to shed traced lines of sensation down my cheeks. My scattered thoughts resisted my efforts to corral them into a plan.

The mental paralysis, not only mine but among the League as a whole, lasted a long time. As I stood at the window, I listened to them trading ideas. *Storm the prison.* Nine young men against a troop of soldiers? *Disguise themselves as jailers and arrange for Percy's escape.* Good plan, but difficult to manage on short notice. Chauvelin had to observe some kind of judicial process, but he would dispose of his enemy as fast as he could. *Hang around until the big moment and rush in to release their leader from the tumbrel.* Andrew vetoed that one too risky, although he agreed to keep it in mind as a last resort.

Their discussion, however unproductive, galvanized me into action. My thoughts coalesced, rendering my fear manageable.

Could we bribe Chauvelin? Not with cash, for sure. Our local villain was ambitious and fanatical but not venal. He would refuse a ransom.

With honors, then? He seemed to care about his appointment to the Committee of Public Safety. I imagined writing a letter that would summon him to Paris on notice so short he would have no time to arrange a suitable escort for his dangerous prisoner, the Scarlet Pimpernel.

It might work. And if it did, what then? A germ of an idea took root in my brain. It had potential, despite some inherent weaknesses. We just had to get the French agent out of the way.

18. Palais de Justice

ANDREW DASHED OFF A LETTER APPRISING CHAUVELIN OF his imminent receipt of an unnamed but prestigious award from the Committee of Public Safety, collectible only in Paris. After filling it with enough bureaucratic flourishes in French to evoke a sigh of amazed appreciation from Marguerite, he dispatched Lord Hastings to deliver the missive. The rest of us then sat around for hours trying not to chew our fingernails to stubs until Hastings—imitating, of all things, a baker—slipped through the window not long after nightfall with a basket of bread and the news we longed to hear. We clustered round him, pelting him with questions.

"Faith, Chauvelin swallowed the bait," he reported. "Hook, line, and sinker. He left this evening—without Percy. We have a day, at most, to spring him from jail before Chauvelin learns the truth and comes haring back here with murder on his mind. For the moment, the locals have stuck Percy in the Palais de Justice."

"The Palais de Justice?" Andrew asked. "I thought that was the parliament building."

"Used to be a prison, though," Hastings said. "The cells may not have the latest improvements, but they'll hold Percy fast until we can release him."

"Who's in charge?" The wool of Marguerite's cloak felt rough in my hands. My scheme depended on Hastings's answer to that question.

"The mayor, I'm told. We may have some leeway there. The shopkeepers in the market say he can be bribed. Likes fine wines and good food, local girls—you know the type." He cast a guilty glance my way, as though he'd just recalled that the League had an additional member at present, and a woman at that.

From my perspective, though, that last sentence contained the very information I'd sought. The hazy outlines of my plan solidified. There was only one problem. To have a hope of making it work, I needed Marguerite.

"You're sure Chauvelin's gone?" I asked. "He's not faking, hoping to lure another of us?"

A reasonable question, but Hastings insisted he'd seen Chauvelin leave. I considered our options, then decided to concentrate on saving Percy. No point in trying to predict the workings of Chauvelin's twisty brain.

I revealed my scheme. A chorus of groans greeted me, although the plan wasn't nearly as risky as Percy's—or their various suggestions.

"We might pull it off," I said.

"And if not?" Andrew asked. "Then we lose you, too."

In which case, Andrew and Tony would win. I hesitated, then decided I could live with that, so long as I went out with a bang. Ian would owe me one if I lost the game for his sake. "Give me something better, then. We don't have much time. We have to free Percy before Chauvelin comes back."

They wasted another hour in arguing, but not one of them could come up with a workable alternative. "We can try those others if this one fails," I said. Having committed myself, I was impatient to get started. The longer I waited, the shakier my nerves became. And given the costs of failure, frankly I wished one of them *did* have a better idea, but I could see they didn't.

At last, they capitulated. "What do you need?" Andrew sounded like a man sentenced to have a dozen teeth pulled at once.

I leaned forward. "Andrew, do you still have the ring I brought from Richmond?"

Securing Marguerite's cooperation took a lot longer. I lost half an evening figuring out exactly the right combination of bullying, coaxing, pleading, and praising. Even then, she nearly backtracked in horror when she saw what I had in mind.

«It's for *Percy*,» I said for the umpteenth time. «No one else can do this. If we fail, Chauvelin will kill him!»

Her mental voice sounded weary. «You're so competent. You do it.»

«No. I need you. You're better at feminine than I am. I'll speak the lines, but you have to handle the mannerisms. Come on! You're an actress, the best in Paris. And you belong to this world. I don't.»

By the time she agreed, I was ready to tear my hair out. Finally, sometime after midnight, according to the town clock, she gave in.

«Thank you,» I said, with heartfelt sincerity. «Believe me, Percy will thank you too.»

There, I thought with satisfaction, she'd needed a definite task. For the first time since we'd left the inn at Marles-les-Mines, she felt fully alive.

With Marguerite on my side, my spirits rose. I recalled once more that this was a game, not reality, and I might as well play my role to the hilt. The next step involved the acquisition of

a low-cut silk gown, which Lord Hastings gallantly undertook
to secure from one of the "hostelries" that edged the market
square where we had lost Percy.

The next morning, he returned and, with the air of a
magician conjuring coins from the air, produced a pale yellow
confection in the *Directoire* style with an inch of lace around
the neck. Since it had been made for someone else, it required
a little strategic padding. A mirror would have helped, but the
expressions on the faces of my co-conspirators when I rejoined
the group reassured me that I'd achieved the effect I sought.

"Good God, Andrew," Tony said. "You can't let her go out
looking like that. Percy will pin our ears to the wall!"

Andrew dropped his head in his hands and didn't reply. His
shoulders shook. I couldn't tell if he was laughing or crying.

After more than a week on the road, I'd come to regard
them both as the brothers I'd never had, so I saw no need to
mince words with Tony. "Percy will do nothing of the sort.
Slay you with politeness, maybe."

"Cut out my liver, maybe," Tony muttered. "At least put
on that fichu."

"Nonsense," I said. "It would wreck the whole scheme."

Andrew's voice sounded choked. "I think that's the idea."

I swirled Marguerite's cloak around my shoulders. "Look,
no one will see a thing till I get to the mayor's office."

"Well, that's an improvement, I suppose," Tony said.
"Maybe you'll make it halfway to the square before someone
decides to molest you. Just don't tell Percy I knew anything
about it."

"Oh, don't be so chickenhearted." I swept out the door.
"We have to get him back before he can cut out anyone's liver.
And if he does, he will probably start with mine."

"Amen to that." Already deep in his role as a lackey,
Andrew slouched into the corridor in my wake.

«This dress *is* quite improper,» Marguerite said as we reached the street. «They were thinking of you, like true gentlemen.»

«Pipe down,» I told her. «I'm scared out of my mind, and I don't want any trouble from you. Get ready to play your part. If it kills us, we're going to pull this off. Because it's certainly going to kill us if we don't.»

Despite my fear, it felt good to take action. By the time I reached the Palais de Justice, Marguerite and I had pushed everything else aside to concentrate on our self-imposed mission, pretending to be Chauvelin's cousin. It took some time to argue and plead our way past the guard at the entrance, but eventually we found ourselves in the office of a florid-complexioned, middle-aged man of bon vivant girth.

Excellent. The mayor wore a tricolor scarf and a black jacket, but his lace collar and cuffs, fine shirt, and ample striped pants would have put Chauvelin to shame. I refused his offer to relieve me of my cloak, flipping the sides back over my shoulders Zorro-style to give him a full view of the confection, and prepared for the role of my life. Andrew stood in a corner, scowling, especially after the confection made its appearance.

The mayor ushered me to a chair. "How may I serve you, Mademoiselle Chauvelin?"

I sat, settled my skirts into place, clasped my hands, and began. With Marguerite's help, I had dressed her hair in tiny curls, threaded through with ribbon to match the gown, and hoped I looked girlish and harmless. "You see, Monsieur, I find myself in a most difficult situation. I do not even know where to start. A man of discretion…" I let the words trail off and blushed into my fan. Fortunately, now that we were, so to speak, on stage, Marguerite had recalled that she loved playing a part. As for me, I was relishing my moment of glory. For the first time, I appreciated the appeal of the gamble, the thrill of a challenge that kept Percy laughing at fate.

"I assure you, Mademoiselle, nothing you say to me will ever leave this place." He patted my hand, and Andrew let out a small snarl. I glared at him over my shoulder.

"It is a family matter, you see." I allowed myself to be persuaded to accept a glass of red wine, took a single sip, and set it on the end table at my side. "My cousin—Monsieur Chauvelin, I mean—oh, really, I cannot talk about it! The shame! The embarrassment! But if I do not tell you, the poor Englishman! Oh, I don't know what to do!"

Anyone well acquainted with me—up to and including Percy—would have given the whole show away at that point by rolling in the aisles and hooting. Andrew, bless him, possessed real self-control. Or perhaps he thought I'd finally come to my senses and started acting like a proper female.

The mayor leaned in again, and I decided I'd better get specific, and fast. My hands fluttered a good deal, for verisimilitude, but mostly to keep him at bay.

I took a deep breath, and his eyes goggled. Marguerite, as I've mentioned, was quite well endowed, and the low-cut gown didn't meet the normal standards for morning wear.

«I told you it was improper,» she said.

«Oh, hush,» I told her. «It's working, isn't it?»

While Marguerite grumbled in the background, I smiled demurely at the mayor. "We fear for his sanity, Monsieur. The last few months, he has obsessed over this Englishman whom they call the Scarlet Pimpernel. Everywhere he goes, he sees the Englishman. My family and I spend almost all our time now following my poor cousin around, trying to save him from himself. I cannot tell you how many he has arrested! And each time, he insists that this one is indeed the Scarlet Pimpernel. Did he not do that here?" I made my eyes big, like Little Red Riding Hood confronting the scary wolf, and leaned forward to give him a better view. Andrew managed not to growl this time.

The mayor tapped his finger against his glass. "He did indeed, Mademoiselle. And you are right, Monsieur Chauvelin does appear unusually concerned about this case, even for the chief agent of the Committee of Public Safety. He seems to detest this Englishman, who does not, to be frank, look dangerous to me. Why, when I merely asked your cousin how he knew he had the right man, he snapped at me and would give no answer. And then he runs off to Paris and leaves the English lord in my care!"

"It is his madness." I made my voice sad. "He sees the Scarlet Pimpernel everywhere. Six times this month, he has arrested some unfortunate Englishman and tried to send him to the guillotine. It is not, you understand, that I have such sympathy for the English, Monsieur."

The mayor looked shocked. "Of course not, Mademoiselle. I would never suspect a lovely girl like you of harboring traitorous sentiments."

"You are kind." I gave a deep sigh. "So I comprehend that the English have not yet reconciled themselves to the existence of the republic and must be regarded with suspicion. But most of those whom my cousin arrests are high-ranking. And although I feel certain that the government can and should eliminate the enemies of France, to arrest powerful men from another country with which we are not yet at war, well, it does seem rather reckless, don't you agree, Monsieur?"

Prompted by Marguerite, I sighed again. The mayor agreed, absently, without lifting his eyes from my bodice. I developed a new appreciation for the advantages of being the most beautiful woman in Europe. The story I was spinning had more holes than a block of Swiss cheese, but some girlish hand wringing and a few well-placed deep cleansing breaths had this seasoned politician eating out of my hand.

"I have even heard of cases," I ventured, "where the real Scarlet Pimpernel has communicated with the authorities *after* Cousin Chauvelin has incarcerated one of these unfortunates, and still my cousin will not believe that he has the wrong man."

The mayor jerked as if I'd pricked him with my brooch. "Indeed, I received such a communiqué this very morning."

So he had. Andrew had written it himself and signed it with Percy's ring. "You see," I said, leaning forward again, "it is my cousin's obsession at work, as before. Surely, Monsieur, you do not wish to send an innocent man to his death! Can you not bring yourself to free the Englishman?"

He sipped wine, twirling the glass between his fingers. "I don't see how I can, Mademoiselle. Your cousin, however deluded, has considerable authority within the government. Your sentiments do you credit as a tenderhearted young lady, but really, the life of one Englishman…" He didn't add, "as compared to my own," but the implication was obvious.

"But of course, you must say nothing." I reached out and clasped his hand, which had strayed perilously close to the lace frill. "Cousin Chauvelin would be furious! He thinks we meddle, and naturally he is right, but we do it only because we love him, to save him from the consequences of his own folly. What will Robespierre say if my cousin keeps arresting different Englishmen and every time claiming he has caught the Scarlet Pimpernel?"

I stood, dropping his hand and backing away from him. "My cousin left Douai yesterday, the guards told me. By now, he will already be on the track of another Englishman. If you say nothing but merely release the one you have here, we will take him to the border and make sure he troubles you no more."

"And if the troops return for him?" The mayor had, like a good gentleman, risen when I did and now circled the desk. Andrew didn't exactly make a threatening move—a lackey wouldn't—but he did manage to block the mayor's way. We had reached the crisis point.

"They will not. But if they do, why, you need only tell them that you sent him on to Paris, as ordered by Citizen Chauvelin himself," I said. "Surely no one will blame you if he does not arrive. And if you show them the note that the Pimpernel sent you, will they not realize that my cousin has made another mistake, and this was not the right man after all?" I prayed that Percy had stayed in fop mode during his arrest. "I saw this one in the marketplace. As you said yourself, he does not much resemble a hero."

This time, my clasped hands gave me some much-needed control. I'd finished my tale, and at that moment the whole story sounded so ridiculous I doubted it would convince a child of three. But I had underestimated the power of male chauvinism. After what seemed like ages, the mayor shouted, "Corot! Get in here!"

A short man in uniform presented himself at the door.

"Fetch the Englishman," the mayor ordered. "Bring him at once."

While we waited for Percy, I dodged around the office, coached by Marguerite, alternately luring and eluding the mayor. In truth, I felt quite ashamed of the exhibition I was putting on, but if the eighteenth century chose to impose so many limitations on its women, I saw no reason why I shouldn't benefit from the few advantages. It wasn't as though running into the Palais de Justice waving a gun would have done either Percy or myself any good.

Tromping feet and an ominous clanking soon signaled the soldiers' return. Two men pushed Percy through the door and came in to stand on either side of him. He had manacles on his hands and feet, and his clothes were torn and dirty. A bruise marked the side of his face. He moved stiffly, and blood stained his shirt. When he saw me in the confection, though, his eyes widened in startled admiration.

At the sight of his wounds, I almost lost my composure. But as I reached out my arms, the mayor stepped in front of me and I remembered that Percy was supposed to be a stranger. Somewhere a horrified segment of my mind wondered if Ian felt the pain of those injuries. What kind of game was this?

"Undo the chains," the mayor ordered. "I have received new information. This man is not the Scarlet Pimpernel."

Ducking around Andrew, I darted toward the mayor, clapping my hands, and kissed him on both cheeks. I thought he would faint from joy. Percy looked like he might faint from shock. Marguerite applauded.

"Oh, Monsieur," I told the mayor, "every angel in heaven will bless you! You have done a good deed this day!" I skipped toward the window and exuded delight.

"It has been my pleasure to serve you, *chérie*." The mayor turned to Percy. "This young lady is Mademoiselle Chauvelin, cousin to the gentleman who arrested you."

Percy treated me to his royal-garden-party bow, and I curtseyed, silk skirts arrayed with grace and eyes lowered. I bit my lip when he stopped in mid-bend, winced, and straightened.

"It appears—" the mayor said.

I interrupted him. "Oh, Monsieur, you promised you would say nothing. I count on your discretion."

The mayor produced a bow of his own, neither as elegant nor as tortured as Percy's. "And I will not, Mademoiselle. I sought only to explain to this gentleman why we are releasing him."

Again he focused on Percy. "As I started to say, Monsieur Chauvelin acted too soon. We have received evidence that the Scarlet Pimpernel remains at large. If you will consent to accompany Mademoiselle Chauvelin, she has promised to see you to the border, which as you perhaps know lies quite close to this region."

Percy, begrimed and battered as he was, had not lost a shred of his aplomb. "I would be honored to accompany Mademoiselle Chauvelin wherever she cares to go," he said, his eyes on the ridiculous neckline. He half-bowed once more, exchanging glances with Andrew, then gestured at the door, as though ushering me out of a London salon.

"You will need this," the mayor said, handing me a slip of paper. It was our pass out of the city.

"A thousand, thousand thanks, Monsieur." I settled my cloak into place, suffered another round of cheek kissing, and left, the slip of paper clutched in my fist. Percy and Andrew followed.

«We did it!» I said to Marguerite. «Thank you, thank you, thank you!» A warm orange glow told me she had heard.

Percy said not a word until we passed into the street from the Palais de Justice. Nor after that, for as I saw him open his mouth, I said urgently in French, "Not here. Let's leave the city while we can."

The words spurted out before I stopped to think, and for a moment I worried that I had offended him. A person so experienced in evading pursuit must have survival instincts better than mine.

Although he didn't *look* offended. He didn't respond, in fact. Instead, he nodded and strode down the street, Andrew muttering directions from behind.

With the immediate danger past and our escape no longer dependent on me, irrational thoughts swooped like bats through my head. I had to assume that Ian, a modern man, could cope with owing his rescue to a woman. But Percy's pride might not allow him to accept what I'd done. I couldn't rule out the possibility that his chivalry hid prejudices to equal the mayor's. And even modern men can go off on a girl when she's not expecting it. I studied his back and his purposeful stride, but they provided no clues to his state of mind. As we walked, my marshmallow cloud of relief and happiness dissolved into dark webs of despair. Marguerite felt betrayed, because I'd talked her into helping me.

«I'm sorry,» I said. «If he's angry, blame me.»

«Don't be silly,» she said. The dark webs untangled. «You got him out. None of the others came up with a plan.» She paused before adding, «We did it together.»

That was sweet. «So we're friends?» I asked.

«Friends,» she said. The image of her beautiful smile lingered in my mind.

When we reached the Couvent des Clarisses, Percy pulled me into a recessed archway and took my face in both hands. Shocked out of my gloom, I stared at him. I'd been expecting chill courtesy or anger, not the aching tenderness I saw in his eyes. "Ah, sweetheart." His thumbs rubbed my cheeks. "Can you ever forgive me?"

"For what? Getting captured?" I said, confused.

"For thinking you wouldn't care." I heard hurt in the husky voice, as I had an eternity past, in the rose garden. "Or that if you did, you'd wring your hands and do nothing."

"Well, I did wring my hands a good bit," I said, to lighten the mood. "I had no other way to keep the mayor on his own side of the desk."

That made him laugh, as I'd intended. "You're a treasure, darling," he said.

By then, Andrew had gone into the convent. Percy took me into his arms and kissed me with satisfying comprehensiveness. If he also disarranged the confection in ways the mayor could only dream of, well, he had the right. He was my husband.

Less than an hour later, again clad in our bourgeois outfits, we hired a simple open carriage and drove out of Douai. No one stopped us, for the pass we carried bore the signature of the mayor himself.

19. Arras

FOR A WHILE WE DROVE IN SILENCE, GLAD TO WATCH DOUAI recede into the distance. Marguerite purred in the back of my mind, emitting a pale-yellow aura, like the sunrise. I reveled in her happiness, her pride. Working together, we had achieved something neither of us could have managed alone. Curled up at Percy's side, I closed my eyes, letting awareness of him wash over me. His arm tugged me closer, and his lips brushed my hair. Time slipped away.

I make no excuses. I heard Percy demand the full story from Andrew. I heard the tale grow in the telling, as the best tales tend to do. And with my knowledge of the eighteenth century, I should have anticipated Percy's reaction. *Had* anticipated it, in fact, when we first left the Palais de Justice, only to have him surprise me.

Because I kept fusing him with Ian—about whom I still had much to learn. And that backfired on me this time. Lost in my euphoric daze, I got my first inkling of trouble when Percy jerked his arm from around my waist. I straightened to find myself facing the supercilious stare that had greeted my confession in the rose garden. Later I realized he'd been directing the stare at Andrew, but in the heat of the moment I missed that part.

"So," he drawled, "nine men in the League, and they allow my *wife* to risk her life to help me escape. Not one of you could put himself in harm's way?"

Andrew twitched in his seat. I ignored him—and Percy's implication that his men had lacked the courage to rally round him. The sorrow and fear I'd suppressed earlier exploded in a blaze of fury. Oblivious to my pleas, Percy had walked into a trap that almost led to his death, and here he had the nerve to act as if what I'd done for him didn't matter, for no other reason than because *I* had done it?

"Why, you ungrateful…" I spluttered, struggling to finish a sentence. "How dare you? When I tried to save your sorry… Chauvelin nearly had your head on the block!"

Percy narrowed his eyes. "Yours, too."

To keep my hands away from his neck, I pressed both palms against his chest. "You should have thought of that, shouldn't you, before strolling into his trap?"

Marguerite had ducked into some hidden corner of my brain; and Andrew, probably fantasizing means of escape, focused on the passing fields.

Percy didn't hesitate. "I didn't expect my *wife* to engineer my rescue. Who asked you to risk your life for me? To spout such a farrago of nonsense? And that absurd yellow dress!" He plucked the skirts of my brown wool robe for emphasis.

I ripped my hands from his chest and scooted to the far side of the coach. "Don't you dare give me grief about the dress. Do you think I liked having that horrid man ogle me? Just to save your ungrateful behind? But the ploy worked. He couldn't take his eyes off the neckline. He didn't notice the holes in the story because he didn't bother to think."

Percy's mouth twitched. "Very clever. But he'd have had no chance to ogle you, would he, had you not thrown yourself in the lion's den."

That's when I lost it completely. "*Thrown* myself? Lion's den? What, exactly, did you expect me to do, Percy? After my own lion made a wild dash into the forest and fell into a pit, it seemed like a good idea not to leave him there! And if my lion cared a jot about me, he would think twice before he did such idiotic things."

I turned my back on him and put my hands over my face. Yesterday I had wanted to cry and couldn't, so naturally, when I would have given anything to match Percy's composure, tears came on like thunderstorms in July. And why could I never find Marguerite's handkerchief when I needed it? Rummaging through the pockets of her cloak turned up nothing.

With one arm, Percy drew me against his shoulder. With the other, he offered me a square of linen. "My dear girl," he said. "I don't want you putting yourself in danger—especially not to save my hide. When I realized the risk you'd run, my heart dropped into my boots. It's one thing for Andrew or Tony to take chances with their lives—they swore an oath when they joined the League—but I want only to keep you safe." His attention switched to his best friend, still studying the landscape. "And what *they* thought they were doing, letting you take the brunt of it, I can't imagine."

Andrew didn't retaliate, just hunched further into his corner. The tips of his ears looked rather red, poor man.

"He's being gentlemanly and accepting responsibility." I took a deep breath so I could speak without sobbing. "They tried to talk me out of it, and when they couldn't, Andrew helped by playing my servant. The mayor would have given me a lot more trouble if I'd gone alone. You know Tony would have insisted on accompanying me if Andrew hadn't volunteered. It's not fair to blame them. We picked the scheme that had the best chance of succeeding. If it had failed, they'd have come up with something else."

"No, Percy's right." Andrew stopped observing the greenery and looked at his chief. "We shouldn't have involved you. Tony and I knew that from the start. But you came up with the best plan."

Wearily, I rested my head against Percy's shoulder. "You're missing the point, both of you. We agreed to fight together, right? Me, you, the kitchen cat—Chauvelin will kill the lot of us if he can. It doesn't matter who takes the risk so long as we live to fight another day. And we did. Game's not over. We have another chance to rescue Suzanne and Armand."

Andrew swallowed. I saw his Adam's apple jump. "Suzanne?"

Percy's chin brushed the top of my head. "Not a word. Wherever he's keeping her, he hasn't confided in the guards at the Palais de Justice. But I saw no women in the jails."

"Damn," Andrew said with feeling, then went back to staring out of the window.

"Yes," Percy said. "I am grateful, you know. Thanks, old chap."

When Andrew nodded, Percy turned to me, his voice silken. "As for your lion caring about you, my love…" He left the sentence unfinished, kissing me with a passion that even for him represented something entirely new.

Later that afternoon, we met up with the League in an abandoned château. Not Percy's. This house hadn't fared as well as the woodland cottage. No fancy carpets, no delicate furniture. No furniture, if it came to that.

The younger members of the League seemed giddy with relief, lying around on parquet floors drinking wine and cracking jokes. Tony and Andrew stood off in a corner with Percy, faces set.

After a while, I left the room. The three of them didn't need me to settle their problems.

Whoever stripped the château had taken the clocks, but I guessed that about twenty minutes passed before Percy tracked me down in a salon.

"You should give it a rest. Andrew and Tony did you no harm," I said.

His eyes gleamed. "Now, Margot."

"Don't you 'Now, Margot,' me." I put my hands on my hips and glared at him. "They saved your life."

He caught my right wrist, pulled it toward him, and kissed my fingertips. "They did indeed. And so did you. Dear Margot, I love you. Forgive me."

Oh, there it was again, that melting sensation. "You never call me Margot," I said, as if that had some significance.

"I used to." His thumb pressed into my palm. "Before we were married. Don't you recall?"

Marguerite's memories increasingly blended into my own. The answer to Percy's question seemed to be yes. My eyes met his. "So what are you trying to tell me?"

My mouth felt dry. He had forgiven her. He would say so, and then...

But as Percy took a step forward, I saw his teeth close on his lip and realized that in the hubbub no one had looked at his wounds, let alone treated them. My petty grievances vanished, and I tugged at his hand. "Show me what they did to you. At the least, we should clean and bandage your injuries."

"Ah, sweetheart." He caressed my cheek. "How would I manage without you?"

Back in the kitchen, surrounded by League members who for once were not acting like schoolboys, I stripped off Percy's shirt and inspected the damage.

"Ouch. They didn't hold back, did they? We're lucky they didn't break anything." The fingers I brushed over black-and-blue ribs made him wince. "Or did they?"

"I don't think so." Percy formed each word with care. "I doubt Chauvelin expected me to talk. This was more in the nature of punishment, I fancy, but he wanted me standing for his moment of glory, so he did rein his minions in from time to time."

"Small mercies, then. I wish he'd reined them in a lot sooner." Andrew passed me a bowl of warmed water and a soft cloth, and I washed the cuts. Although I dabbed as gently as I could, the sweat had broken out on Percy's brow before I finished.

"Give him some brandy," Lord Tony suggested, and Hastings passed Percy a glass.

"Where did you get that?" I asked. "But don't give it to him. It won't do him any good."

That amused them no end. Even Percy recovered enough to smile.

"For the pain," Tony said.

I shrugged and let it go. Eighteenth-century medicine prescribed many worse potions than brandy, and this might not be real cognac anyway.

Although I had to admit, those cuts and bruises looked both real and painful. Poor Percy!

A good night's sleep combined with Percy's formidable constitution had worked a near-miracle by morning. He winced when he moved, but the bruises had already shifted toward the mottled green end of the color spectrum, and the cuts had started to close. I felt I could relax for a bit—until Chauvelin surfaced again.

Marguerite had faded once more—waiting for her next task, I supposed. I'd have to think of something soon, but our journey didn't make it easy. The woods of northeastern France provided few opportunities for a society lady, even one with a republican past.

At breakfast I discovered the real reason behind Percy's tense discussions with Andrew and Tony: sending men out to scout the area.

"We need to discover where Chauvelin sent Armand after he captured me," he told the League, gathered in a circle on the floor around a cloak doing double duty as a table. Coarse bread and ale—not my idea of breakfast, but I ate what I could. Wispy memories of mango smoothies and pancakes hovered at the edges of my awareness until I banished them.

"I saw nothing of him in the prison at Douai," Percy went on, "and it had only a few cells, so I don't think he could be there. No sign of Suzanne, either."

"Odd," Hastings said. "Chauvelin left for Paris within the hour in response to the summons we sent, purporting to come from the Committee of Public Safety. I saw him leave. He didn't take any prisoners with him."

"Did Chauvelin's whole troop accompany him?" Percy asked.

Hastings shook his head. "Three men only," he said. "And the four of them rode out of Douai under their own power. Whenever we've seen Armand, they've had him surrounded. Only sensible thing to do. Armand's a Frenchman. The minute they lose track of him, he's gone. He could blend into the nearest town and disappear. Suzanne, too."

"Then we must assume the remaining soldiers took them both," Percy said. "The question is where. And we'd better find them soon. Two failed attempts already. One more, and the Scarlet Pimpernel's reputation will suffer, what?"

By ten in the morning the League had completed another round of inquiries. Chauvelin's troops had moved Armand to Arras, another walled town of ancient lineage not far from Douai. Still no trace of Suzanne, but we hoped for the best.

"Arras?" Percy said. "What's in Arras?"

The question sounded rhetorical to me, but Andrew answered it. "Tapestries, once upon a time. Robespierre, before he went to Paris to sit on the Estates-General. Trade."

A strand of blond hair escaped its black ribbon. Percy brushed it back impatiently. "Yes, yes, my dear fellow, but why would Chauvelin take Armand there? Why not go on to Paris?"

"Perhaps he wants to avoid Paris for the moment," I said. The men responded to my interruption with amazement. I seldom contributed to their discussions.

The more I considered it, though, the more sense it made. As they sat there, perplexed, I tried to explain, working it out as I went along. "Think about it. Chauvelin had a reason to take *Percy* to Paris: to execute him in a way that no one could miss … oh, Percy!"

I'd almost lost him. A few hours' delay, one mistake in the mayor's office, one circumstance I couldn't control—and no more Percy.

I couldn't stop shaking even when Percy wrapped his arms around me. The world tumbled in until I couldn't see or feel, although I heard Percy talking. Marguerite reached out a tentative hand, but she sought as much comfort as she offered. I clung to her.

"Courage, my darling," he murmured. I flinched. He'd used almost the same phrase on the street in Douai.

"No, no, she's fine," he told the League. The words I hadn't heard must have been them expressing concern. "She's realizing what a close call she had. She was so brave when it was happening. Not surprising that she'd give way now that she sees how much danger she was in."

"Not me." How could a smart man miss such an essential point? "*You*."

His lips brushed my hair, a touch feather-light, precious. The maelstrom of voices retreated. I buried my face in Percy's warmth.

"Give me your handkerchief, Tony, there's a good chap." Soft linen touched my cheek. "Don't cry, sweetheart," Percy said. "I'm right here. Thanks to you."

The trembling slowed, then stopped, but I stayed within his arms and let the League talk over my head. Percy picked up where I'd left off. "Margot may be right," he said. "If Chauvelin takes Armand and Suzanne to Paris, he loses control of the situation. Robespierre and the tribunal take over, and there goes Chauvelin's sole means of getting what he wants from us. He has no chance of recapturing Margot, and now he's let me slip from his grasp." Still pressed against his shoulder, I felt him relax against the wall. "Ergo, if Chauvelin needs to stay out of Paris and has stationed Armand in Arras to await developments, we have, for a change, the luxury of time."

"Not a lot of time," Tony said. "Chauvelin hasn't shown much patience so far."

"True," Percy said, "but we need only a day or two."

"You have a plan," I said, recognizing that tone. I pulled back to get a better look at him, only to wish I hadn't. The disturbing light was back in his heavy-lidded eyes. I was beginning to recognize it as anticipation of a challenge to come. "It had better not involve you sacrificing yourself this time."

The gleam intensified. "Not at all, m'dear. Any more appearances of you in that yellow dress, and the mayors of northern France will be falling over themselves trying to arrest me, what? My life won't be worth living."

He was incorrigible. Amid howls from the League, I hissed in his ear, "I'll make sure it's not worth living anyway, if you don't behave." Which merely sent him into further paroxysms, the wretch.

Percy sent Hastings and Bathurst, dressed as artisans once more, to investigate the situation in Arras. At my request, they returned with a set of men's clothes. Percy needed it. My brown wool gown could stand multiple rewearings, but his suit bore the stains of Chauvelin's mistreatment. I couldn't stand to look at it.

It took us several days to reach Arras by a circuitous route that included more barns and hedgerows than I ever want to see again. Andrew and Tony had gone on ahead, with Lord Hastings to carry messages from the city. Hastings also unearthed—he didn't say how—an innkeeper who pretended to serve the republic but harbored royalist sympathies. For a suitable reward, the innkeeper would host a merchant and his wife and agree not to notice any unusual changes of costume. Percy and I, still in disguise, slipped into Arras ten minutes before the gates closed for the night. There Andrew, dressed as a coachman, met us and led us to the inn where he, Percy, and I would prepare for our third attempt to rescue Armand. And Suzanne, if we could find her.

The innkeeper provided us with a nice private room on the second floor. Chauvelin's troops, if they came, could search one room as well as another, so there was little point in our hiding in an attic. We had to hope that in a pinch, our disguises would buy us enough time to get away. The location of the room helped: it opened onto a small ironwork balcony with tubs of pink geraniums at either corner. If necessary, Percy could drop into the side street below. I might even let him drop me, if the alternative was facing Chauvelin's troops. My fear of heights had been fading ever since I had learned where it came from, and I could stand on the balcony without wanting to curl into a fetal ball. I looked even more kindly on a large feather bed with clean sheets and, better yet, a copper bathtub discovered behind a screen.

Coachman Andrew dumped our one bag and retired below stairs. Hastings had secured the required change of clothes for Percy and me during his trip into Arras to research innkeepers. Two changes, in fact: one suitable for our merchant guises, and the other for the necessary but dangerous moment when we would have to resume our real identities if we wanted to gain access to Armand. I opened the bag and peered inside, trying to figure out what I could safely put away and what should remain stored until we needed it for our rescue plan. For a crucial half-hour, Sir Percy and his lady had to make an appearance, but timing was everything. With luck and good planning, Chauvelin would learn of our presence after we'd left.

The few clothes that had to be unpacked lay at the top of the bag. I began transferring them to the dresser drawers.

"You'll have to make do with me as lady's maid," Percy said. "No time to find a girl we can trust."

"Some lady's maid." I looked over my shoulder and smiled. It was good to see him at ease for once. Our journey often felt like an endless hunt in which we were both predators and prey. "Lolling on the bed while your mistress unpacks. You'd be dismissed before sundown."

"True, Madam. Leave that and come over here. I'll show you where my skills lie." That sounded a lot more entertaining than emptying the suitcase, so I put the stockings I'd been folding into a drawer and joined him on the bed.

"Weren't you injured?" I asked as he pulled me down.

"As you see, m'lady, I am fully recovered." And he proceeded to convince me he spoke the truth.

For two days, we stayed at the inn, watched only by Andrew. Percy sent everyone else to hunt for news of Chauvelin. We couldn't make our move until we knew for sure where he and his troops were stationed and, if possible, what they planned to do next—unless we wanted to chance them showing up exactly when we most needed them to be elsewhere. They weren't easy to pin down, either. From the reports that filtered in, our adversary was roaming the countryside like a hungry and rather bad-tempered wolf.

Armand and Suzanne remained in captivity. Marguerite had relapsed into catatonia. Percy kept his inimitable cool. I worried, my nerves becoming tauter by the hour. My only relief came from exploring Arras with Percy—in disguise, of course. Tense or not, I enjoyed being with him.

Arras is an ancient town—really ancient. It was founded by the Atrebates, a Celtic tribe that lived in Gaul before Julius Caesar came and saw and conquered (58–51 BCE, if you care). None of the Celtic settlement remained by the eighteenth century, although pieces of the Roman town popped up in odd corners. For most of the Middle Ages Arras belonged to the Netherlands—more accurately to Spain, which controlled the Netherlands—and it had, as Andrew noted, specialized in tapestries. When old Polonius was stabbed behind the arras, the word "arras" referred to this town. In Shakespeare's day, people used it as a synonym for "tapestry," the same way that these days we use "google" to mean "Web search."

When the revolution came, the town had been French for about 150 years, but it had Dutch-looking houses and wide streets and pretty flowers, not to mention a thriving commerce with the Low Countries. Strolling it with Percy gave me an unadulterated pleasure. His impeccable courtesy, wry humor, and quick intellect made him an excellent conversationalist. He knew everyone in society (and could tell tales about most of them). He had traveled and read widely and spoke three or four languages. He liked opera and concerts, art and horse racing, good food and wine. He felt comfortable at all levels of society: he could walk into a restaurant or a taproom and know just what to do. When I was with him, I felt beautiful and charming and completely secure. And often enough to keep me comfortable, I encountered Ian's familiar sparkle or heard his characteristic turn of phrase.

Each day I fell further into the world of *The Scarlet Pimpernel.* More than two weeks had passed, and we remained inside the simulation. I could no longer tell whether the game would end—or when. But I wanted to cherish my happiness while it lasted. The future would intrude soon enough.

20. Hôtel de Ville

AND INTRUDE IT DID, THE VERY NEXT DAY. IN THE FORM OF Lord Tony, who arrived with news not long after sunrise. I scrambled into my clothes behind the screen, where I could hear him and Percy talking.

"Hastings tracked down Chauvelin's troops. They're a good six hours' march from here, but they're coming to collect Armand. My contact at the Hôtel de Ville expects them today, tomorrow at the latest." Tony sounded tired. I wondered if he'd spent the night seeking information.

"Good work," Percy said. I could hear him buttoning trousers and pulling on boots. "We need to move fast, then. Are the others here?"

"Outside the city," Tony said. "Do you want them in Arras?"

"No. Hand me that shirt, will you, old fellow?" The next sentences came out muffled, as though Percy were talking through linen. "Keep them where they are. Who's commanding?"

"Bathurst?" Tony asked.

"Better you, I think," Percy said. "You know what to do?"

Tony didn't answer in words. As I peeked around the screen, trying to attract my husband's attention, I saw Tony nod.

Percy reached for his cravat. "Tell Andrew to report here before breakfast. We'll need the three costumes and the packet I gave him yesterday. Oh, and tell Bathurst to hire a carriage. It's time Margot paid a visit to her brother in the Hôtel de Ville."

"I can't go anywhere," I said from behind the screen, "until my maid comes and buttons this gown."

"Be right there, m'dear," Percy said. "Soon as I tie my cravat."

The riskiest part of our mission was about to begin. The anticipation of a challenge thrilled me, even as tension cramped my stomach, leaving me nauseous. This must be how astronauts feel just before the rockets fire.

For those unfamiliar with French, *hôtel de ville* means "city hall." As a place of confinement, this one struck as me as no more secure than its equivalent in Boston or Philadelphia. Keeping Armand there made sense only if Chauvelin wanted to fool the Scarlet Pimpernel into carelessness, but since we assumed that was exactly what our opponent wanted, we didn't waste time overthinking the decision. Coached (and accompanied) by Percy, I set off to beard another set of officials in their dens. Even he admitted we could not afford a repetition of the incident in Douai, which might have handed Chauvelin an unconditional victory. If I and my yellow dress hadn't intervened, that is.

The yellow dress wouldn't have done us much good here. I realized that two minutes into my conversation with the governor. You couldn't call him a Chauvelin clone—he lacked the malice and the keen intelligence that, in combination, made France's special representative so formidable an adversary. He had the puritanical streak in spades, though. No lace ruffles or wine bottles here. The cravat hung so pathetically starchless that even I considered it a fashion abomination. I prayed that Percy would keep his opinions to himself.

"I am Marguerite Blakeney," I told him when he finally agreed to see us after an interminable wait. Although Marguerite seldom emerged these days, I had not lost access to her French. "*Née* St. Just. I learned this morning that you have my brother, Armand, imprisoned here. Monsieur Chauvelin has invited me several times to visit him, but until now I have found it difficult. Chauvelin moves Armand so often! I no sooner arrive in one place than I find that the troops have spirited him off once more. Please, I beg of you, permit me to see him. He is my only relative."

I pointed to Percy, reclining in the chair next to me and exuding bored sophistication from every pore. "Other than my husband, of course." Percy bowed over his steepled fingertips in acknowledgment.

The governor leaned back, considering. "Hmm. Chauvelin left no orders regarding visitors." His eyes roved over my face. "But I recognize you. Comédie Française, was it not? Quite the sensation, as I recall. I saw you in *Misanthrope*."

"I am honored that you remember me." Which was true. Marguerite had missed the excitement and adulation of the stage—until I'd arrived to pitchfork her into one scrape after another. These days, she yearned for the quiet life.

The governor pondered a while longer, while I smiled and Percy stared at the ceiling. Perhaps that air of total cluelessness tipped the scales, because at the point when I was deciding that I couldn't keep the smile going another moment without its turning into a death mask, the governor tipped his chair forward. "Well, I see no harm in allowing a short visit. Chauvelin sent word this morning to prepare St.

Just for another transfer, and then, Madame, you would have to chase him again."

He called to the guard. "No more than fifteen minutes," he said as we left the room.

I blew him a kiss. It had worked when Jane Seymour did it in the BBC's *Scarlet Pimpernel,* and it worked now. The governor blushed like a teenager. For a split second, you'd have thought he was human.

Armand looked worse than when I'd last seen him: thinner, more worn, and radiating a sense of hopelessness. This even though his physical surroundings weren't bad. The town government had converted an interior office into a cell, so it didn't smell worse than any other building in Arras that housed a lot of men and no bathrooms to speak of. They'd replaced the original furniture with a cot, but compared to Percy's descriptions of the cell in Douai, it seemed reasonably comfortable. So I guessed that prolonged stress and hunger, as well as sleeplessness, explained Armand's deteriorating state. In one sense, I hated to see it, but it would help our plan succeed.

After the usual round of effusive greetings, which the guards tolerated with much greater sympathy than Chauvelin had mustered in the market square, we got down to business. Percy's foppish manner had already instilled something between astonishment and horror in the guards; it took little for my husband to focus their attention on him. As I leaned in and grabbed Armand's arm just below the elbow, I could hear Percy making lame jokes in his abominable French, the guards too stunned, more often than not, even to attempt a reply.

I handed Armand a small packet, until then tucked in the bodice of my gown. Lady Luck had favored us: the governor of Arras did not yet search female visitors, as those in Paris were reported to do. "Swallow these pills as soon as we're gone," I said in a near-whisper. "They'll knock you out. Percy's a 'doctor' and I'm his 'assistant.' We'll be back the minute the guards call us. But don't delay. Chauvelin's men will arrive in a few hours."

He nodded and slipped the packet into his cuff while Percy and I blocked the guards' view. I touched his cheek, moved by that aura of despair.

"Go," he said, catching my hand in his. "I'll find a way."

"*À bientôt.*" I hugged him.

"Time's up," the guard announced. One last embrace for Armand, and I followed Percy out the door.

"Oh, dear," I said to the apparition that presented itself in the inn an hour later. "I wouldn't let you near me with a razor, never mind a scalpel."

Percy twisted and turned before the mirror. "I think I look rather fine, Madam. Quite the man to inspire confidence."

Confidence in what, I shuddered to think. The long, full-sleeved black gown, if more suitable to an academic doctor than a medical one, conveyed a certain gravitas, as did the curled white wig and the black velvet cap. All had seen better days, but they projected the desired image—a once-prominent representative of one of the professions. Not necessarily the medical profession, but people in those days weren't so fussy about cleanliness that they expected doctors to wash their hands before conducting an examination, never mind showing up in spotless white coats.

"It's the nose," I explained. "It's so ... red. You look like someone who drinks brandy for breakfast." Indeed, I couldn't decide whether the bulbous monstrosity obscuring the center of Percy's face reminded me more of Rudolph the Reindeer or the winos I'd seen around the Port Authority Bus Terminal in New York. But I had no doubt that I'd give my kidney to an Internet surgeon before I let someone with a nose like that anywhere near me with a medical bag.

"That's the idea, darling. I've seen surgeons whose hands shake when they reach for the knife, and doctors who take a swig themselves before dosing the patient. And we don't want the guards remembering the cheerful gentleman who traded jokes with them an hour ago, what?" He pasted an eyebrow that resembled a centipede over one eye, regarded it critically, and made an adjustment. "Besides, isn't this a case of the pot calling the kettle?"

I joined him at the mirror. "Lord, you've made me into a hooligan. I should be robbing banks, not healing the sick."

"Precisely." Percy pasted the matching centipede and turned to his fingernails.

"I think there's a hole in these pants," I told him.

"Several, probably," he said, still studying the fingernails.

"No, you don't understand. This one's embarrassing." I showed him, provoking a shout of laughter.

"Here." He tossed me a needle and thread. "A little domestic embroidery, I think, m'dear."

When the message came, we were ready. Tony's carefully cultivated friendship with the guards at the Hôtel de Ville paid off, so the summons for a medical man to treat Armand, taken suddenly and inexplicably ill, went not to the local barber/ surgeon but to the illustrious retired doctor from Toulouse who had decided to visit Arras the day before. We piled into a cart driven by Andrew and headed back into the center of town.

"First hurdle crossed," Percy said as we set off. "Tony must have sown those rumors well. Usually, they wouldn't bother saving a prisoner destined for Madame la Guillotine."

"What rumors?" Andrew asked.

"That Chauvelin had threatened to gut anyone who let Armand come to harm," I answered. "I bet he would, too. A dead Armand wouldn't make much of a hostage."

Andrew nodded, and we slipped back into our roles.

For sure, the guard who met us at the gate appeared concerned. He wrung his hands as he greeted us and hustled us up the stairs before explaining why he'd called. "The young man seemed well this morning, Citizen Doctor," he said to Percy. "A bit listless, perhaps, but such is normal among prisoners. His sister came to see him earlier today"—I shrank deeper beneath the enveloping hood that increased my resemblance to a gangster—"and even after she left, he showed no particular symptoms. Then, perhaps thirty minutes ago, the guard on duty saw St. Just turn pale. He fell over, rubbing his stomach and moaning, then passed out. Now he just lies there."

"Is he breathing?" Percy asked, in a guttural voice so bizarre it nearly threw me out of character.

"Barely," the guard answered. "Pass a hand in front of his face, and you can feel the breath, but you wouldn't know to look at him."

"Poison?" Percy barked.

The guard jerked. "We found none, Citizen Doctor." Good, Armand had managed to destroy the packet, then. "And how would he obtain it? Unless his sister—but no, the guards did not leave them for a minute."

"Very well," Percy said. "Lead me to him, and we will see."

And see we did. If I hadn't been in on the plot, I'd have written Armand off as a goner. I couldn't believe how much he'd deteriorated in the short time since we'd left. Could I have given him the wrong potion? The wrong dose?

As the guard had warned, Armand lay in a coma. Until Percy placed a mirror in front of his nose, I would have sworn his breath had stopped altogether. I saw no signs of life.

Percy looked grave, shaking his head. As he snapped commands, I passed him one item after another from the medical bag. He prodded and poked and muttered while Armand lay in his stupor. I half-expected him to call for a cow so he could examine the entrails.

"You have waited too long." He growled at the guard hovering at his heels. "The humors are severely unbalanced. Earth dominates. With no air or fire in the room, earth cannot dissipate. Water merely heightens the effect of earth. Think of mud."

I choked, started to laugh, turned it into a cough just in time. Percy was winging it. Eighteenth-century medicine produced some pretty wacky theories and lost more patients than it saved, but the mud theory of illness topped the lot.

Except one. "We must bleed him," Percy announced. "Pierre, fetch the leeches."

Mine not to question why, et cetera. I dug a disgusting jar from the recesses of the medical bag and handed it to Percy, together with the cup he requested next.

The doctor jerked his head, and I rolled back Armand's sleeve. His arm felt limp as a rubber chicken in my hand. My concern deepened. It would get worse, Percy had warned, before we saw any improvement.

Percy dropped leeches, one by one, onto Armand's arm as I held it over the cup. The whole experience created a horrid fascination, and I tried without success to tear my eyes away.

"Enough," he said at last, returning fat but reluctant leeches to their cup and handing the cup to me. With indecent haste, I tipped the leeches back into their jar. A series of reddened circles, like giant flea bites, marked where they had latched onto Armand's arm.

"Now I will burn incense to remove the foul humors," Percy announced.

At the best of times, incense has a cloying quality. I'd attended enough Eastern Orthodox church services and New Age gatherings to anticipate the smell, but Percy's idea of incense knocked those preconceptions out of the park. If you imagine the back of a barn meeting a week-old egg, you can get a hint of its awfulness. Without a doubt, it would push Armand over the edge. The question was whether the rest of us would remain standing to rescue him.

In the corridor, the guard gagged and protested. "Citizen, must you? If we scrub for a month, we'll not rid the room of that stink."

Percy wrinkled his centipede brows. "If you had kept the humors balanced from the beginning, I could have avoided such extreme treatments. You waited too long. See, even my skills are proving insufficient. Look, you!"

Armand's pallor had degenerated into a waxen rigidity that indeed resembled death. No sign of breathing appeared, even when I reapplied the mirror at Percy's command. The doctor shook his head, saddened by the evidence of human folly.

"He is gone," Percy said. "I can remove the body, thus sparing you the blame."

The guard didn't seem to hear. He pounded his head against the door until I stopped him. We didn't have room in the cart for two corpses.

"Calm yourself, Citizen," I said. "We have come to assist you, and assist you we shall. I can see the dead man was a prisoner. Can you not say that his execution took place sooner than expected or he died trying to escape?"

The guard frothed at the mouth. His eyes had the wild look of people in demon-possession films. "You do not understand," he said. "This man was under the charge of Citizen Chauvelin, chief agent of the Committee of Public Safety."

"Right-hand man to Citizen Robespierre," he added, in case we hadn't gotten it the first time. "Citizen Chauvelin has sent troops to collect the prisoner. What shall I tell them when I cannot produce him?"

"Hmm." Percy stroked his chin and pretended to consider this. "A pretty problem. Perhaps best to take a well-earned holiday, don't you think? Starting immediately." He poked Armand for emphasis. "Because if you're not here, your Citizen Chauvelin will have to take out his anger on someone else." Not waiting for an answer, Percy nodded at me. "Go fetch the driver, boy, and tell him I require his assistance."

As I went down the stairs to inform Andrew, I heard him telling the guard, "Lots of work for a man of your abilities in the South, 'tis said."

Andrew and Percy lugged Armand down the stairs and laid him in the doctor's rickety cart while I arranged the obligatory note, signed with Percy's pimpernel emblem, to inform Chauvelin that his adversary had defeated him again. I'd protested that Chauvelin didn't need yet another reason to send us to the guillotine, but Percy overruled me. The note was part of the Scarlet Pimpernel's modus operandi. End of story. So I took charge of the note, hoping to speed up our escape, only to discover that positioning the thing chewed up an indecent amount of time. I had to locate the perfect spot: a place the French would not find it before we had made good our escape but where they would stumble on it later.

By the time I folded the paper and tucked it under the bowl used for bleeding Armand, the knots in my stomach had tightened to the point where I could have profited from some medical attention myself. I dashed downstairs to join Marguerite's comatose brother in the cart. The men had wrapped Armand in blankets to conceal his identity, further increasing his resemblance to a mummy. At another nod from Percy, I took my seat in the back, trying to settle my nerves.

With excruciating slowness the cart rumbled toward the gates that separated us from the town. Armand didn't move, even when one of the soldiers peered into his face. Another man examined our papers and passed them back. I'd just decided we might make it when the soldier who'd done the peering turned away. His rifle butt thumped the cart. The cart jerked, throwing me sideways and onto Armand. He moaned.

The tiniest moan, but enough.

"Hey, he's not dead," the soldier shouted.

"That was me," I called. Too late. Booted feet smacked the ground as the garrison woke up and came to investigate.

Percy snapped the reins. The cart weaved, knocking me from side to side. Hot air whizzed past my ear as a bullet thudded into the wood. Searing pain lanced my shoulder, and I collapsed onto the old sacks that lined the cart.

A voice yelled, "At ease, Citizens. We have them." In an instant, a band of soldiers in the blue and red uniforms of the French Republic surrounded us. Their spurs jangled and their white artillery straps caught the light. Despite the pain that streaked down my arm, I hauled myself upright and clung to the side of the lurching wagon.

The troops urged us toward the street outside the city hall. My head was spinning. In my blurring vision, the soldiers multiplied, pushing their horses in and out but never creating an opening through which Percy could escape. Inexorably, they drove us toward and through the town gates, hurling insults at us and at the guards who demanded their papers.

"What's wrong with you?" their leader shouted. "Can't you see that we serve the republic? This villain is wanted by Citizen Chauvelin! Stand aside, or your head will roll!"

Nursing my injured shoulder, I collapsed once more onto the sacks, no longer concerned. I had recognized the man yelling commands.

It was Lord Tony.

21. English Channel

WE STOPPED AS SOON AS WE WERE WELL AWAY FROM THE guards. "You've been shot," Percy said. He stood at the back of the cart with his hands on his hips. I couldn't read his expression, but I didn't much like the look of it, either. Then again, perhaps that was an effect of the ridiculous nose.

"I'm sure they were aiming at you," I said, more than a little cranky. My arm hurt like the dickens. "Can't you take off that dreadful nose? And the eyebrows! I feel like a character in one of Molière's plays."

"Tut, tut, Madam." He was laughing, the beast. "Lucky I'm a doctor, what?" His voice softened. "Let's find out what they've done to you." Over his shoulder, he added, "See to Armand, Tony, there's a good chap."

Armand looked terrible, ashen and drawn. Sweat beaded on his brow. Tremors ran through him—an improvement, I suppose, over his former near-coma. Still unconscious, he groaned.

Tony beckoned to Andrew, and the two of them propped Armand up enough for Lord Bathurst to squirt liquid into his mouth, one drop at a time. Gradually the color returned to Armand's cheeks. He sputtered, gurgled, and opened his eyes.

"Margot, you're bleeding," were the first words out of his mouth.

"So she is," Percy said. "And refusing to let me look at that wound. Come here, darling."

Armand held out a shaky hand. I edged my way over the sacks and clasped it. "You're happy again?" he asked softly. "All is well there?" He jerked his head in Percy's direction.

"Very well." I kissed his cheek. "Just get better, my dear, and quickly. Lord Tony will take you to the shore, and I'll see you on board the *Day Dream*."

I could feel his dark eyes following me as I eased my way back to the tailgate, wincing each time I had to use my right arm. Just before Percy lifted me down, I turned. For the first time since I'd met him, Armand was smiling.

The charcoal burner's hut that huddled next to the town walls boasted few amenities, but it did have a fire pit smack in the center. No chimney, so the smoke swirled around, getting in ears and eyes and pretty much everywhere. You'd be hard put to imagine a less suitable emergency room.

Percy insisted on carrying me into the hut. Quite unnecessary, but I suspected he felt guilty about my taking a bullet, so I didn't argue. When he put me down, my head spun. Blood loss was already making me dizzy. Maybe I *had* needed his help.

While Andrew built a fire, Percy stripped off my hooded jacket and shirt. I yelped. Exposed to air, the wound ached more than before.

"Not bad," Percy said with professional detachment. I hoped he remembered he hadn't actually trained as a doctor. "The bullet didn't hit anything vital."

"Excuse me," I said with what composure I could muster under the circumstances. "Skin strikes me as vital." The shot had seared its way across my collar bone, from about six inches below the neck up through the upper part of my right arm.

"True, m'dear." The bubbly quality had returned to Percy's voice. "Sink me if I'm not thoroughly devoted to yours." His lips brushed my forehead. "'Tis more easily replaced than muscle or bone, however, not to mention heart or lungs."

His calm acceptance of the situation made me feel infantile. I opened my mouth to apologize, but the room made a huge circle around me and I found myself staring at a dirt floor.

"Damn," I heard Percy say. "The place is filthy. Where can we put her so I can clean this wound?"

Straw tickled my ear. The room continued its orbit, but after a while I identified the cloth underneath me as the doctor's gown Percy had worn during Armand's rescue. I lay face down. The pain at the edge of my shoulder had transformed into throbbing discomfort. I probed it, but a wad of cotton blocked my way.

Strong, gentle fingers caught my questing hand. "Don't poke at it, sweetheart. You'll make it worse."

I turned my head toward the voice. Percy had abandoned the nose and the centipede eyebrows and no longer looked like Vincent Price on a bender.

He handed Andrew a basin. "Feeling better, m'dear?"

"It doesn't hurt as much," I said, flexing the shoulder and earning myself another rebuke, "but the room keeps going round in circles."

"Hmm." Percy's arm came around my shoulders as he raised me to a sitting position. He pressed a flask to my lips and I drank it, trusting him. Fire burned my throat.

Coughing and furious, I pulled away from him. "What was that?"

"Cognac." He had the nerve to grin.

Still choking, I scowled. "Never mind, darling," he said. "You'll feel better in no time. Let me help you. We need to leave before your friend Chauvelin shows up."

"He's not my friend," I said, but the effort of getting me on my feet consumed our attention, and my comment went unremarked.

According to Percy's carefully laid plans, horses and a change of clothes lay hidden in a field a mile or so from Arras. My taking a bullet had detoured us to the charcoal burner's hut. Now I struggled to sit, never mind walk, and the cart had gone off with Armand to the coast.

"I should have sent you with them," Percy said. "Tony would have kept you safe. Now we have to deliver you to the *Day Dream* before we can make a last-ditch effort to rescue Suzanne."

There wasn't much I could respond to that. We couldn't leave Suzanne in limbo, and little as I wanted to sit on the yacht while the men took care of things, my spinning head and aching arm would only slow them down, if not stop them in their tracks.

"You can escort her while I go after Suzanne," Andrew offered. Generous of him, but Percy turned him down flat. I'd have expected nothing less of the Scarlet Pimpernel.

"Chauvelin's a tricky beast," Percy said. "You'll do better with help. And if we ride to Calais, we can collect Tony and the others. Armand and Philip can guard Marguerite on the *Day Dream* for twenty-four hours. But first we need horses."

That, however, was the problem. Inside the city walls we could find livery stables that rented horses and carriages, but was it worth taking the risk of going back there?

"I'd have to carry you," Percy said.

Again with the carrying. I did my best to ignore the room dancing before my eyes like raindrops in sunlight. "Don't be ridiculous. You can't carry a young man into town and expect no one to notice."

"You can't walk that distance on your own if your head's spinning."

So much for trying to keep the room under control. "I might make it if you gave me your arm."

"My dear girl, if I saunter into Arras with my arm around a young man's waist, it will cause more talk than carrying you." He picked a grimy pile off the floor and shook it at me. "Besides, my mistake. You can't go anywhere in this shirt. The guards will be looking for someone injured." He frowned at the shirt, shifted his gaze to me, and finally settled on Andrew.

Andrew didn't wait to be asked. "I'll collect the stuff from the field. If I don't run into trouble, I'll be back in thirty minutes."

Percy nodded. "Thanks, old chap."

I muttered my gratitude, but I'm not sure Andrew heard me. As he slipped out the door, I buried my head in my hands and begged the room to stand still.

In due course, Andrew returned, leading a spare horse. From the saddlebags he pulled two bundles of clothes, which he handed to Percy. The doctor disappeared, and a merchant took his place. Percy rolled the doctor's outfit into a ball and stuffed it under a pile of straw near the back of the hut. Then he turned his attention to me.

With a lot of assistance from him, I managed to clean up most of the grime and produce a reasonable semblance of the merchant's wife. The tight sleeves of the current style added to the throbbing in my arm and shoulder, but I gritted my teeth, determined to shut out the pain. The hair proved my biggest hurdle; in the end I braided it and pinned it into a knot and hoped it would pass muster.

Andrew had also brought bread and wine. The food counteracted the swirling quite a bit, although I refused the wine. It wouldn't help the dizziness, especially after the cognac Percy had already dumped down my throat.

We moved outside. Andrew handed me off to Percy, who settled me on the pommel in front of him. I wrapped my arms around his waist and closed my eyes. The simulated bullet wound hurt like hell. Which meant that Ian had felt every blow of that interrogation in Douai.

Even so, our situation had improved. Armand was on his way to the coast, and I would join him in a few hours. I hated to think of Percy and the League heading into danger again, but with any luck, they would soon rescue Suzanne. If we escaped, the game would end. We would have won— wouldn't we?

We almost made it. Fifteen miles from Calais, as we rode into the inn where we planned to change horses for the last leg of our trip, Chauvelin caught up with us. We'd talked about hiring a carriage: it would put less stress on my injured shoulder, and the horses would move faster and tire less easily if one didn't have to carry a double load. Then Percy remembered that horses could travel cross-country if necessary, and that put paid to the carriage idea.

I agreed with his reasoning. I, too, wanted to reach the coast as soon as possible and evade pursuit. But by the time we reached that last inn, I felt like I'd been forced through an old-fashioned mangle.

Chauvelin opened the inn door as Percy pulled the horse up in the yard. I jolted upright, fingers clutching the soft cotton of his shirt. He kissed my cheek and murmured, "Courage, darling."

I flinched. That phrase again. And it didn't take an Einstein to see that we'd need more than courage this time. A dozen uniformed French soldiers poured from the stables. One grabbed the reins of Percy's horse while another seized Andrew's. I tightened my grip on Percy's shirt. He covered my hand with his and squeezed.

Only then did I sense his tension. Watching him, I recalled the impression I'd had of him in Douai: perfect composure on the outside, muscles taut, ready to spring. I couldn't tell whether I found that reassuring. He had my back. He was competent in the extreme. Yet we had lost in Douai.

I felt no impetus to play into Chauvelin's hands by offering him a courteous greeting, but Percy chose to keep up the pretense. He doffed his hat and bowed his head. Chauvelin responded in kind. Percy unclenched my fingers from his shirt, dismounted, put his hands around my waist, and lifted me down.

"Your servant, Mon-soo-er," he said, his voice affable and careless, the London fop well in evidence despite his merchant clothes.

Shivering in the October breeze, I checked the Weasel for clues. The height of the sun suggested late afternoon. Hours had passed since we left the charcoal burner's hut. Chauvelin must have learned of Armand's escape, or why the soldiers?

"A pleasure, Sir Percy, as always," the Weasel said. "You left early last time. I'd hoped to spend more time with you." His oily smile flashed. "Lady Blakeney, are you quite well?"

"Yes, Monsieur. The day's journey has tired me." I heard the tremor in my own voice. Percy moved closer, and I leaned against his side, drawing on his quiet strength.

Chauvelin bowed again, his sinister streak well in evidence. "I'm sorry that *la belle France* has proven so inhospitable that you wish to leave us. And in such haste that you had no time to find clothing appropriate to your station!"

I caught Percy's hand and pressed it against my stomach, which seemed to be turning cartwheels. "Don't be silly, Citizen Chauvelin," I said. "We chose clothes that wouldn't draw attention to ourselves. Your revolutionary guards can be overzealous when they think they've discovered an aristocrat. Even an English one."

"Look at 'em now, m'dear fellow." Percy snaked his arm more tightly around my waist as my knees buckled. "Trying to steal our horses, what?"

"Arrest them!" Chauvelin shouted. The soldiers moved in. A sob escaped me, but Percy elbowed them away.

"Arrest us for what?" He gave Chauvelin his most supercilious stare. "Wearing the wrong clothes?"

"For helping a condemned prisoner to escape!" Chauvelin, his face pinched with disgust, waved his arm at the soldiers. They stopped trying to pull me away from my husband. I shifted my feet enough to wrap both arms around him and looked up, memorizing the lines of his face. Was this, despite everything, the end?

Percy removed a hand from my waist to stifle a yawn. "Do calm down, dear fellow. Prisoner? Escape? What *are* you rambling on about?"

"Don't play games with me, Sir Percy." Flecks of spittle rimmed Chauvelin's mouth. "I know who you are! The Scarlet Pimpernel! You arranged your own escape. And Armand St. Just's. You'd have freed Suzanne de Tournay too, I don't doubt, if my men hadn't executed her on the spot. Your fine intelligence didn't reveal that, did it?"

He'd killed Suzanne? How could he?

But I knew the answer to that question. Those were the stakes of the game. Chauvelin had set the rules himself.

At the first mention of Suzanne, Andrew roared and lunged, but the men holding him dragged him away and pinioned his arms. Not before I saw the way his hands curled, though. He'd have strangled Chauvelin, given half a chance.

Percy, frowning, regarded his furious lieutenant, then returned his attention to Chauvelin. His puzzlement appeared genuine—that disarming stupid expression he'd worn when I first saw him with the vicomte in Dover. The arm that pinioned me against his body told a different story, but his voice remained perfectly steady, almost bored. "You killed a young woman, given succor by a foreign country, who posed no threat to you? Not sporting, dear chap. Not sporting in the least. No wonder you French can't run a government. Although at least that mayor of yours had the sense to release me when evidence of your lunacy came in."

Chauvelin twisted his hands till I was sure they'd fall off. "Don't give me that. You subverted the mayor of Douai— that's obvious. How you freed St. Just I have yet to discover. No one in Arras was even coherent. Dead men and doctors—a fairy tale for children, but none of that matters. We found the Scarlet Pimpernel's note boasting that he freed St. Just, and the governor can swear that you and Lady Blakeney visited him this morning. You can explain the rest to the tribunal." He nodded at the soldiers surrounding us. "Take them in!"

"No!" I stumbled as Percy released me to pull his rapier from its sheath.

I lunged at Chauvelin. In my head, I executed the maneuver perfectly, grabbing him round the neck and forcing him to call the troops off. In reality, two guards caught me as I toppled forward, dragged my wrists behind my back, and clapped handcuffs around them.

The remaining troops, at least a half-dozen men, had Percy surrounded. Sword in hand, he dispatched them one by one.

In the hubbub, Andrew's guards lost track of him. He pulled his own rapier from its scabbard, broke through their line, and spun so that he and Percy stood back to back. My captors yanked me forward, the pain in my wrenched shoulder became excruciating, and my already shaky grip on reality loosened. As the men picked me up and threw me into a wagon that stood near the stables, I saw Percy and Andrew, swords clashing against those of the troops as they fought their way toward me. One man swung a gun butt toward Percy's head, and he dodged it just in time. Two more tripped Andrew and held him down as they bound him in chains.

With Andrew out of the picture, the troops could concentrate their efforts on Percy. Even the Scarlet Pimpernel could not stand against so many opponents. Within minutes, the soldiers dumped him and Andrew next to me.

Tears ran down my cheeks. This was the end. Chauvelin had won.

Percy's eyes were a liquid blue. His smile glowed with tenderness. I caught my breath, realizing this was goodbye. Whatever happened next, the end of the game meant that I would lose Percy forever.

Chauvelin walked toward us, rubbing his hands, the weasel smile plastered across his face. I slumped into the straw, distraught. We had lost.

❀

Percy couldn't hold me because of the manacles, but he kissed the top of my head. "Never mind, *mignonne*. We'll think of something."

I rested my cheek against the soft wool of his jacket. Who was he kidding? The three of us lay bound, and I lacked the strength to move even if someone released me. The League was escorting Armand to the coast. We might think of something, but we had no one to carry out the plan.

The horse pulling the wagon plodded toward Calais. Chauvelin had taken a seat next to the driver. He stared straight ahead.

Any minute now, we'd leave the town where we'd expected to change horses and would enter open fields. As soon as we reached a spot where there were no eyewitnesses, Chauvelin could shoot us and claim we'd been attempting escape. Wasn't that how he'd treated Suzanne? If he'd executed her on the spot, as he claimed, I couldn't imagine why he'd risk turning us over to the tribunal. He'd do nothing but give the League time to rally its forces.

My shoulder throbbed. I wondered what it would be like to die. Everything that happened in the game felt real. The thought made me shudder. Death at twenty-four—even simulated death—was not what anyone anticipated. I remembered how casually I'd tossed off plans to get guillotined early in the game, not understanding what that would mean.

If I kill you, you lose—David's words, clear and unmistakable. And yet I'd had no idea, then, how bad failure would feel.

The horse trudged along. The wagon rocked. I watched Percy, the wisp of hair that fell over his brow. The curve of his lips, the tenderness in his face. I wanted to throw myself into his arms, brush my fingers across the bruises left by the soldiers, but my fetters kept me immobile. I could only gaze into his eyes.

The cart shuddered to a halt. Someone gave a strangled croak. I jerked awake. Percy rolled away from me and sat up, although hampered by his chains. Andrew had propped himself against the side of the wagon. I pushed my cuffed hands against the planks below the straw and struggled onto my knees.

A fourth body, bound and gagged, tumbled into the wagon. I recognized Chauvelin, who looked as stunned as I felt. Two soldiers unlocked the iron cuffs binding Percy's and Andrew's arms. While I stared at them openmouthed, I heard a sharp metallic click as the cuffs slid from my wrists.

I glanced over my right shoulder. The troop captain greeted me with a broad and very familiar grin. Lord Tony, in the soldier's uniform he'd worn in Arras, had somehow pulled *another* fast one on Chauvelin, with the help of the League.

"What, did you think we'd abandoned you?" He lifted me out of the wagon and kissed my cheek. I gaped at him as though he were a ghost who had materialized out of thin air. "As soon as we put Armand in the dinghy and saw him on his way to the *Day Dream*, we circled back. Military uniforms make a great disguise, especially when you're traveling. Chauvelin assumed we were the troops he'd asked for, and we played along. We've been biding our time until the right opportunity appeared."

I shut my mouth, vainly reaching for the words that had charged out of my head. Tony chortled at my stupefied expression and beckoned to the remaining League members. One of them led two horses from a nearby copse.

"What about Suzanne?" Tony asked. "Are we going back for her?"

Andrew swore. "No. That bastard Chauvelin killed her."

Tony glanced at Percy for confirmation. "Really?"

"So he said." Percy's voice was grim. He slapped Andrew's shoulder in a sympathetic male way. "You'll see her again, old chap." It sounded like spiritual counseling, but he meant that we'd be reunited with Suzanne outside the game.

"Yes, we're done here," Andrew said. He took the reins of one horse from the man leading the pair and handed them to Percy. "For God's sake, let's finish this and go home."

Surrendering Chauvelin to the League's tender mercies (although no one interfered as Andrew exacted a few minutes' revenge on behalf of Suzanne), Percy, Andrew, and I mounted the horses and made a dash for the sea. Tony promised to ditch Chauvelin in one of the fishermen's huts near Calais and meet us at the yacht. Percy refused to countenance murder, even of his archenemy, but he wanted to leave no doubt we had won.

Even without pursuit, the ride took us almost an hour, although I found that out only later. The time spent with my hands cuffed behind my back had taken its toll on my injured shoulder, and the effect of pounding hooves proved too much.

The next thing I heard was the sea lapping the beach. White-topped waves met my gaze as far as the eye could see, and the smell of salt filled my nostrils. Not far from the shore, the graceful *Day Dream* rocked at anchor. Armand waved from the deck. As I watched, two sailors pulled a dinghy onto the sands.

The horse stopped. Percy lifted me down. The minute his hands closed on my waist, I tumbled into his arms. "We made it!"

He swung me around, laughing. He said, "Margot, I love you," in the soft, husky voice that turned my insides to mush.

"I love you, too," I murmured before he kissed me. The sailors on the dinghy cheered.

In a flash, the shift happened. I wasn't in France anymore.

22. Terra Nova

BRIGHT LIGHTS. CLICKS AND BUZZES. APPLAUSE? THE chatter and laughter of perhaps thirty people swirled around me, replacing the sound of the waves. The tang of salt spray gave way to the aroma of coffee. The coastal breeze dissipated amid hot, stale air. The pain that had inflamed my shoulder vanished as if by magic, and my exhaustion went with it.

I opened my eyes. Percy's blond hair had turned light brown, his blue eyes hazel, but the attractive smile lingered. Ian—his face lit with tenderness and passion, his arms wrapped around my waist. Who would have believed this was my *bête noire* of two weeks ago?

"We're home!" I could hardly believe my luck, and I meant more by that than making it out of the game in one piece. "We won!"

He ran one finger down my cheek. "Yes, love, we are. We did." He leaned toward me, as if to kiss me again, only to stop midway.

I tugged him toward me, then let go as I realized that we stood in the midst of a crowd of people hugging and shaking hands, decompressing after weeks spent inhabiting bodies and minds not their own. An impromptu cast party was taking place in the middle of a huge warehouse that could have passed for an airline hangar while a dozen blue-shirted Dreamlife employees shoved cubicle dividers against one wall and others circled with tea trays containing snacks and cups of liquid. One couple wielded mops and brooms.

My senses reeled. Nothing around me resembled Dover, Richmond, London, Calais, or anywhere in northeastern France.

A wave of nostalgia swept over me as I realized that Percy and Marguerite were gone forever. I would have to readjust to modern life with no smart, funny French companion at my side.

But I had Ian. The glint in his eyes hinted at unspoken but intense desire. My skin tingled. I wished myself—and him—elsewhere.

Two of the blue-shirted technicians appeared and stripped the computer disks from our temples and wrists. One reached down to pull off the sensors attached to my ankles, then pinned a name tag to my shirt. The other did the same for Ian. We thanked them, and they left as quickly as they'd arrived. I glanced around, looking for my classmates.

A tall, good-looking man with dark brown hair and gray eyes held hands with a beautiful brunette with loose curls halfway down her back and an animated face. She gestured as she spoke. Simon and Suzanne—alive. I rushed toward her.

As I drew close, she ran forward to intercept me, Simon at her heels. She kissed me on both cheeks, French style. As I responded, I felt Marguerite's presence and stopped, puzzled. Where had she come from, since I no longer wore the sensors?

Simon shook my hand. "Nice job, Marguerite. You too, Mighty Leader." He slapped Ian's shoulder. That was when I realized Ian had kept pace with me. Simon grinned. "Was that fun, or what?"

"Wasn't it, though?" I said. "Thank you so much for not deciding to go it alone. None of us would have made it if we hadn't stuck together."

"Same here," he said. "Tony came through for us, too. I had my doubts about him, but he proved me wrong." His smile broadened. "And David has a problem. Five students, two slots. That'll teach him to play games with us."

"Four students," Suzanne said. "David killed me, so I'll be looking for another adviser." She pulled her face into a very French moue. "Think I can sneak out of here? I'd rather not have to face him again. Ugh!"

I hugged her. "It's our fault he got you. We shouldn't have left you in London. It sounds lame to say that I had no idea you were in danger, but it's true. Chauvelin didn't capture Suzanne in the book, so the possibility didn't occur to me." I could have gone on about how I'd believed she'd dumped me while she took off for France on her own, but the comment seemed superfluous. "And after the way you handled Lord Grenville's ball, I think you deserve the prize as much as the rest of us." I glanced at Ian and Simon, who nodded. "See," I said to her. "We stick together, and we win."

Suzanne stopped looking like a person anticipating an eight-hour oral exam. "Thanks. Worth a try, I guess. Where is David, anyway?"

Ian and Simon, tall enough to scan the crowd, did so. "No sign of him," Ian said. "That's odd. He can't still be tied up somewhere, can he? I suppose I'd better go see, since I'm the one who ordered him put away."

He'd taken about three steps when Tony appeared out of nowhere and lifted me off my feet. "Aren't you the one? I'll treasure the image of Marguerite in that yellow dress as long as I live."

Tony, my brother in spirit forevermore. His face glowed with mischievous affection. I laughed like a child as he swung me around. No sooner had my feet skimmed the ground than he turned to embrace an attractive brown-haired woman in glasses. Her name tag identified her as pretty Sally, the barmaid from the Fisherman's Rest. "I enjoyed that," she said with a slight British accent. "My ancestors would be proud. Have a tankard of ale on me, only I think it's coffee."

Coffee ... I hadn't had a cup since entering the simulation. Like a bee scenting nectar, I headed for a tray held by one of the blue shirts. "If I see David," I called over my shoulder, "I'll tell him where we are."

Ian raised a hand in acknowledgment. "You go that way. I'll try over here."

I agreed, my thoughts focused on coffee, not David. I was closing in on the tray when the haughty comtesse, a beautiful Japanese girl who couldn't weigh more than eighty pounds, crossed my path. Giggling, she poked her son—a balding, slightly pudgy gentleman in his fifties—with what looked like Marguerite's cane. A slim woman with short dark hair and an intelligent, humorous face strolled by, her hand on "Armand's" arm. Her tag identified her as Louise, Marguerite's maid. He came from Delhi—tall and slender, with long-lashed black eyes the same color as his hair and smooth brown skin. I stopped to say hello. The coffee moved away, and I had to hunt for it once more.

The cubicle movers had rejoined the crowd. Jellyband and the butler, most of the League members, and the Prince of Wales, doffing an imaginary hat with royal aplomb, wore the blue Polo shirts that marked them as simulation staff. Nonetheless, the computer must have generated most of the bit players. There weren't enough humans in the room to account for every one of the farmers and shopkeepers and soldiers we'd encountered on our journey.

Ian's shout of laughter caught my attention just as I grabbed the sought-after coffee and palmed a second cup for him. I turned to discover what had caused his outburst. He, Simon, and Tony formed a group on the other side of the room. Simon said something—they stood too far away for me to hear what—and the pair of them doubled over. Remembering some incident from the game, probably. Ian straightened, grabbed a broom from a passing employee, and went into a fencing lunge, handle extended in front of him like a long, unwieldy sword. He must have been demonstrating a thrust, because Simon took the broom from him and repeated the move. Ian corrected him, and Simon tried again. The business part of the broom stuck out behind, giving him the faintly ridiculous air of a peacock with a bargain-basement tail. As I chuckled, Ian looked across the room at me, mischief in his face, and winked, exactly as Percy had in the fisherman's hut near Calais.

My face softened. I'd started toward him, keeping an eye on the cups as if that would prevent a spill, when, like a genie popping out of a bottle, David emerged from the throng. "Get the others and meet me in the main office," he said.

His grim expression crushed my high spirits. I hadn't expected him to enjoy losing, but fury twisted his face into a semblance of Chauvelin's. As I headed back to collect my fellow-students, I felt an unpleasant tightening in my stomach. I couldn't help wondering what David had in mind.

Jeb's office was every bit as chaotic as the last time I'd seen it, if not more. I experienced déjà vu as I entered it, coupled with an odd sense of disjunction in time and space. The room's technological jumble emphasized how far I'd traveled from Percy's elegant mansion—or even the fisherman's hut.

As I came in, I caught a glimpse of myself reflected in the darkened computer screen and realized for the first time that I no longer wore Marguerite's brown dress. Instead a rather dumpy young woman with badly cut chin-length hair and an army green turtleneck stared at me. I gulped. Where were the glorious red curls, the exquisite taste? Surely I didn't have to look *that* bad to have people take me seriously as an academic!

At the same time, I could see that the person on the screen had potential. She wasn't ugly, as I'd always believed. Rather, she'd chosen to undermine her own looks—almost as if she raised a barrier against attractiveness. Not hard to figure out, in retrospect, that she had gone overboard in her quest to avoid resembling one of Dad's bimbos. I decided then and there that, graduate stipend or no, I'd go home and throw out my thrift-store clothes and try again. I swear, I heard Marguerite let out a cheer.

Ian took over a couch in the far corner and—unfazed by my horrible appearance, as far as I could tell—beckoned to me. I handed him the second coffee, by some miracle still in its cup, and received warm thanks in return. I kicked off my shoes and curled up on the seat next to him, relishing the touch of his hand on my waist.

Suzanne, Simon, and Tony piled in. "The prisoner's dilemma," Ian reminded them. Suzanne looked puzzled (she had missed his previous explanation), but when Simon pulled her close and whispered into her ear, she nodded.

Just in time. David barged through the door. Chauvelin's furious expression distorted his teen-idol handsomeness, creating a curious hybrid. He grabbed the nearest chair, slung it sideways, and straddled it, his elbows across the back. One foot kicked the office door closed.

"Miss Henderson," he said, "you lost. You may leave. Meet the rest of us in the parking lot in twenty minutes."

Suzanne's mouth dropped open, but she didn't move. David's brusqueness irked me. He had no right to chastise us. He'd set *us* up, not the reverse. I saw Simon clench his fists, felt Ian tense at my back, but I didn't wait for the men to take charge. After two weeks or more in the eighteenth century, I'd had enough of the passive female bit.

"I don't agree," I said. David's weasel glare swiveled in my direction. "For one thing, she's part of the class. She belongs here. And for another, she made an important contribution, so she didn't lose. She prevented Marguerite from learning the truth about the Scarlet Pimpernel's identity, and in that sense she thwarted Chauvelin as much as any of us did. You captured her because the rest of us failed to protect her. We didn't think far enough outside the novel to realize she was at risk."

"Or you," Ian said over my head. "Ninel's right, David. You can't select among us four"—he included Simon, Tony, and me with a sweep of his hand—"because we defeated Chauvelin together. Why pick on Suzanne?"

"Besides," Simon interjected, "we won't accept that ruling. We decided mid-game that we would sink or swim as a team. And the team includes Suzanne. So you take the five of us on, or nobody. To be honest, I don't much care which. Chauvelin, if you'll excuse the expression, was a complete bastard. Good research material, whether or not he was an accurate portrayal, but not the dissertation adviser of my dreams."

I couldn't have said it better myself. Ian's face remained hidden from me, but I guessed from the way his hand tightened on my waist that he felt the same way. Suzanne looked shellshocked, although a small smile tugged at the corner of her mouth. "That's telling him," Tony said as he punched the air.

David gave us one more round of the weasel glare. We scowled right back at him. Then, like the sun blazing through clouds, his natural sense of humor took over. Chauvelin disappeared, and he burst out laughing, our drop-dead gorgeous professor again.

"You five take the cake," he said when he could speak. "Admittedly, this is the first time I've had this good a setup"— his arm encompassed Jeb's cluttered sanctum and the wall between us and the warehouse—"but I've run versions of this game for years, and no one ever figured out the trick. No one defeated Chauvelin before. The students fought one another, and I picked them off at leisure. The last two left standing won."

"Ian got it first," I said, out of fairness. "He convinced the rest of us, so if anyone wins, he should."

"All for one, one for all." Ian pulled me closer. "They rescued me, the three of them, when they didn't have to. And that was Ninel's scheme, from start to finish. Percy almost had a heart attack when he walked into that office and saw her dolled up like a lady of the night."

David grinned at me. "So I deduced from the mayor's story. Sorry I missed it. You must have put on quite a performance, crazy cousin included." I blushed, remembering the yellow dress, but he'd already passed on to the next thing. He stood and saluted us with a bow almost worthy of Sir Percy. "You're right. The five of you earned it. You wrote spectacular papers, which you can pick up from outside my office tomorrow morning, and you defeated not only Chauvelin but the game as well. You all get an A, and it will be my privilege to supervise each and every one of you."

My jaw dropped. Tony led a ragged cheer, and I recovered enough to add my hands to the applause.

David headed for the door. "Anyone who wants to ride the van back to Cambridge, meet me in the parking lot with your suitcases in ten minutes. We have one more class on Friday as a debriefing session, then we're done for the semester." With that, he left.

Suzanne hugged Simon. Tony hugged them both. Ian kissed my cheek. "I have a car," he said. "May I drive you home? We have a few things to catch up on, I think."

The understatement of the decade. I twisted my head so that I could gaze into his eyes. Hazel, not blue. Ian, not Percy. "Yes," I said.

So, when Suzanne, Simon, and Tony finished their congratulations and goodbyes and filed out to collect their suitcases, Ian and I stayed behind.

But it wasn't so easy to switch gears. I wriggled around to face Ian, my mouth clogging with sand as I gazed at him, unable to decide where to start. Among other problems, the office was a disaster for the kind of conversation I wanted. Cluttered, geeky—a poster board for the dangers of emphasizing the technological above the emotional. You'd be hard put to dream up a less romantic scenario.

But of course, the office wasn't the big problem. I didn't know where to start because I'd reached a place where intellect alone couldn't help me. I no longer trusted my sense of how Ian and I related to each other, either before or now. We weren't enemies—even fake ones, as we used to be. We weren't competitors, with the game over and David's acceptance assured. We'd succeeded—independently, but together as well. I felt happy, relieved, anticipatory, anxious, and at sea. I had changed, in ways I sensed but couldn't yet articulate. And Ian had done much to bring that change about. In eighteenth-century Europe, we'd become lovers, partners, companions. Friends. I wanted to give him my heart, to share his life. But how well did I know him, when push came to shove? How much of Ian had gone into Percy, and how much of Percy remained in Ian?

I decided to start there, if in a roundabout way. "What was the simulation like for you? Did you enjoy playing Percy?"

He regarded me through narrowed eyes, as if trying to read my mind—or perhaps my emotions. "Yes, I did. I found it quite freeing, at first, being able to make witty, even outrageous remarks that weren't really mine. The preoccupation with clothes bothered me until I realized they were just another disguise. He spent as much time figuring out how to represent the perfect hag as the perfect dandy. The driving and dancing, even things I wouldn't normally do, like gambling—it was quite entertaining."

"And the dueling? You can't have enjoyed that." I trembled at the memory of him and Simon, back to back against Chauvelin and his men. I'd forgotten, then, that I was taking part in a game. It had felt 100 percent real, as if the man I loved could die. And that hadn't come from Marguerite.

Which told me everything I needed to know about what he meant to me, but I couldn't face that yet.

He collapsed against the arm of the couch, chortling. When he didn't answer, I sighed. "Don't tell me. You're an Olympic fencer, or something."

"Not that good, no." The mischievous gleam in his eyes gave him an elfin expression. "But I was state champion in high school. I haven't kept it up since I left Chicago, so I'm out of practice these days, but it was great. Although Chauvelin didn't strike me as a worthy opponent, except in the intellectual sense. I might have done better with the vicomte."

Fencing. How apropos. And I'd thought he wasn't an athlete until I saw him outside the Dreamlife warehouse. Was there anything I had gotten right about him?

He rubbed my temple with his thumb. "But the best part was spending time with you, trying to figure out when Ninel would appear. Not a lot, at first, I think. I hadn't realized you were afraid of heights."

"Oh, yes," I said. "Quite dreadfully, although at least by the time I left I could sit on a horse without cringing. Not ride a horse, but that was mostly lack of knowledge. You helped a lot. Thank you for that."

"My pleasure," he said. "I wish I had done more, sooner, but I had difficulty getting Percy to trust Marguerite." He grinned at me. "Until you pushed him into the goldfish pond. I didn't have much trouble with him after that. The baroness hadn't prepared him to handle strong-minded women."

I couldn't help but giggle. "He looked so funny, sitting there. I can still see the look on his face. Did he fade, too? Marguerite did, after Chauvelin's men knocked me out, but with you, I couldn't tell. After I had no book to judge him by, the two of you seemed so much alike it became difficult to separate you."

"No," Ian said. "If anything, he became stronger as the Scarlet Pimpernel. But we did fuse more, I think, in the second half of the game. When Chauvelin kidnapped you, Percy and I reacted in exactly the same way."

A knock sounded at the door, and Ian called, "Come in." I didn't welcome the interruption, although I didn't resist it either. I needed time to consider what to say next.

Jeb poked his head round the door. "You're still here," he said. "Lock up when you leave, will you, Campbell? Everyone else has gone." He pushed the door further ajar and beckoned to someone unseen, who turned out to be another blue-shirted technician delivering our battered suitcases. The technician dumped the bags against the nearest wall and departed at a nod from Jeb.

"Sure," Ian said, accepting the keyring Jeb held out. "Good game."

Jeb glanced at me, then Ian. "Yes, I thought so. Stop by tomorrow and we'll discuss the programming. I could use your help, if you're willing. The six of you pushed the game to its limits. I couldn't have asked for a better test, but I need to make some adjustments before I let this beast out into the wild."

"Ten?" Ian asked. "This is my last course. I have most of the summer free, except for my research."

Jeb agreed, said his farewells, and left. Ian and I had the warehouse to ourselves. And I still hadn't found a way to introduce the topic that occupied my mind.

Ian left the couch and bent over the computer. As I tested this idea, then that—rejecting each one as too lame, too dramatic, too something—I watched his fingers play a symphony on the keys. After a few minutes, he stood and held out his hand. "Will you join me in Richmond?"

Richmond? Blakeney Manor? In the back of my mind, I felt Marguerite stir to life. But I hesitated. I wanted to talk with Ian as myself, even in a mud-green sweater. I'd loved being gorgeous, but Marguerite was not me.

"I didn't change our faces," he said. "Just the setting. This office is dreary as hell, don't you think?"

I couldn't disagree. So I let him apply the sensors, then walked with him down the hall to the open room we'd left such a short time before.

This time, I was prepared for the shock of entering the eighteenth century. On the other side of the door, I tumbled into Blakeney Manor at its finest. A grand ballroom, with crystal chandeliers glittering in the light cast by hundreds of candles, brimming vases filled with narcissus and peonies and yellow hothouse roses, parquet floors polished to a fare-thee-well, painted and gilded Rococo walls worthy of the Winter Palace in St. Petersburg. Chamber music swirled around us in a dance rhythm, but we were alone in the room—no musicians, no servants, no other dancers. Ian appeared in Percy's cream satin suit, the one he had worn to the opera house and Lord Grenville's ball. And no more camouflage green for me—I sported Marguerite's gorgeous *Directoire* gown.

Ian raised my hand to his lips. The music changed to a slow, sensuous tune. "The *minuet à deux*, darling. Will you honor me?"

My jaw dropped, and I forced it shut. Marguerite whirled with joy inside my head. The *minuet à deux* was the wedding dance of eighteenth-century Europe, and throughout the simulation—since their wedding, in fact—Percy had refused to perform it with her.

I let her guide my steps as we moved into the dance. «But don't interfere,» I told her. «This is my romance, not yours.»

«Oh, Nina, don't be silly,» she said. «Haven't you figured it out yet? I *am* you.»

Which sounded close enough to the truth that it made my skin prickle. I concentrated on Ian. "Didn't you tell me you found the minuet tedious?"

We were walking side by side, one way, then the reverse. He turned to face me and lifted my hand above my head. We stepped toward each other, retreated. "Percy said he found it tedious. You can't imagine Percy admitting he couldn't stand the agony, can you? It made him want to grab Marguerite and carry her off, like a caveman in a cartoon. Not the act of a true English gentleman."

"Not Percy's style," I agreed. Marguerite had subsided, leaving me to handle the conversation with Ian while she directed the pattern of the dance.

Ian lowered my arm, and I sank into a curtsey. As I returned to standing, he placed an arm around my waist and we began the promenade again. An idea occurred to me, and I voiced it, not waiting for doubt to silence me. "I thought you hated me. I told you that at the cottage. In class, in the game. Until—oh, Covent Garden at least. Even then, I felt sure that was Percy, kissing Marguerite. Or you kissing Marguerite." I stopped, fighting the lump in my throat. The music swirled around me. "Was I right?"

He raised a Percy-ish eyebrow. "Let's forget this cursed dance, shall we?" Without waiting for an answer, he swept me off the floor and through a pair of French doors at the far side of the room. We stopped on a balcony. The grounds of Blakeney Manor spread to the horizon, where the Thames River gleamed. I didn't even notice the height until later.

"No, Ninel, you didn't get it right." He steadied me with one arm around my waist. "I thought *you* disliked me. I said that, too, at the cottage. Even my compliments made you prickle like a porcupine."

"It's because you insist on calling me Ninel," I said. "Why not Nina, like everyone else?"

"Because Ninel's such a lovely name. It's different. Like you. Anyone can be a Nina." When I stared at him, speechless—he considered Ninel pretty, distinctive?—he tapped the tip of my nose with his free hand. "If you insist, I'll call you Nina. But I much prefer Ninel, and not least because no one else uses it. Are you really not aware that I've been smitten with you for two years? You, not Marguerite." I heard laughter in his voice as he finished, "Although I did tap Percy for the courage to kiss you, intimidating woman that you are."

"Intimidating?" I asked. "Me? You're joking. *You're* the star of the graduate program. How could I intimidate you?"

"How could you not?" he said after a pause. I stared at him, unable to believe my ears. "You're bright and beautiful and thoroughly adorable. I fell in love with you the moment I met you. So naturally, everything I said came out wrong. The game gave me an opportunity to start fresh."

As his words sank in, I felt a warm glow ignite in my chest and spread outward. He had fallen in love with me. He had seen the game as an opportunity to woo me. He loved me, not Marguerite. And I had misread him from the beginning. Time to hit the reset button.

I touched his shoulder. He responded immediately, clasping my fingers with his free hand, but his face had the grim lines of a miner pondering a cave-in. "That's not the whole story, sweetheart."

What had I expected? Of course, it wasn't. Life couldn't be that easy. Not if it involved me. I was Henry VIII's daughter, doomed from birth. I pulled away from him. Or tried to—he refused to let go. In fact, his arms tightened around me in a way that sent the butterflies in my stomach turning cartwheels. "You're married," I said, struggling to remain analytical despite my body's betrayal. "You have AIDS. Or some other incurable disease. You're gay, but we can be friends. You have six kids."

He brushed my lips with his. Amusement again lit his eyes. "Goodness, you make me feel better. None of the above."

"What, then?" A stray breeze from the window made me shiver—well, I told myself it was the breeze.

"In the cottage. You accused Percy of having a mistress, and I lost it. Remember?"

I did. I'd thought it weird at the time. The one thing he'd done that didn't make sense, even if he loved me. Not that I'd wasted two minutes worrying about it since, what with eluding Chauvelin and getting shot only to wind up captured, followed by that dramatic last-ditch escape at the end. But if Ian wanted to explain, I'd listen. "Yes," I said. "What was that about?"

"That's what I'm trying to tell you, *mignonne.*" Oh, that word. "I'm not married, but I was. For three years. It broke up because my wife accused me of infidelity. Once a week or more, even though I gave her no cause. Nothing helped. She refused to see a counselor because she insisted everything she believed was rational. When I couldn't take it anymore, I filed for divorce. And applied to Harvard. Where I met you. But I didn't want to cause another car crash, so I stayed away from you at first. Then turned you off, without meaning to. At the cottage, I panicked. Things seemed to be going well—until I discovered that you didn't trust me either. But I soon figured out that was my problem. Nonsense. An old wound."

A wife. I'd never heard about the wife—or the divorce. So that was why he'd clammed up whenever I asked about his past. I didn't know enough about him as an individual, distinct from Percy. I couldn't love him. It was insane.

And yet, compared to my father, a past-tense wife and no life-threatening diseases didn't sound like *such* a bad deal. He'd flipped out for a few minutes, but under the circumstances I didn't think I should hold that against him. He'd revealed his Achilles' heel, which I could avoid kicking in the future. And his explanation covered more ground than he'd admitted to. "You kept me at a distance," I said. "You weren't really intimidated."

He burst out laughing. "That galls you, does it? But I was, Ninel, I was. And it backfired on me! Forgive me, darling, please. I have flaws like everyone else, but I promise to work on them."

I sighed, and not from distress. The man could charm a swallow from the trees. "Oh, I suppose, as a special favor, because you asked so nicely."

"Thank you, Madam." His arm went around my waist, and I leaned against his pearl-studded chest. "So, Lady Blakeney, may I take you to dinner? Take you home? Will you trust me to love you?"

Words worthy of the Scarlet Pimpernel. Nina the Analytical put up one last fight, but my heart had already declared victory. My mother was right. Why chase all the nice boys away? I wanted a career, yes, but not to live alone in my ivory tower forever. It wasn't the eighteenth century. I didn't have to choose between love and self-fulfillment.

Ian's ivory satin coat gleamed in the computer-generated moonlight. The froth of his cravat brushed my cheek. From Blakeney Manor's exquisite gardens, the scent of lilac wafted on the late spring breeze. He had programmed this setting. He sometimes worked for Jeb's company. We could return to this mannered past, to Percy and Marguerite, whenever we liked.

But we also had Cambridge, and a future that I longed to explore. And he had offered me his love, asked me to trust him. I wrapped both arms around his neck and stood on tiptoe to kiss him. "Sink me, Sir Percy, I believe I will."

Acknowledgments

WRITE A NOVEL, AND YOU SOON DISCOVER WHY ACTORS give forty-minute speeches at the Academy Awards, ignoring the band's attempts to play them off the stage. They don't want to slight one of the many wonderful people who helped them, long before they won anything—and neither do I. My gratitude to those who read the book in its early (sometimes infant) stages: Irina, Liv, Susan, and Terry—fellow toilers in the editorial and translation trenches; Andrea, Gay, Mary, Pam, Perky, Sally, and Sharon; Allan, who offered his help even though I had called him out of the blue on the recommendation of the friend of a friend; and my mother, who does not resemble Nina's, even though the story about rheumatic fever comes from her childhood.

Special thanks to Annick Applewhite, who made sure I knew how to pronounce Arras (Ah-RASS, with a rolled "r" and final "s") and generally oversaw my French. To Carol Craig, for more good advice than anyone has a right to expect, and her assistant Janice Hussein; Leslie Daniels, for graciously tolerating my ineptness and pushing me to think through Nina's character; and my critique partners Kathryne Andrews, Diana Holquist, Colleen Kelley, and Janet Olshewsky. And most of all to my family, who soldiered on while I wrestled with my imaginary people—especially my husband, who assures me that such classroom simulations do take place at elite universities, if without the immersive technology that complicates the challenge facing Ninel and her comrades.

The Author

As a child, C. P. Lesley thought everyone told themselves stories to help themselves fall asleep. It never occurred to her that anyone would pay her for them, and for a long time, she was right—no one would. But after years of producing horrible prose, reading books about novel writing, and pestering hapless fellow-writers and friends to read her drafts, some of the advice stuck, and she finished *The Not Exactly Scarlet Pimpernel*.

Since publishing this book in 2012, she has produced four other novels: *Desert Flower* and *Kingdom of the Shades* (Tarkei Chronicles 1 and 2—a pair of science fiction romances that reexamine two of the world's great ballets), as well as *The Golden Lynx* and *The Winged Horse*—books 1 and 2 of Legends of the Five Directions, a series set during the childhood of Ivan the Terrible. She is currently working on Legends 3, *The Swan Princess*. Find out more about her and her books at www.cplesley.com.

When not thinking up new ways to torture her characters, she edits other people's manuscripts, reads voraciously, maintains her website and blog, and takes classes in classical ballet. She also hosts New Books in Historical Fiction, a channel in the New Books Network (http://newbooksnetwork.com).

Desert Flower

An Excerpt

FABRIC GLEAMED IN THE FLICKERING CANDLE FLAME. Shadows danced on the cave walls. Blush pink ribbons slid through her fingers—soft and smooth. Once, before her mother died, she had stroked a *m'retta* with fur like this.

"What are these?" Entranced, Choli held out her find to the man who sat cross-legged in the corner, who had watched without speaking while she rummaged through his few possessions. Tall and slender, dark-haired, dark-eyed, olive-skinned, austere in his charcoal robe, he looked like the men of her world. But no man of her world would have tolerated her presence, never mind giving her free run of his home. This one sat, still as the rocks at his back, hands folded like a scholar or a priest. Or so they said, the people of the caves.

Choli wondered how they knew. Scholars were rare among the Kazrati. In her thirteen years, she had not met a single one. Priests were not so rare, but they were intimidating. Danion, of course, was not Kazrati, although he appeared to be.

His deep, cool voice answered the question she had almost forgotten asking. "They are shoes."

A lock of straight dark hair fell into Choli's eyes as she squinted at the shoes. Restless hands pressed them, prodded them. The uppers were soft, the soles like blocks of wood in her palms. "They're so hard. Who wears shoes like that? Are they yours?"

"Not mine." The man before her did not smile; he seldom smiled. Still, a note of something that might have been amusement tinged his voice. "Ballerinas wear them, so they can stand on their toes, like this." He took one shoe from her and stood it on its toe, balancing it with a long slim finger, then handed it back. "As you see, that one is not new."

Examining it more closely, Choli saw he was right. Someone had scraped satin off the toe, scored the sole with a knife, sprayed the front with varnish. The ballerina, she assumed. Whatever that might be. She asked.

"A human dancer," Danion said. "Usually, anyway. Not necessarily human." He flicked the shoe. "It is difficult to dance on your toes. The shoes must be just right—not too hard, not too soft. They prepare a dozen pairs at once, wear each one for a single performance, then throw them out."

"I have never seen a ballerina." Under the pressure of her hands, the shoes became more malleable: warm, flexible, alive. What would it be like—to dance on her toes? "These were not thrown out."

"No," Danion said. "Because she cannot wear them again, the ballerina sometimes gives them away, to mark a special performance. That is how they came to me."

As though they had a will of their own, the shoes turned in her grasp, ribbons spilling toward the floor. Anxious, she leaped to catch them, but Danion stopped her with a touch. "It's all right, Choli."

Someone had written on the pink satin, flowing passages of Tarkei script. Choli put her head on one side and pondered.

Would Danion be angry if she asked what they meant? But he was teaching her to read, so perhaps he would not mind.

She held out the shoe with the writing on it. "What does it say?"

In the candle flame, garnet flashed in one diamond-shaped ear. Danion reached for the shoe. He did not look at it, but his long fingers encircled the satin, caressing it. With his thumb, he pressed the heel inward, winding the ribbons into a neat circle around the arch. "Come here," he said. When she stood beside him, he pointed the letters out to her, one by one.

"'For thee, *kaleita*,'" she read, "'may the stars always smile.' I can't read the rest. It's not Tarkei."

Choli looked at her mentor, eyes wide. "Who wrote it?" Then, considering what he had taught her, "Stars don't smile."

For an instant, she was sure, his lips curved. "Not literally," he said. "But life is not always literal, my child, even on Tarkei. The shoes were given to me, long ago, by a great ballerina. Some say the greatest ballerina of the century."

"Really? But who was she?"

"Her name was Alessandra Sinclair. That is her signature, the part you can't read."

Alessandra Sinclair. A name like music. A human name. And Danion sounded sad, more sad than she had ever imagined he might feel.

The child stared at this teacher who never failed to surprise her. "And you knew her? But how?"

"Sit down," he said, "and I will tell you."

FIVE DIRECTIONS PRESS

THIS BOOK WAS TYPESET USING GARAMOND, A BODY FONT dating from the early days of printing, with headings in Edwardian Script ITC to evoke the mannered world of *The Scarlet Pimpernel*. The type ornaments come from Poetica (pimpernels) and Type Ten Embellishments.